A NOVEL OF THE MARVEL UNIVERSE

BLACK PANTHER

WHO IS THE BLACK PANTHER?

A NOVEL OF THE MARVEL UNIVERSE

BLACK PANTHER

WHO IS THE
BLACK PANTHER?

JESSE J. HOLLAND

ADAPTED FROM THE GRAPHIC NOVEL BY
REGINALD HUDLIN AND **JOHN ROMITA JR.**

TITAN BOOKS

MARVEL

Who Is the Black Panther?
Print edition ISBN: 9781785659478
E-book edition ISBN: 9781785659485

Published by Titan Books
A division of Titan Publishing Group Ltd
144 Southwark Street, London SE1 0UP

First Titan edition: April 2018
10 9 8 7 6 5 4 3 2

Black Panther created by Stan Lee and Jack Kirby
Interior art by John Romita Jr. and Klaus Janson
Cover art by Gabriele Dell'Otto

Editor: Stuart Moore
VP Production & Special Projects: Jeff Youngquist
Assistant Editor: Caitlin O'Connell
Manager, Licensed Publishing: Jeff Reingold
SVP Print, Sales & Marketing: David Gabriel
Editor in Chief: C.B. Cebulski
Chief Creative Officer: Joe Quesada
President: Dan Buckley
Executive Producer: Alan Fine

A CIP catalogue record for this title is available from the British Library.

Printed and bound in the United States

For Carol, Rita and Jamie.
The best is yet to come…

CHAPTER ONE

A TRIO of black SUVs rumbled down a dirt road. The late fall wind whipped leaves out of the swaying trees and across the road, the fluttering yellows and oranges contrasting sharply with the gray, billowing clouds racing across the sky.

The trucks kicked up a cloud of dust behind them as they cruised down the lonely Virginia road. Other than the occasional curious look from a grazing cow, the SUVs were alone and out of place in the remote countryside. After cresting a couple of hills and maneuvering around potholes in the road, the SUVs one at a time swerved sharply into an opening in the trees, where the road looked more like dual indentations in the grass. Branches whipped the sides of the SUVs until they entered a clearing with a small, ramshackle farmhouse. Slowing to a crawl, the trucks followed the grassy path around the house to a massive antique barn and slowly drove through a set of open double doors.

Shielded from the sky by a canopy of enormous oak trees, the brown- and-green dappled barn blended in perfectly with its surroundings…except for the satellite dish hidden under a back eave of the roof, and the surveillance cameras hidden in the overhanging branches and around the perimeter.

Inside the barn, the SUVs idled. Trios of dark-suited men disembarked, looking around at the banks of high-tech monitor screens hung around the multilevel structure. Surrounding them on ground level, in what apparently were former horse stalls, were overall-clad men, some with dirty-blond or red beards, assembling and mock-firing rifles, AK-47s, and other weapons.

In the back of the barn was a makeshift firing range, where other men in jeans and T-shirts discharged bullets repeatedly at dark-colored mannequins. One of the black-suited drivers nodded at his compatriots and slowly walked up to one of the men on the firing line. Tall, with a scraggly, reddish-blond beard, the man's body shuddered as he fired repeatedly at the target dummy, shredding the head and shoulders. While his clothes were quaint—his jeans were torn, his sweaty T-shirt declared "The South Will Rise Again," and a Confederate-flag bandanna around his head kept his eyes clear of sweat—his intelligent eyes shone with a frightening intensity.

The black-suited man considered this as he adjusted his Armani tie. Luckily, in the arms business, those kinds of men didn't haggle over price.

When the clip was finally empty, the dark-suited arms dealer tapped him on the shoulder. "Carson Willabie III?"

Willabie slowly turned around, his eyes giving the man a clear once-over before speaking. "Could be. And you are…"

"Someone who doesn't have time for games, Mr. Willabie. If you have my cash, I have your order."

Willabie smiled an enigmatic grin, a piece of hay dangling from his mouth. "There's always time for games, Mr. Blackthorne."

Blackthorne snorted, and then coughed as the rancid scent of mansweat and gunpowder invaded his body. Breathing out of his mouth, Blackthorne retorted, "Find someone else to play with, then. I don't want to be out here any longer than I have to be. Give me my money, get your merchandise off my truck, and let me get back to my city."

Willabie laughed, his Southern drawl becoming more apparent as he talked. "You hoity-toity city slickers have never been able to stand the appearance of a real man, have you? You make all of this noise about making this country great, but when it comes time for the dirty work, you can't do anything but get out of the way of real men."

As Willabie talked, the bustling activity around the barn halted. Men shuffled toward their leader, who grew more animated and wild as he spoke. Flecks of spittle gathered on his ragged beard as his arms began to flail about.

"We're the real Americans! Us! And we're gonna take our country back from these foreigners and immigrants! No one's gonna put up a temple to them in my country if we have anything to say about it, right, boys?"

A ragged cheer and whoops from his men led

Willabie to raise his hands as if he were a prizefighter celebrating a victory. Blackthorne just looked bored. Willabie exulted in the praise for a few seconds, then nodded his head toward a secluded stall that had been converted into a makeshift office. He wandered over, followed by the still silent Blackthorne.

Willabie sat down behind an antique desk and propped his boot-clad feet on top of the dirty surface. "Shut that door so we can have some privacy to conduct our financial dealings, will you, Mr. Blackthorne?"

Blackthorne hesitated outside the door for a second, wary of the situation. Taking out a radio earpiece, he coiled it around his ear and spoke into the microphone. "If I'm not out in 15 minutes, go to plan Omega 5. Full sweep. Maintain radio silence until I return."

"Don't trust me, huh?" Willabie cackled, hocking a huge glob of spit onto the dirty floor.

"Just keeping my options open," Blackthorne said. He pulled the door closed and yanked his radio out of his ear. Silence filled the room for a couple of seconds. Then Willabie slowly stood up and walked around the desk to look directly at Blackthorne, who set his feet and curled up his lip in a sneer.

The two men then laughed as they hugged each other.

"Johnny-boy," Willabie patted him on the back. "Good to see you in person again. How's the arms business going?"

Blackthorne chuckled. "Just about as well as the

secret-agent business, Car. Have you talked to Dad lately?"

Willabie snorted. "That old coot? The last time he deigned to talk to his youngest child, he was still Scrooge McDucking his way through the Fort Lauderdale social scene." He held up his hand and sat back down in his desk chair. "And before you ask, yes, we're still cut out of the will."

"Damn." Blackthorne pulled a rickety chair out of the corner and brought it up to the desk. "I was hoping he had dementia by now and forgot he'd disowned us."

"No such luck. We're on our own for a while longer. You bring the goods?"

"Yep. It took a little doing, but our Belgian contact came through. Got some machine guns, a few grenade launchers, and some older Brownings from the gray market. All dirt cheap, but pretty good profit margin on the resale market. Your men ready?"

Willabie leaned back in his chair, chewing on his straw. "Those idiots? They're as ready as they're ever going to be. All you have to do is mention the white man is losing in America, and they're willing to do any old stupid thing I can think of. And this one will be a doozy…"

Blackthorne chuckled. "Whatever. Just get them down to the Mall and kick up a ruckus. I'll take care of everything from there. We need to get people riled up—and hell, if this doesn't do it, then I don't know what will."

"Don't worry, bro. I'll get them fired up and ready to go."

"Be sure you're not down there, okay? In case things go sideways." Willabie chuckled again. "Believe me, when I'm done they'll be begging me to stay behind to carry on the glorious fight. Mix a little racial pride with a lot of disoperation, and you've got a ready-made army, bro." He sighed and sniffed at his clothes. "Now I have to get back in character, bro. I just wish I didn't have to get so…fragrant on this gig. Put your secret-agent face back on, and let's get underway."

CHAPTER TWO

DEVONTE Wallman ran as fast as he could, darting around people on the Washington, D.C., sidewalk, all seemingly more concerned with their daily lives than his urgent mission. He was late, and the doors would be locked soon if he didn't hurry. And these tourists—with their Witness Protection T-shirts and smartphones and stuff—were in his way. But an elbow here, and a shove there (and a couple of words that would make Gramma tan his hide if she heard them coming from his mouth), and he could see clear space in front of him. His goal was in sight: the entrance to the Smithsonian National Museum of African Art.

He could see that security was tighter than normal, even for the nation's capital. Men with earpieces wandered the perimeter, and news crews jostled for position near a microphone stand on the sidewalk, as if they expected someone important to give a speech soon.

Normally, Devonte would hang around to see whether the person speaking was famous (he'd gotten to see his favorite wrestler, The Rock, that way before the guy started making Disney movies). But today was too important. Two more steps, and Devonte burst through the door, panting hard. An elderly lady at the front desk smiled bemusedly at him as he bent over trying to catch his breath, his chest heaving as sweat dripped from around the drenched New York Yankees baseball cap he had stuffed around his unkempt dreadlocks.

"You okay, hon?" She peered over the desk as Devonte struggled to stand upright again. Unable to make his lungs and mouth work at the same time, Devonte waved his ticket frantically at a poster on the wall.

"Ah, the Wakandan exhibit. Downstairs, son, and hurry. They're starting any second now."

After clearing security, Devonte staggered toward a set of stairs in the middle of the room and headed down two steps at a time, security guards glaring at him just in case he posed a danger. Skidding around a corner on the slick marble floor, Devonte saw a crowd gathered at the door of a gallery with a red ribbon blocking the entrance. At the back of the crowd, looking anxiously at her watch, stood his mom, who was in the process of pulling out her phone. She was tall and lean, with her long braids tied up in a halo around her head and secured with a white headband that contrasted with the mahogany color of her skin. Devonte thought his mom was the most beautiful woman in the world; at 10, his buddies had started teasing him about how cute his mom was. He didn't like thinking about his mom that way, and he definitely didn't like his friends thinking that way, even if they were right.

When she saw her son skidding around the corner, a look of exasperation flickered across her eyes before she sighed. "Why are you late?" she hissed good-naturedly as she gathered him in her arms and began a futile effort to try to straighten his clothes into some semblance of acceptability.

Devonte shrugged and squirmed, trying to free himself from his mom's insistent efforts at grooming him. Out of the corner of his eye, he could see some girls about his age in the crowd, and he knew he was losing major cool points with members of the opposite sex by having his mom smooth down his shirt and use a baby wipe on the corners of his eyes. But he also knew she'd only get louder and more insistent if he fought against her mothering instinct, so he suffered through it.

"This is important to me, right?" his mom whispered in his ear, finally satisfied with her efforts. "It's been years since we've seen the king, and after all of your grandfather's stories, well, this is important. I need you on your best behavior, okay?"

Devonte smiled, knowing his mom's moods as well as anyone else did. He gave her the puppy-dog eyes, knowing that would make her melt. "I promise to be good. And we're going to the new museum next, right?"

She snorted and gave him a quick hug. "I know that look, mister. Better men than you, including your dad, have tried that with me."

"And it worked, too, didn't it, Mom?"

The sound of wood chimes cut off her good-natured retort. An elderly, gray-bearded docent shuffled in, escorted by two of the most powerfully built women Devonte had ever seen. One was tall and wiry with dark bronzed skin. She was built like a professional basketball player, but she moved impossibly light on her feet. A scowl seemed permanently imprinted on her face, and her dark eyes locked on each face in the entranceway from behind dark sunglasses, looking for danger.

Her companion resembled an Olympic gymnast, compact and quick. Her head moved from side to side, sweeping the room and casting quick glances at an impossibly thin, smartphone-looking device wrapped in a lycra-looking band on her arm. She was as dark as her partner, but her skin seemed to glow with her smile, as if she had a secret that would make her laugh out loud if she were to share it.

Both women were bald and dressed in matching skintight, blue-black pantsuits. Devonte could see the quiet communication between the two as the taller one nodded, then disappeared into a nearby anteroom. The elderly docent cleared his throat.

"Ladies and gentlemen, the Smithsonian is pleased to welcome you to the National Museum of African Art, and to the opening of our new Wakandan exhibit. This collection—whose pieces were empowered to counter physical, social, and spiritual challenges—were commissioned exclusively for this exhibit by our guest, who graciously took time out of his busy schedule to come join us here today." The man coughed briefly, and grinned broadly, his white teeth shining brightly. "I could continue talking, but I'm just as excited to hear from our speaker as you, so I'm going to get out of his way. Ladies and gentlemen, I'm proud to present to you our benefactor: the Black Panther of Wakanda, His Royal Highness King T'Challa!" Devonte heard his mother's sharp intake of breath. He desperately tried to stand on his tiptoes to see through the crowd, which burst into applause. As Devonte peered around arms and over heads, he could barely make out the slender dark-skinned man now walking next to the bald amazonian bodyguards. When he got a better look, Devonte was slightly disappointed. He'd been expecting a king. This man looked like a magazine model.

The man's walk to a small dais set up in front of the ribbon was graceful, like one of those Harlem dancers his mom had made him see at the Kennedy Center. Instead of crown and robes, he wore what Devonte assumed was an expensive black business suit with a Kente-cloth sash draped around his shoulders and chest. In fact, now that the applause had died down, Devonte could see that King T'Challa wasn't much older than some of the recently graduated teacher's assistants at his middle school. A hint of a beard covered his face, and the smile he gave the crowd didn't quite seem to reach his piercing brown eyes, which darted around the room, locking gazes with the adoring audience members.

T'Challa raised his hands for silence as he settled

in next to the beaming docent. One of the bodyguards handed him a few notecards and whispered something into his ear, which made him smile, his white teeth contrasting with the darkness of his skin. He shuffled the cards for a second, and then placed them inside his suit pocket. As he leaned forward, a strong African accent infused his soft tones.

"Thank you, my friends, and thank you to the Smithsonian for inviting me here today for the opening of this exhibit. As some of you may know, I recently ascended to my honored father's throne in our homeland of Wakanda. But even before becoming king, it was my fondest wish that our country become a more active participant on the world stage, and I can think of no better way to introduce ourselves to the world than through the glory of art." T'Challa turned and gestured smoothly at the gallery behind him. "In here you will find representation of some of the greatest artists and craftsmen of our country, commissioned by me for the royal palace in Wakanda while I was still crown prince. But I thought it would be a better gift to the world and to our friends here in the United States to share them, as a sign of friendship and honor.

"For decades, we Wakandans have embraced isolationism, content to let the rest of the world live as it would. But we have only one Earth, and her children can little afford not to share the glories and the tragedies of our collective existence much longer. I hope these small tokens of Wakandan culture will signal a greater openness and a renewed partnership between our two countries, a partnership that will lead our world into a better future for all mankind. Thank you."

Applause filled the room as the young king stepped away from the podium and approached the red ribbon. The docent produced a large pair of silver scissors, leading the taller of the king's guard to move protectively toward her charge while the smaller one placed her hand on the elderly man's arm. His eyes widened when he realized what he had done, but an easy grin from T'Challa put him at ease.

"We won't need those." The king pulled some kind of black glove from somewhere inside his suit. With a single swipe, the ribbon fluttered to the ground, and the crowd cheered again.

The old man waved his hands at the crowd again. "When you registered for this opening, several of you were specially chosen to tour the exhibit with the king and his retinue. The ones who were chosen were contacted by phone earlier. I need you to step forward with a photo ID if you're part of today's party."

Devonte felt his mom's hand on his shoulder. "That's us, kiddo. Surprise!"

His eyes widened in shock. "We get to meet the king? Too cool, Mom!"

"I knew if I told you before today, you'd have bugged me about it all week, baby boy." She chuckled as they moved toward the front of the crowd to be wanded at a security line. "I don't know if we'll get to meet him, but we'll be in the same room. That's still cool, right?

Devonte and his mom made their way through the extra security and wandered into the new gallery. Even though his mom endeavored to direct his attention to the fine art, Devonte spent most of his time spying on the king. T'Challa walked with his two female companions, the elderly docent, and a couple of business-suited white men, conversing about each piece they passed. Occasionally, they would be joined by an African woman or man— the artist or craftsman, who would take over the conversation about the piece.

Devonte didn't hear any of his mother's lectures about the pieces. Once, while peeking around his mother's back, he noticed the shorter of the two women was looking right into his eyes. He blushed and turned away, only to peek back to see a wide smile on the woman's face. She winked at him, and turned back toward the king and whispered quickly in his ear.

Devonte froze as T'Challa turned to look at him. His mother was still talking about the statue in front of them, oblivious to the movement behind her as the king and his companions approached them. Devonte had to tug on her jacket to get her attention, and she froze as well when she saw T'Challa.

"Beautiful, is it not?" T'Challa's soft voice was comforting yet commanding at the same time. He held out a hand. "King T'Challa of Wakanda. And you are?"

Devonte had never heard his mother stutter before. "S-Synranda Wallman, Your Highness."

T'Challa locked gazes with Devonte, a small smile on his face. "And this young gentleman?"

His mom nudged him forward. Devonte gulped and held out his hand. "Devonte Wallman, sir. Nice to meet you."

The taller woman frowned. "Address him as 'Your Royal Highness.'"

T'Challa waved her off as he shook Devonte's hand. "No need to stand on ceremony with the young, Okoye. So, Mr. Wallman, what do you think about the exhibit?"

Devonte looked down at his shoes bashfully and eked out a quiet "It's okay." His mom gave him a no-nonsense nudge.

"Ummm, I think the art's great. My mom says I need culture and need to know where I came from but I wanted to go to the new black museum and see the music exhibit and we made a deal to come here first and see this and then we can go to the museum and…"

Devonte saw the look in his mother's eyes and trailed off. T'Challa saw the unspoken communication between the two and laughed. "Yes, mothers can be trying sometimes, can't they? But believe me, a mother's wisdom is irreplaceable." T'Challa leaned over and whispered in Devonte's ear. "Even though I am king, I still have to listen to my mother. That's how I keep out of trouble."

T'Challa straightened up. "I suppose this could be a little boring for a child. I assume by 'new black museum,' you're talking about the Smithsonian National Museum of African American History and Culture? Nakia, is that on our itinerary?"

The shorter of the two women tapped at her arm, which Devonte could now see bore a glowing keyboard and miniature screen. She spoke a few words to T'Challa in a language Devonte didn't understand before T'Challa stopped her. "In English, please. Let's not be rude to our hosts, Nakia."

Nakia grinned. "We have a few minutes after this event before our appointment at the White House, your highness."

T'Challa rubbed his hands together. "Then it's settled. Devonte Wallman, Synranda Wallman, would you like to be my guests at the 'new black museum'? It would be my honor to experience this museum with you."

Devonte's eyes widened. He looked up at his mother, who was just as astonished. "Please, please, please," he silently mouthed to her.

"Your highness, we wouldn't want to impose on your time…" his mother began.

T'Challa waved his hand. "It wouldn't be an imposition at all. In fact, I insist. Nakia will take care of the details, and we'll meet at the museum. Now, if you'll excuse me, I need to continue with my tour before my countrymen start painting pictures of me with devil horns for ignoring their fine work."

T'Challa winked at Devonte, kissed his mother gently on the hand, and was escorted off by the docent, artists, and museum officials. Devonte and his mom looked at each other in astonishment. "What just happened?" she whispered.

"He does this all of the time. Just roll with it," Nakia grinned at them. She thrust her hand out toward Devonte. "I am Nakia of the *Dora Milaje*. I am pleased to meet you. If you would follow me…"

She escorted them to the door and back up to street level. The afternoon sun was beginning to set as the three of them wandered across the National Mall. Devonte, hanging on his mother's arm, was bursting with questions for the young Wakandan woman, but he knew his motormouth would get him into trouble with his mom. But after a couple of steps, Nakia's twinkling eyes caught him trying to be on his best behavior. "My elders tell me that I don't take things seriously enough sometimes, but I find that an open mind makes interesting times, don't you? So go ahead and ask, young man. I won't be insulted."

Devonte looked up at his mom, and she nodded. "What's the king like?"

Nakia laughed. "King T'Challa…" she hesitated for a second, as if trying out unfamiliar words on her tongue. "I've known His Royal Highness my whole life, and I still wouldn't be able to describe him properly in just a few sentences. He's…intense, but kind. He's one of the smartest men in the world, but so gentle…"

Nakia trailed off, lost in thought for a second before snapping herself back to formality. "King T'Challa is the heart and soul of Wakanda. It is an honor for the *Dora Milaje* to serve him."

Devonte looked at her questioningly, rolling the unfamiliar words off his tongue hesitantly. "*Dora Milaje?*"

Nakia ruffled Devonte's head. "What's the best way to explain this to you? We are like—what's the English word?—bodyguards for the king, chosen from the many tribes of Wakanda. We receive special training and live in the palace with the king to serve his every need."

Synranda quirked her eyebrow. "His…every need?"

Nakia's dark skin flushed. "Nothing like that. He says we're more like…daughters to him than anything else. Okoye and I, we won the honor of representing the *Dora Milaje* in public with the king, while the rest of our sisterhood trains for their day."

Devonte wrinkled his nose. "All girls?"

Nakia chuckled and patted him on the head. "All girls. Someday, that'll sound good to you."

As she talked, Devonte could see the Smithsonian National Museum of African American History and Culture looming before them, its multi-tiered, bronze-colored walls reflecting the setting sun.

Devonte's mom excused herself to make a phone call, and Nakia and Devonte stepped off the sidewalk to wait and watch the people queuing up for tours. The museum had been open for months, but there were still lines of people trying to get in. Cars and taxis drove by as commuters made the evening rush out to the suburbs, while tourist buses slowly meandered by in the setting sun.

"We don't have anything like this at home," Nakia whispered. "This is so…cool."

A chirp quietly sounded on Nakia's arm wrap, and she spoke in an unfamiliar language into her wrist as they joined the lines heading into the museum. "The king will be joining us soon. Tell me, Devonte, is there something we should be sure that the king sees before he leaves?"

Devonte had studied the exhibits online for weeks, and he had an entire itinerary ready for his visit. He started to answer when he felt Nakia's hand tighten quickly on his arm.

"Ow," he complained. But Nakia didn't seem to hear him. Her eyes were locked on a white tourist bus that had just pulled up across the street from the museum…

THE EVENING sun reflected off the window, preventing Nakia from seeing anything more than the driver's outline, but something felt wrong. It was a Friday, but she was sure their security brief said buses weren't allowed to unload in front of the museums...

"Move!" Nakia screamed as she threw Devonte to the ground and covered his body with her own. The bus's doors opened, and two men in full ski masks charged out, firing assault rifles into the crowded sidewalks. Pandemonium ensued. The masked men rushed across the street, pushing screaming people aside as they riddled a nearby guardhouse with bullets, killing the unsuspecting man inside.

Across the street, two guards ran out the door of the museum, both holding Uzi submachine guns. There was noise and confusion as people ran for cover inside the museum and ducked behind walls. The guards tried to site the attackers through the crowd. They crossed the lawn, expertly hurdling the people huddled on the ground, but they never had a chance. From 50 yards away, shooters from the bus aimed and fired, smashing out the windows and dropping both guards.

Nakia pushed her young charge as close to the ground as she could. She peered up to see another of the bus's windows smashed out, a shoulder-mounted grenade launcher being prepped on the inside.

"Stay low," she hissed at Devonte. She began to speak into her communicator in Hausa, a language only spoken by the *Dora Milaje* and their king. *"Okoye, keep Beloved away! Several armed men in body armor are attacking the museum from the east."*

Nakia knew that if she did nothing, the boy

might be safe from bullets, but a destroyed building could still fall on their heads. As Devonte squirmed on the ground, Nakia heard screams piercing the air around her as vacationing parents threw themselves down to the ground hoping to shield their children. She saw one mother frantically crouch down behind her child's stroller with a baby in her arms, as if the massive black plastic conveyance was going to provide any protection. Nakia looked again at Devonte, who was old enough to follow instructions to stay down, wasn't he? Someone had to do something, and there was no one there but her. *"I'm about to engage the heavy artillery, located on the east side of 14th Street inside a bus."*

"Nakia, are the boy and his mother okay?" She glanced down at her communicator, surprised to hear the king's voice.

"I have the boy, but I don't have eyes on the mother." Nakia looked around but could not see Wallman among the people covering their heads on the ground. The guards were clearly dead, but as far as she could tell, there were few fatalities among the civilians so far.

"Find her. She and the boy are under my protection. I will take care of the rest." Nakia could hear the soft whine of machinery in the background.

Nakia began to argue. *"Beloved, our first concern is your safety…"*

A silence permeated the line. *"That is an order from your king, Nakia. No harm is to come to the boy*

*and the mother. Use whatever force necessary. Okoye
and I will take care of the rest. On site in five."*

Nakia looked down at her charge. *"Yes, Beloved."*
Switching to English, she nudged the boy underneath
her. "Everything's going to be okay, Devonte. How
are you doing?"

Devonte whimpered slightly, a hint of tears
welling in his eyes. "Where's my mom?"

"We'll find her in a minute. She'll be fine. The
king will handle everything," Nakia hoped she was
telling the truth. She watched the men assemble the
rocket through the bus window.

All of a sudden, screams could be heard from
inside the vehicle, as a black shadow appeared within.
Bodies were flung around, and Nakia could hear
the telltale crunch of bones, followed by unheeded
pleas for mercy. One by one, three men were thrown
from the broken bus window into the street—long,
bleeding scratches across their faces and chests. They
writhed on the street, moaning and holding broken
arms and hands, as their weapons, including the
grenades, followed them out of the bus.

The two gunmen who had killed the security
guard froze and looked back at their comrades in
shock. The bus door slowly opened, and a cowled
man wearing an all-black, tight-fitting bodysuit
gracefully stalked off. The dark, cloth-like armor
rippled around his muscles as it seemed to absorb
the fading light. His hands were gloved in the same
hue, and he flexed metallic claws at the tips of his

fingers. His face was concealed in a catlike helmet with glowing white eyes, leaving no indication of his identity or intention. Silver, metallic lines covered the entire suit, running through the mask, over the chest, and down to the boots, which made no noise as the Black Panther stalked across the street toward his masked prey.

The two remaining gunmen looked at each other, then whipped up their machine guns and fired at the Panther. Sparks shot off the Panther's costume as the bullets fell at his feet, their momentum halted upon contact with his armor. The Panther's cold white eyes turned to the men, and he leaped across the street with effortless grace toward the nearest gunman. Crouching down, the Panther sprung up at the gunman, slamming his fists into the man's chest, knocking the gun free. He raked back down with his claws, shredding the gunman's chest armor, sending blood gushing through the cracks. A black-gloved backhand drew blood from the man's jaw, spun him around, and dropped him to the ground.

THE PANTHER stretched gracefully, looking around for the second gunman. He stepped over the prone body at his feet, sunlight glinting off of his polished black armor, and stole a quick glance at Nakia, still crouched on the ground protectively over Devonte and trying not to bring attention to herself. A quick nod from her assured him of her safety, and he began to scan for the remaining gunman among the screaming and moaning people strewn about the landscape.

A soft growl emerged from his throat as he saw the gunman drag a terrified man to his feet and jam his gun into the back of the man's hair. The Panther took a couple of steps across the street, toward the gunman. The man swung his hostage around between himself and the black-clad hero, attempting to shield himself from the Panther's wrath.

The man moaned, leading the gunman to shake him roughly. Spittle flecked out of his ski mask. "Another step, and he's dead, Cat-man."

The Panther took a couple more steps forward. The gunman jammed the weapon even harder against his hostage's head, pushing the man's head sideways. "I mean it, dammit," the gunman insisted. "You're killing him."

The Panther never stopped, spitting out words in a slightly modulated tone through the helmet. "Kill him, then. You will join him shortly, but your death will not be as quick."

"You won't kill me, hero. Your kind don't do that."

"Your life means nothing to me. I am a king. I can kill you here in the middle of the street and be at home in Wakanda by sunrise."

The gunman shook his hostage. "What about his life?"

With a shrug, the Panther moved forward. "He

is not Wakandan. His life is meaningless as well."

The gunman began to shake as the Panther stalked toward him. Pushing his hostage toward the king, the gunman started to drop his weapon and raise his hands in the air. "I give up, I give up!"

But as soon as the gun cleared the hostage's head, the Panther pounced around the sobbing hostage and landed on the gunman, dragging him to the pavement. Rapid blows to the head stunned the gunman, and a quick swipe across the face left blood dripping through the ski mask. The Panther grabbed the man's head and pounded it into the pavement until he was clearly unconscious.

The Panther stood, cocking his head at the sirens starting to wail in the background. Looking around, he saw Okoye using plastic zip ties to bind the hands of the gunmen left behind in the street. Nakia slowly rose, Devonte clinging to her arm as she moved the terrified boy toward the Panther. The boy's frantic mother rushed across the street, wresting her son from Nakia's care and smothering him in kisses.

The Panther unbolted his helmet, revealing T'Challa's concerned visage. He walked over to the still-sobbing man, knelt down next to him and placed his hand on his shoulder. Traumatized from his brief hostage experience, the man tried to rally himself, wiping his eyes and nose on his garish Hawaiian shirt. He looked up as T'Challa spoke with a kindly voice.

"Are you okay, sir?"

The man nodded a reply. "I-I think so."

T'Challa smiled. "Good. Stay here, someone will be along to take care of you shortly."

T'Challa started to walk away when the man spoke softly, voice betraying a slight Southern twang. "That was a bluff, right? You didn't really mean that you didn't care if I died, did you?"

T'Challa looked at him with a twinkle in his eyes. "What did you think?"

"I thought I was going to die," the man admitted.

"That's why I was successful in saving your life," T'Challa said. "So did your attacker. Now sit still. Help is on the way." As he watched the Americans, Nakia moved over to his side.

"The boy and his mother?" he asked the *Dora Milaje* agent in Hausa. *"They are fine, Beloved."*

Scowling, Okoye walked up behind them. *"Respectfully, Beloved, what passes for American police will be converging on the scene soon, and leaving will become a chore. We should return to the Embassy."*

"Not until we make sure the Wallmans are okay. Gather them and bring them with us. They will be treated with all due hospitality until they are emotionally ready to return to their domicile."

The mother was still sobbing as Okoye hustled her toward the waiting Wakandan limousine. Devonte, however, was in awe as Nakia dragged him toward the car next to the Panther. T'Challa spared a second to smile at the boy before they hustled into the car and headed toward the Wakandan Embassy.

CHAPTER THREE

THE SUN was shining particularly bright this morning, General Willie "Bulldog" Matigan thought as his limousine crossed the 14th Street bridge out of the nation's capital and into Virginia. From his seat, he could see the Washington Monument, the Jefferson Memorial—and there, just ahead, was his new home: the Pentagon.

Glancing up to make sure his driver wasn't looking, Matigan quickly caressed the two stars on his new shoulder straps and smiled to himself. The short, stocky 62-year-old Oklahoman knew he was supposed to act like he wasn't still excited about his promotion. But sometimes, even when he was in public, he just had to stroke his stars, to be sure they were still there. He'd wanted to find a second to do so while in the White House earlier, but there were too many cameras in the well-guarded mansion, and he didn't want the embarrassment of some Secret Service jarhead watching him in the bathroom and wondering what the new co-chair of the Joint Task Force on African Affairs was doing.

The limousine pulled off the highway and eased its way through security. A lowly lieutenant—a bedraggled, limp-haired blond with a chunky, Iowan corn-fed look about her—scrambled up to the door and opened it for him. Matigan stepped out of the limousine and never broke stride, forcing the lieutenant to hustle to catch up. Matigan smiled to himself. His orders were to shake things up, and they'd better learn to move at his speed or get out of his way.

"General," the lieutenant squeaked in a high-pitched voice, struggling to keep up with him and balance the massive notebooks in her arms. "I'm Lieutenant Carla Wilson, your new attaché." Refusing to stop, Matigan waved his identification at a couple of guards, almost losing Wilson again as she reassured the already tense guards and caught back up with her new boss.

Matigan stalked down the massive corridors. "Are they ready for me?" he growled over his shoulder as he neared a pair of oaken double doors.

"Sir?" Wilson tried to maneuver in front of Matigan to steer him farther down the corridor. "Dr. Reece thought it might be best for you to take a few minutes and read the briefing books before joining the meeting."

Matigan stopped, and froze Wilson with a glare. "Are you insinuating, *Lieutenant,* that I am not already prepared for the assignment my president has personally given me?"

The young lieutenant withered under his gaze for a second, and then rallied. Matigan was slightly impressed, knowing that his buzzcut and steely blue glare had intimidated much braver men than this pencil-pushing, horn-rimmed geek. He'd have to find some other way to make her knuckle under.

"No, sir. But after the incident yesterday, Dr. Reece thought—"

"I don't care what Dr. Reece thinks, Lieutenant. If the meeting has started, that's where I need to be. If they knew what they were doing, the president wouldn't have sent me over here."

Smirking, Matigan pushed his way through the double doors into a massive conference room lined with monitors displaying cable news and satellite feeds from around the world. Sitting around the table were men and women from all the different branches of the military, some of whom he recognized. There were a smattering of business-suit-clad men and women sprinkled around the edges of the room, whom he assumed were either intelligence officials or subject-area experts. He felt free to ignore them, since they didn't know the might of the military the way he did.

At the front of the table, a beautiful black woman peered at him over a pair of reading glasses, seemingly annoyed at his interruption. Long black hair with streaks of sliver cascaded down her shoulders and framed her attractive face while contrasting with her white business suit. Matigan smiled to himself. He had bought his stay-at-home wife the same Donna Karan suit the year before. The woman stopped mid-sentence and stared at Matigan as he walked around to take the seat nearest to the head of the table.

Reclining back in the chair, he waved his hand

regally at the woman. "Continue, please."

The woman calmly placed her laser pointer down on the lectern in front of her and stared at him, hands on her hips. "General Matigan, I presume? I'm Donde Reece, civilian chair of this committee. I expected you later today."

Matigan locked gazes with Reece. "I bet you did. But given what happened earlier today, and my brief from the president, I thought it was prudent I give the committee the benefit of my experience in these matters as soon as possible."

"Did you, now?" Reece looked over at Wilson, who shrugged almost imperceptibly. "And you feel you're…up to speed on this area of the world?"

Matigan smiled, chomping down on an unlit cigar as he spoke. Like all other government buildings, the Pentagon was now nonsmoking, a point of contention for some of the older generals.

"Ms. Reece, you'll find that there aren't many problems that can't be solved with the judicious application of American military might. All I need to know is who is causing the problem, how many assets I have under my command, and whether y'all need it to be covert or loud. The name and history of this Podunk little African country doesn't mean a hill of beans to any decision I make here."

"Hmmmm." Reece adjusted her glasses and looked down at Matigan. "General, I feel that you would make a more…worthwhile contribution to this conversation if you availed yourself of the intelligence we've painstakingly gathered on Wakanda. But if you feel you're able to keep up, by all means, feel free to listen in and share any thoughts you might have."

Matigan snorted as Reece turned back to the screen. "And General?" she said over her shoulder. "It's Doctor—not Ms., Mrs., or Miss. My rank was earned as well."

Reece clicked her laser pointer back on and aimed it at the map of Africa on the main screen.

"As I was saying, since Wakanda is centrally situated in a crucial part of the African diaspora, their airspace would be the ideal place for sorties into several terrorist havens on the continent. Ideally, if we could get cooperation from the new Wakandan government or perhaps even establish a joint task force, we could strike a crippling blow against Hydra, Boko Haram, the remnants of Al-Qaida, or any of several other groups we know are trying to set up safe haven in Africa. The fact that King T'Challa is here and was willing to help means there's an opportunity—"

"Excuse me, *Doctor* Reece," Matigan interrupted with a frown. "I know I'm new to this committee and all, but when did the United States of America start *asking* for permission to use an African country's airspace? We should tell them that United States military aircraft will be flying overhead, and that they should stay out of our way. End of story."

Reece sighed. "General, I understand you're trying to impress the president and your bosses. But if you'd read the briefing books, you'd know that you can't treat Wakanda like that. They require a… special touch."

Matigan chuckled and stood up out of his chair. "A special touch? The only thing special they're going to get is the 12-man Special Forces outfit that we're going to use to destabilize and overthrow their government if they don't get out of our way. Am I right, people?"

Matigan looked around the room, expecting nodding heads and laughs. Instead, all he got were frowns on their faces and disapproving murmurs—even from Wilson, who should have known better.

"What?" he said, looking back at Reece. She was shaking her head sadly at him. He glared back at her and looked out across the conference room.

"We're the United States of America, people. We break braggarts and spit steel. No one, and I mean no one, gets in our way for long."

He looked derisively at Reece. "Just because she's soft on her Af-rik-an brethren," he spit out with emphasis, "doesn't mean that we need to tiptoe around them and their grass huts in the name of political correctness and one-worldism." He gave a mock bow toward Reece. "No offense meant, *Doctor.*"

The room went deathly silent. Eventually, Reece cleared her throat and placed her reading glasses on top of the lectern before speaking.

"Everyone, we'll continue this briefing later today at 1600. I'll want plans from your working groups on how to convince King T'Challa of the benefits of working with us or at least turning a blind eye to our operations—or maybe S.H.I.E.L.D.'s. Thank you, thank you all."

Matigan stared as the room quietly began to empty. Even his military friends refused to meet his eyes. He started to turn toward the door when Reece spoke again in a soft voice. "General, would you mind staying behind for a second?"

Reece glanced at the wide-eyed Lt. Wilson, who was hovering nervously at the edge of the room next to a blond, dark-suited man. "Lieutenant, he'll catch up with you down at his office in a few minutes. Go get yourself some coffee and wait. Ross, I'll want you to stay for a few minutes as well."

"Ma'am," Everett Ross nodded, and ushered the almost trembling Wilson out the doors, quickly closing and locking them after pushing the young officer out. Ross, a smirk on his face as he twirled a gold ring on his finger, walked toward Reece and stood at her side as she and Matigan glared at each other.

"Listen here—" Matigan started.

"No, Willie, you listen," Reece interrupted, poking a well-manicured fingernail into Matigan's chest. "You EVER question my loyalty to my country again, and you will find your career in Washington coming to an inglorious ending. You don't know me, you don't know what you're talking about, and you're the type who gets American military operatives killed just to prove a point. And that's what you'd be leading them into in some stupid macho attack against Wakanda."

"Lady, I've commanded troops in Iraq, Afghanistan, Niganda, Sokovia, Carpasia, and hundreds of other off-the-book operations YOU don't have clearance to know about," Matigan huffed. "You're not part of this man's army, so you don't know what we're really capable of. If I say that a couple of American badasses can pop a cap in some no-name African dictator's skull and set up a puppet government in two weeks, then that's what'll happen, diplomacy be damned. And I don't give a damn if you think they're some long-lost cousins of yours. They're not Americans, and we can take them without breaking a sweat."

Ross reclined against a wall. "No, you can't."

Matigan turned on him with a snarl. "Did I ask your opinion, college boy?"

Reece frowned at Matigan. "General, this is Everett K. Ross. He's the State Department's expert on Wakandan affairs, and probably the best-informed person alive about that area of the world. There's no one with more intelligence about Wakanda who isn't living there as a subject of King T'Challa right now. You might want to listen to what he has to say."

"Bulldooky. I make two calls over to Langley, and we'll have someone inside their rickety castle reporting back to us in two weeks."

"It. Can't. Be. Done." Ross spoke slowly, as if he was talking to an infant.

That just made Matigan madder. "Don't contradict your betters, son. You don't know what assets I have at my command."

Ross smirked. "Call Langley and ask them about the package they received from Wakanda two years ago, on July 4th. Somehow, the Wakandans knew exactly how much of whatever knockout juice they use to give those three CIA agents. They woke up and started beating on the crate just as it was being delivered by FedEx through the doors of the CIA's holding facility in Virginia."

A small red scar on top of Matigan's left eye began to throb as he visibly tried to keep himself under control. "Give me a couple of Marines, a few of those crazy boys from Fort Bragg, and a fleet of drones, and we'll bring that postage stamp of a country to its knees in no time."

"It's been tried by the best, General. Did you even glance at the briefing books the White House sent over? I missed a weekend with this beautiful softball coach from Georgetown getting that information together."

Matigan harrumphed, leading to an amused smile from Reece. "Broad-stroke it for our dear general, please."

"Yes, ma'am. You see, General, Wakanda is notable for the simple fact that it has never been conquered in its entire history. Not once. When you consider the history of the region, the fact that the French, the English, the Belgians, and any number of Christian or Islamic invaders were never able to defeat them in battle… Well, it's unprecedented."

Ross looked up at one of the screens, which flickered in and out of focus. Words scrolling across the top of the screen declared "Live feed: Birnin Zana."

"They have a technological superiority that defies explanation. None of our spy satellites seem to be able to get a usable image from inside their borders. So even if we decided to go in with force, we'd have no idea of the terrain, the infrastructure, or the manpower that'd be waiting for us."

"Where'd they get their tech from? Russia? China? Latveria?" Matigan asked.

"I covered this quite extensively in the briefing book, General. No Cold War alliances with either side, and no contemporary alliances with the Arab world, including OPEC. Despite geological estimates that they have large oil deposits, they don't even pump it."

"One of the Roxxon boys mentioned that this morning," Matigan said thoughtfully.

"What the hell are Roxxon reps doing in a White House briefing?" Reece glared at Matigan, who had the courtesy to look sheepish for a second.

"Never mind. Continue, Ross."

"Wakanda doesn't need the oil as an energy source, or what could be billions in revenue as a financial base. They have a variety of eco-friendly alternative power sources like solar and hydrogen.

They've turned away every overture from every oil company in the world."

"That's just un-American," Matigan muttered.

Ross quirked an eyebrow at him. "They're not American. They're Wakandan, and that's what matters. They reason differently; they have a different religion and a different history from the rest of the world, and a warrior spirit that even some of the world's most vicious martial cultures fear."

"What does this have to do with the price of tea in China, Ross?" Matigan snorted. "Once again, with the right 12-man black-ops squad…"

Ross sighed. "I cannot emphasize how stupid an idea that is, General. America has sent its best to Wakanda before, and come up short."

Matigan thrust his finger into Ross's face, turning bright red. "A pencil-neck geek like you wouldn't know America's best if he came up to you and slapped the spit out of your mouth."

Anger flickered in Ross's eyes for a second, but he retreated to pick up a leather briefcase from the corner of the room. Pressing his thumbprint on a security lock, he shuffled some papers around before pulling out a USB thumb drive and walking back toward Reece.

"Doctor, if I may?"

She hesitated slightly before smiling at Ross. "I think we're stuck with Willie here for a while. Might as well open his eyes to reality." She turned back to Matigan. "You understand that the information you're about to see is classified Top-secret Q Level?"

"I'm on the National Security Council, Doctor." Matigan sputtered. "There's nothing on God's green earth I'm not authorized to see."

"You think so?" she said as Ross stifled a laugh. "I do love it when they send us newbies, Everett. General, you even think about talking about what I'm going to show you, and you'll not only find yourself demoted, but also likely manning a radar tower in Alaska somewhere by the end of the week. Understand?"

Matigan watched as Reece placed her thumb in an indentation on the flash drive. It hummed, and when it glowed green, Reece walked over to a computer bank and plugged it in. Mousing around one of the larger screens in the room, Reece clicked on a video file and called up what looked like a colorized digital film of a silent jungle clearing. A camera apparently had been set up in a tree, looking down with a wide-angled shot of swaying brownish-green grass

She nodded at Ross, who began to narrate as a clock started counting down in the screen's top-left corner. "The Wakandans shared this with us during one of the more…tense periods in our relationship. This was shot during World War II."

Matigan snorted. "No one had color-film technology that good back then. Even our best stuff was in black-and-white."

Reece shook her head, her long hair forming a

dark halo. "The Wakandans already had color-film technology and were working on digital. But that's not what's important, General. Keep watching."

The clearing stayed silent for a few seconds more. Then, at the edge of the dense underbrush, a triangular shield with a familiar red-white-and-blue motif slowly emerged. The camera slowly zoomed in as the Sentinel of Liberty crept out of the bush, apparently unaware that he was being watched. An extremely young Captain America, his shiny new duralumin scale uniform perfectly matching his shield, hesitated for a moment before waving for someone to follow. A couple of green-helmeted soldiers slowly crept into the clearing with Cap. They were heavily armed with M2s and grenades, and they hauled heavy rucksacks. The three men hesitated, then knelt down to begin consulting a map.

Ross narrated as they watched the men pore over the map. "On one of his very first missions, Captain America was sent into Wakanda to track down and capture a special Nazi science unit. Allied military intelligence believed this unit was attempting to infiltrate the country and exploit one of the most promising caches of scientific weaponry on the planet. We couldn't let the Nazis get their hands on it, so we sent our best to get there first—or, failing that, to covertly take the Nazis out before they could cause any damage."

Matigan relaxed. "I love watching old footage of Cap kicking ass. That's what a real American son looks like, boys and girls."

Reece cocked an eyebrow at the general. "I could tell you things about the Super-Soldier program that produced Steve Rogers that would change your mind about its 'American-ness,' General. But we'll save that for another time and watch the 'ass-kicking,' shall we call it. Mr. Ross?"

"Yes, ma'am. You see, what Cap didn't know was that the Wakandans caught and beheaded the Nazi invaders within 12 hours of them crossing their border. And the American attempt to covertly 'assist' the Wakandans was considered an invasion as well."

On the screen, the jungle clearing was suddenly filled with Wakandan soldiers. They surrounded Captain America with what looked to be grass shields and spears humming with some unknown type of energy. Cap slowly stood and raised his hands above his head, waving for the other soldiers to do the same. One seemed unwilling, and began to reach for his weapon. A Wakandan soldier made a gesture, and an electronic current warped from the metal tip of his spear to the soldier, causing the man to freeze, jerk, and collapse to the ground.

"Holy crap, was that a taser? In 1941?"

"Something like that, sir," Ross said calmly.

They watched Captain America ignore shouts from the Wakandan troops, dropping down to his knee to check on the soldier. Cap felt for a pulse; when the man stirred, the American Super-Soldier stood again and began shouting at the assembled Wakandans.

"The sound quality's piss-poor, but the captain's report said he was trying to explain to them that they were only there to help, and that his man needed medical attention. The on-site Wakandan commander is telling him that they're not going anywhere until their king arrives. Cap's not going to take that well."

Cap and the Wakandan commander continued to shout at each other. Then, almost faster than the camera could follow, Captain America slugged the African soldier, grabbed his uniform by the lapels, and swung him around between himself and the surrounding soldiers in a massive headlock.

"As you can see, General, by slowly turning him in a circle, Cap used the soldier as a shield in the front while using the *actual* shield on his back as protection. It was a standoff."

"A standoff, my ass." Matigan growled at Ross. "I've seen Cap take on worse odds than that and come out on top."

Reece interrupted before Ross could retort. "Be that as it may, here's the important part. As far as we know, this is the first known footage of the Black Panther in action."

The Wakandan soldiers parted quickly and dropped to one knee. The Panther strode confidently up to the clearing, bare-chested, with a full-face cat mask, black tights, and a black cape billowing behind him. Captain America and the Panther gestured toward each other, an intense conversation going on outside the range of the camera's microphone.

Ross narrated again. "Cap is telling him that his man needs medical attention, and the Panther is explaining that the penalty for invading Wakanda is death. But they're going to come to an agreement."

On screen, Cap pushed the captive Wakandan toward the Panther. The commander immediately dropped to one knee before the Panther, who placed a hand on his head and dismissed him with a whisper. The Panther took off his billowing black cloak and began to stretch cat-like in the clearing as Captain America did the same on the other side.

"Cap later told us what the Panther had said. If Cap agreed to face him in one-on-one combat, he would give Cap's compatriots medical attention and an escort to the border. If Cap won, he could go as well. If he lost, well, the penalty for invasion was death."

The two men bowed. Then, at some unknown signal, they charged at each other. Captain America swung a powerful haymaker at the Panther, who lithely dodged it and kicked at the American's head. His heel missed by less than an inch. Cap's frantic duck below the kick allowed him to swipe his leg toward the Panther's legs. A high leap by the Panther followed, and the impact of his feet against Captain America's shield knocked the hero back on his heels. A backflip, and the Panther brought his fists toward Cap's head again, only to be blocked by the triangular shield again. Sparks flickered from the shield as the Panther raked it with his claws in an attempt to pull it away, but Cap held on tight.

Again, at some unknown signal, the two men broke away from each other and began to circle. The cheering Wakandans formed a human ring.

"Cap later said that he'd never fought anyone as fast and dangerous as the Panther," Reece said admiringly. Matigan glared at her and was about to speak, when the two men locked grips again.

Cap feinted left and suddenly charged at the Panther, clearly hoping to use his greater size to overwhelm the slimmer man. The Panther flipped over the charging Captain America, using the man's momentum to push him into the surrounding soldiers, who shoved him back into the ring. Cap charged again, shield first—but this time, the Panther stood firm and waited. Just before impact, the Panther slid down and twisted himself between Cap's legs, tripping the red-white-and-blue-clad soldier into the ground. When Cap hit the dirt, the Panther pounced, driving both of his knees into the star on Cap's back and striking at the unprotected back of his head.

The Panther continued to press his advantage, striking again and again as Captain America struggled to flip over and get back to his feet, swinging his shield wildly to regain the fight's momentum. But a simple feint to the side left Cap's midsection open, and the Panther drove both fists into Captain America's sternum, doubling the man over and leaving him open for a fist to the jaw that dropped him to the ground.

Ross, Reece, and Matigan watched as the Panther stood above Captain America silently, seemingly not even breathing hard. Then, with a gesture, he sent medics running toward the injured American soldier. The unhurt soldier was hustled away with his injured friend. The Panther lifted Captain America, shield and all, like a child, slung him over his shoulder, and walked out of camera range back into the jungle, his cheering soldiers following. A few seconds later, the video file ended.

Matigan stood silently for a minute, then cleared his throat. "Obviously, the Black Panther didn't kill Cap. What happened?"

"A few days later, Captain America and the two soldiers showed up in a private luxury plane from Wakanda with the very first shipment of Vibranium for the American government. Apparently, Cap impressed the Panther." Ross shrugged. "While he couldn't convince them to join the Allied effort, or share the bulk of their technology, the Wakandans signed a nonaggression treaty with the United States and agreed to let our scientists examine the rare metal found in their country that's the source of much of their tech. Cap's circular shield, the one he carries nowadays? That's a Vibranium alloy made from that very first shipment."

Matigan dropped into one of the leather-bound chairs. "That was World War II, Ross. We're much more badass than we were back then."

"Yes, General—and so is Wakanda. According

to Cap, the Panther he faced was named Chanda. The current Panther is T'Challa, his grandson. And as you can see from today's footage, he's just as much of a fighter as his grandfather. But unlike his grandfather, T'Challa's spent extensive time outside of Wakanda, so we know a little more about him than we did about his father or grandfather."

Ross pulled a file out of his briefcase and slid it across the table at Matigan. "I had Dr. Richards over at the Baxter Building do a profile of T'Challa for us, since they seem to be friends."

Matigan began flipping through the pages, but slammed shut the folder in frustration. "I don't have time for this, Ross. Give me the bullet."

Ross sighed again. "No one reads anymore. General, T'Challa is apparently the ultimate in brains and brawn. Richards thinks he's a polymath with an eidetic memory, putting him in rare company on this planet. In fact, Richards feels T'Challa's on par or maybe even smarter in some ways than Anthony Stark, Victor Von Doom, even Bruce Banner. And he could take them all in unarmed, or maybe even armed, combat.

"For about 10 years, then Crown Prince T'Challa dropped off the radar. Oh, he'd appear at royal functions and international soirees, but what was he doing with the rest of his time? It took the CIA forever to figure out where he was. During that time, a 'Luke Charles' earned master's degrees in science, physics, and international politics from colleges around the world, including here in the United States. We even think he took a couple of summers off to teach high school in Harlem. The last thing we were able to find out about was his PhD in physics from Oxford University, which he earned before heading back to Wakanda to take the throne."

"So he's an egghead, too," Matigan sneered. "Then he should know better than to prance around in dancing tights."

"You just don't get it." Ross's voice lost its mocking tone and became flat, devoid of emotion. "Those aren't tights or a super-hero costume. As chieftain of the Wakandan Panther Clan, T'Challa's panther habit is ceremonial regalia that marks him as the leader of his country and head of their religion. In fact, the best way to think of him is as something like a cross between the president, the pope, and the chairman of the Joint Chiefs of Staff."

"So," Matigan interrupted, "if we can get that costume off him and on someone else, they'll be leader of the Wakandans?"

"Black Panther is a hereditary title, but it still has to be earned. There's a series of tests that are so arduous, only candidates who have had special training since childhood can survive them. But just so everyone has a chance, we've heard that the Panther, once a year, allows Wakandans to challenge him in personal combat for the right to the throne."

Ross smiled, watching the wheels turn in the

general's head. "It's been tried, General. T'Challa and his ancestors have won every single year, going back centuries. Short of nuking them, and I wouldn't put it beyond T'Challa to have defenses prepared for that, our best option is to talk to them. Negotiate with them as equals."

Matigan frowned, and stood again to start pacing around the room. "So what we have here is a pagan, militaristic country with unknown technological capacity. Basically, a rogue state."

Ross looked over at Reece before continuing. "Well, General, before you go declaring them a member of the Axis of Evil, keep in mind they've never invaded another country. They only take hostile action when defending their own borders."

"You just said that a member of their royal family was an illegal immigrant in this country, didn't you? And I can't believe that he came alone, so you have members of a foreign government in disguise on American shores. Sounds like a possible terrorist threat to me."

Reece glanced at Ross before taking command of the conversation again. "I think we're getting a little ahead of ourselves here. King T'Challa is a guest of the United States right now, and we have an unprecedented opportunity to improve relations between our two countries through negotiations. We need their airspace. We just have to find out what they need from us."

Matigan began to throw papers into his attaché

case. "A regime change would eliminate any need for negotiation. I think I know what the president would say if we brought our options to him. But anyway, Doctor, isn't it standard operating procedure to have a military option in place for any potential threat to the United States?"

Reece hesitated, bringing a smile to Matigan's face. "And do you have a military option in place?" he continued. "If I'm not mistaken, isn't our brief to be prepared for any situation, whether far-fetched or not?"

Reece shook her head. "Wakanda is not an imminent threat to the United States, General. I'm afraid any raised posture would be taken as a hostile act by a country that should be an ally to our interests."

Matigan smirked. "Keep in mind, Doctor, I'm the military liason on this task force, not you. You advise on political tactics, I advise on military tactics, and the White House decides which one they prefer. Since you failed to have a military option ready, that's what I want presented at the 1600 briefing. Get some of the nerds around here on it. And feel free to bring in some of the people from Military Sci-Ops. I don't care what it takes, we need to be able to bring Wakanda down if we have to."

Matigan looked over at Ross as the general walked toward the doors. "You've convinced me, Mr. Ross. This conflict isn't appropriate for conventional troops. This is a job for special forces. Very special forces..." With that, the general walked out and slammed the door behind him.

Reece sighed. "He's going to be trouble, isn't he?"

CHAPTER FOUR

AT DUSK, a crowd began to gather at the outskirts of the royal palace in Wakanda. No one had announced that T'Challa's royal Quinjet would be landing soon, but somehow, word had spread throughout Wakanda's capital city.

From the window of his aircraft, T'Challa shook his head as he saw the thousands of cheering people waiting for him to land. The Quinjet settled down softly on the outskirts of the royal palace, and was greeted with a roar from the gathered Wakandans, who waited to see their young king disembark from his first successful trip abroad as ruler of their kingdom.

"How did they know?" T'Challa mock scowled in Hausa, the *Dora Milaje*'s native tongue. Across the cabin, Nakia tried to look innocent.

"They missed you, Beloved." Nakia couldn't hide the twinkle in her eyes as she lowered the Quinjet's hatch and peered out. She and Okoye had changed into the *Dora Milaje*'s traditional light armor, short-handled swords and long barreled rifles slung across their backs. Okoye still sported the red sunglasses she had become enamored with from one of the embassy's staff members.

They still spoke Hausa, knowing the pilot could

overhear their every word. *"It has been a long time since the Black Panther prowled outside of the kingdom's borders, and…so publicly. I suspect they were worried about you,"* Nakia continued.

"As were we, Beloved." Okoye spoke for the first time. *"Jumping into a firefight on foreign soil may not have been the best idea for the king of Wakanda, especially after ordering his bodyguards to protect someone other than His Royal Highness."*

"Do you think I was ever in any danger?" T'Challa sat back in his chair, frowning at the *Dora Milaje.* *"Did you think for one second I needed assistance in that situation?"*

The two women looked at each other for a second. *"No, Beloved,"* Okoye said quietly.

"No, I did not. I put you to the most important use I had for you, ensuring that the Wallmans, who had been honored by the representative of the Panther God, were not harmed. Are you questioning my decision?"

Nakia was about to speak when a look from Okoye quieted her. *"Of course not, Beloved,"* Okoye said instead.

T'Challa tugged down his business jacket and disembarked to a roar from the crowd.

"Next time, Nakia, you might want to consider the security repercussions of leaking the king's whereabouts, especially considering the Americans' reaction to the king's assistance," Okoye snarled at the younger woman quietly as they disembarked behind the king, who waved at the crowd.

"Our king is cherished by all of his people," Nakia whispered back as they scanned for threats in the crowd. *"Especially after time in a divided country like America, I thought it would be appropriate to remind him of that. And that's not what you're mad about."*

"We'll talk about that later," Okoye hissed.

Throngs of Wakandans cheered as T'Challa wandered through the crowd. He whispered blessings to children, placed his hand on the tops of the heads of those who kneeled, and shook hands with those who pressed forward in an attempt to touch his suit.

"Panther God! Panther God!" the crowd chanted in Wakandan. As T'Challa made his way toward the palace garden, a small girl rushed forward with flowers. The *Dora Milaje* gave worried glances, but a slight wave of T'Challa's hand put them at ease.

"Did you pick these, my child?" T'Challa asked, turning and examining the bouquet of African violets. "They're lovely."

"Thank you, Panther God," the child whispered, eyes locked steadfastly on the ground in fear.

T'Challa reached down and placed his hand under the girl's chin, and directed her eyes upward until they were locked with his own. "I am not a god, my daughter. I am just a man like any other who speaks for the Panther God. I breathe, I cry, I sleep—just as you do."

The fear in the girl's eyes never diminished as she stumbled to find words. Finally she mouthed, "Yes, Panther God."

T'Challa sighed, and waved the girl back toward her waiting parents.

"She will talk about the day she was blessed by the Panther God for the rest of her life," Nakia whispered to the king as she and Okoye escorted him into the interior palace grounds and away from the crowd.

Standing outside the master bedroom, next to a massive ebony panther totem that signified the traditional entrance to the Panther's personal suite, were two women in flowing Kente-cloth dresses. The older woman walked toward T'Challa with restraint and confident grace, her long gray hair blowing in the slight breeze. The younger one's short-cropped hair was held in place by a small silver tiara. She walked with the same confidence as T'Challa, but with her beauty as armor and the swagger of untested youth.

"Mother! Shuri! I didn't expect you to greet me so quickly." T'Challa swept up the Queen Mother in his arms and hugged her tightly. He then tried to give a playful shove to Shuri, who laughingly dodged and punched him on the arm.

"What did you expect after we saw you prancing about, dodging bullets in the United States?" Shuri laughed. "I almost started measuring the throne room for new drapes."

Queen Mother Ramonda glared at her daughter. "Shuri! That is not funny. T'Challa could have been seriously hurt." She looked over his shoulder at the trailing Nakia and Okoye. "And where exactly were the *Dora Milaje* while their new king was facing a hailstorm of bullets?"

Nakia looked down at the ground, while Okoye remained impassive. T'Challa glanced at them over his shoulder for a second before turning back to his mother.

"They were doing as I ordered, but that is a conversation for later, Mother. I need to get changed and prepare for the debriefing of the security council. Are you available for dinner after the council meeting?"

"Of course," Ramonda looked at Shuri. "And you, my daughter. Are you available tonight?"

"Well, I suppose I could make myself available," Shuri huffed. "It's not like I'm busy with my seat on the ruling council."

Ramonda groaned as T'Challa grinned at this familiar argument. "Not this again. Your seat will be waiting for you when you come of age. You're only 19."

"T'Challa got his seat before then, even before anyone knew for sure he would receive the blessing of the Panther God," Shuri pointed out, studiously avoiding her brother's smirk.

"I was the eldest son of the deceased king," T'Challa said. "Wakanda needed continuity after Father's death. You know this." "What I know is—" Shuri began, before being shushed by her mother.

"That is enough, Shuri! Let your brother shower and change, and we can rehash all of these old arguments later tonight. Nakia, Okoye, we will walk you to your sisters."

Seeing their replacements securely in place at T'Challa's door, the four women started off down the corridor in silence to the *Dora Milaje*'s wing of the royal palace. Nakia looked over at Okoye as they walked, hoping to catch her eye for a signal of what was going to happen, but her partner kept a stoic face as they walked down the ornate halls behind the two royal figures. Her expression matched that of Ramonda, who also kept her face blank. Shuri paid no attention to any of them, scrolling furiously on her wafer-thin Kimoyo card, oblivious to the waves of unspoken anger rolling off her mother.

Finally, Ramonda stopped them, glaring furiously at her son's bodyguards. "Tell me how the *Dora Milaje* allowed the king, my only son, to endanger himself in a street brawl in America," she hissed at the two women, startling Shuri.

"Your Majesty…" Nakia started, but halted at Okoye's raised hand.

"The king ordered us to stand down," Okoye said calmly. "Even with that order, he was never in any danger."

"Because of his skills, or yours?" Ramonda retorted. "The *Dora Milaje* was founded—"

"We do not need you to tell us about our history," Okoye interrupted though gritted teeth.

"Or your failures?" Ramonda looked Okoye in the eyes, daring her to continue.

Open-mouthed, Shuri watched the two women glare at each other. Then Okoye dropped her eyes and took a step back. Nakia stepped up and inserted herself between the two women.

"No, you don't, your majesty," Nakia said.

Ramonda took a deep breath and composed herself.

"I wanted to have this conversation out of range of T'Challa's extraordinary hearing. The council is very disappointed in the actions of the *Dora Milaje*. They, and I, are concerned that the king may continue to throw himself into these situations, and the *Dora Milaje* will not be able to insert themselves between the king and those who would harm him."

Ramonda looked over at Shuri, who was still wide-eyed. "I understand the need for the *Dora Milaje*, and the perilous position your potential dismissal would leave this country in. I know I am not one of you, but I want to make certain that the *Dora Milaje* maintain some connection with the royal family. Therefore, I want Shuri to begin training with you to ensure she keeps her fighting edge, and to cement the *Dora Milaje*'s relationship with the royal family."

Okoye was almost trembling with anger, and had to fight to regain control before speaking. "Has this decision been made? What does the king have to say?"

Ramonda studied the tall woman. "He…has not ruled yet. And I have yet to speak to your elders about Shuri's training."

Nakia reached up and placed a hand on Okoye's shoulder, calming her partner. "Thank you, your majesty, for bringing this to our attention," she said quietly. "We will discuss this with our sisters, and bring back a plan of action for your and Shuri's approval."

"Thank you, Nakia. We will speak of this again. Come, Shuri." Ramonda started off down the hallway, a stunned Shuri trailing behind her.

Okoye stared after them, while Nakia drew a deep breath. *"Come, sister, we have plans to make."*

Nakia took Okoye by the hand and walked up to a set of double doors that led to their dormitory in the palace. *"The elders must be informed, and we will have to make our report."*

"They will blame us, sister." Okoye warned.

Nakia shrugged. *"We will walk into the fire together, then, and die fighting like true* Dora Milaje. *No fear, sister."*

A grim smile spread over Okoye's face. *"Sometimes I forget why I put up with you, little sister. And sometimes I remember."*

Nakia grinned. *"We never surrender, big sister. And we won't now, either."*

T'CHALLA reclined on his chair and looked around the council room at his closest advisors, seeing grim determination on their faces. Sitting at the head of a v-shaped table, with two armed *Dora Milaje* at his back, T'Challa easily commanded the attention of those present. But his last words made everyone in the room uncomfortable—even Queen Mother Ramonda, who sat immediately at his right.

"The president was…indisposed for our scheduled meeting at the White House, and offered a meeting with his vice president," T'Challa said calmly. "We declined, and returned to the embassy. Further contact will be at ambassador level."

The men and women around the table began whispering among themselves. "My king, forgive me," one of the councilors said, wringing her hands. "But Ambassador Abayomi has worked for years cultivating conservative politicians to get that meeting inside the White House for Wakanda."

A grizzled bear of an old man adorned in gold, leaning on a staff, looked across the table at the woman and snorted. "The king is correct. The Black Panther does not meet with underlings," he proclaimed.

"Still, your highness, increased contact with the outside world is an idea you have pushed as crown prince for years. This was a good chance to assert to the world Wakanda's place in the hierarchy of nations."

The old man shook his head. "The world only needs to know that Wakanda will not be insulted, disrespected, or intimidated by anyone. Meeting with a vice president does none of those things."

T'Challa sat silently as his ministers argued

around the table. Ramonda was also quiet, keeping her eyes on her son. T'Challa shifted in his seat, and the room soon quieted.

"I will make myself available to the president if he wants to meet," T'Challa said quietly. "Otherwise, our capable diplomats can handle negotiations between Wakanda and the United States."

Ramonda looked at T'Challa with barely disguised impatience. "Any idea whether the cancellation was meant as an insult, or was truly unavoidable?"

One of the men sitting near the end of the table leaned forward. "Perhaps your interference in their domestic law-enforcement procedures had something to do with it," he suggested.

The room went silent.

"What do you mean, General H'llah?" T'Challa never moved, but his eyes went cold.

H'llah squirmed in his seat. "I beg your forgiveness, my king. But we have talked around it this entire meeting, and it is time we get to the heart of things. The Black Panther is the heart and soul of Wakanda. *Wakanda,* my king, not America. You risked everything we are in a battle that meant nothing to our people."

H'llah sat back, studiously avoiding T'Challa's eyes. Looking around the room, the king saw the same question repeated in the others' eyes.

T'Challa leaned forward and strummed his fingers on the onyx-colored table. "When I pray to the Panther God, I pray for the wisdom to lead our people. I pray for the courage to do what needs to be done. I pray for my people to be prosperous and happy."

He stood, and something stirred behind his eyes.

"I do not pray for cowardice, or self-preservation. I do not ask the Panther God to sacrifice the innocent for my sake, or even for the sake of Wakanda. I do not ask for our nation to lose its honor again as we stand by and protect ourselves while our brothers and sisters are sold, kept in bondage, raped, beaten, or repressed.

"We will no longer cower behind our walls. We will not be bowed. We will stride boldly out into the world and declare that we are Wakandans. If anyone disagrees, I thank you for your service and expect your resignation on my desk."

T'Challa stalked around the room, staring at each of his ministers in turn. When he caught Ramonda's eyes, he could see the pride hidden behind her stern expression.

T'Challa returned to his seat, and looked over at the tall grizzled man who sat quietly in the corner of the room. "W'Kabi. You served under my father as his war counsel. You shall be my regent when I leave the Golden City, which will be as infrequently as possible."

T'Challa pointed at Ramonda. "My mother speaks with my voice until my sister comes of age and takes her place on the ruling council. This gives

Wakanda continuity if something happens to me. But I will not sit idly by and dishonor she whom we serve by preserving my own life instead of working to serve all mankind. Is that clear?"

The ministers murmured their agreement.

T'Challa smiled. "Good. Next order of business?"

WAKANDA is a clear and present danger to American interests," a red-haired man hissed, slamming his fists down on the expensive cherry table.

Matigan sighed and looked around the boardroom. From his vantage point, he could clearly see the White House through the floor-length windows at the other end of the room. He almost laughed aloud. That drafty museum was merely a symbol of American strength, while the true power in this country was sitting around this table with him.

He knew most of the faces looking back at him, having served with some in the military and others on the president's campaign. Honestly, he despised most of them, but they were friends of the president so he tolerated their presence. Some of them were captains of industry, while others were spooks in suits.

He hadn't bothered to commit their names to memory, just as they wouldn't have bothered with his. But they all knew why they were there. Matigan turned back as the redheaded man continued his frothing condemnation of everything Wakandan.

"Those, those Africans…they don't tell us how to fight the war on terror," he snarled.

"And we're not letting them," Matigan said patiently. "Our forces are more than capable of waging war with or without the Wakandans' help. But honestly, we'll save more of our boys' lives by working through Wakandan airspace."

"Then let's announce that we've discovered a terrorist camp on site, gravity-bomb the heck out of them, and build the forward operating base from there," the redheaded man said, smiling. "That's what we do best."

"Now hold on," a gray-haired man drawled. "Let's not get too trigger-happy here. There's some… stuff we'd like to acquire before the walls come tumbling down."

"Getting your greasy hands on their Vibranium is not the goal here," Matigan leaned forward with his brow furrowed. "Our goal is the security of our country."

"And our goal is the security of our bottom line." The man's Texas drawl made his laugh sound drawn out and brittle. "But it seems as if our aims are similar here. You can get what you want at the same time that we get what we want. We just need to be… smart about it."

"What do you mean?" Matigan hated smug storytellers like Saunderson, who leveraged every bit of information they could for their own benefit.

"We're not looking at any immediate need for action, are we? We can play the long game." Saunderson looked around the room, eyes finally focusing on a quiet man sitting at the edge of the table, his posture screaming nonchalance as he chewed on a toothpick. "Destabilization, destruction. That's what YOU do best, right?"

The toothpick flicked around the man's mouth for a minute. "This can't be an in-house job. Technically, they are still an ally, and any mistakes would lead to months of nosy congressmen poking around in things that don't concern them. I'm thinking we may need some foreign talent on this one."

The redheaded man adjusted his glasses. "I haven't been impressed with your choices so far. Or did I miss the fact that we're in charge of Latveria now?"

The toothpick moved even faster. "Some nuts are harder to crack than others, I will admit. But the man I have in mind is a professional, and has experience dealing with the royals of Wakanda. As long as we can afford him, that is."

Sauderson snorted. "Whatever he costs, we'll make 100 times that if we can get our hands on Wakandan technology. Make the call."

CHAPTER FIVE

T'CHALLA smiled to himself, listening to the *ooos* and *ahhhs* as he somersaulted over the royal gymnasium's pommel horse with one hand, not missing a beat. Children brought in to tour the royal palace were told that the viewing booth was soundproofed, so they wouldn't be disturbing the king during his twice-daily exercise period. They were told to feel free to cheer or applaud the outstanding movements they would see. However, no one knew that T'Challa's keen ears could hear right through standard soundproofing—so, for years, he had privately enjoyed the adulation of his viewers. It was one of the few times he unabashedly indulged in the admiration of his subjects without the embarrassment that always ruined it for him in public. And he could allow himself to show off a little, he thought, just for the children.

The cavernous gym had all the normal exercise equipment—speed bags, treadmills, and free weights —as well as gymnastic accoutrements like Olympic-class balance beams, tumbling mats, parallel bars, and midair rings. But people were always most impressed when he headed up top to what he privately called the Iron Jungle: a ceiling-mounted set of rings, poles, and platforms. There he could really stretch out his muscles and test his specialized Panther training.

Uncle S'Yan had been after him lately to put safety nets under the jungle, just in case, but T'Challa believed the slight hint of danger kept his instincts sharp. Plus, he thought—as he vaulted from platform to platform, and easily flipped through a web of protruding poles—this had to look really cool to anyone watching.

A few minutes later, after giving a slight wave to the awestruck children, T'Challa lazily dropped down to the mat on the floor and began an intricate set of cool-down stretches while scrolling though palace business on a holopad screen. He had just agreed to a proposal for a new dam outside of Serpant Valley when Shuri wandered into the gym, tapping on her own screen and sipping on a bottled water. Dressed in black workout gear similar to his, she ignored T'Challa and began her own stretching regimen. T'Challa grinned, knowing their familiar routine.

"Morning, Shuri-bear," he teased.

"Whatever, kitty-cat," she groused, bending backwards in an arch to delicately place her hands on the floor. The two kept stretching silently for a minute until Shuri dropped to the floor in a huff. Always a good judge of his sister's moods, T'Challa dropped down at her side and let her put her head on his shoulder. After a few minutes, Shuri giggled.

"Stinky," she teased.

T'Challa laughed. "That's because one of us has done our exercises, while the other one was a lazy slug-about this morning." He nudged his sister slightly with his hip. "Now, tell me what's wrong."

Shuri sighed. "Mom doesn't trust me. She wants me to train with your future baby mommas now. Thinks it'll give me structure."

"Be sure they NEVER hear you calling them that, or the structure they'll give you will include a place six feet under." T'Challa began massaging his sister's shoulders, working out the tensions that radiated off her like body heat. "Our mother wants what's best for you, and we should respect her wisdom."

"She wants what's best for *you*, T'Challa," Shuri grumped. "And she's not even your birth mother. I'm supposed to be her favorite, not her stepson."

T'Challa stood up gracefully and threw a towel over his shoulder. "She loves us both, Shuri-bear. But I am the king. And if you'd like, I can make your training a royal order instead of a mother's request."

Shuri squinted up at him. "This…was your idea, wasn't it?"

T'Challa looked up at the now empty viewing platform. "I've been considering a change for the *Dora Milaje*, a new role in which they can serve. Them getting used to you being around is the first step."

Shuri raised her eyebrows. "Seriously? You're thinking about taking their guardian roles away from them? Or disbanding them completely?"

"The *Dora Milaje* have kept the peace in Wakanda for years. I would not interfere with such noble tradition lightly." T'Challa flexed his arms and looked back at

Shuri with a serious expression. "But with the blessings of the Panther God, do I really need the protection of mortal women, even those as extensively trained as they? Might they not be of better use somewhere else?"

"You're not thinking of sending them back home?" Shuri gasped.

"The *Dora Milaje* was formed from the 18 tribes of Wakanda, to ensure that each tribe had an equal chance of providing a suitable bride to the king. Their more martial pursuits came later. But only one *Dora Milaje* has become a bride of the Panther in decades."

"Your mother," Shuri whispered.

"Perhaps it's time we faced facts. The *Dora Milaje*'s time in service to the king has passed. Mayhap they can find a new place in the sun, and perhaps their princess can help them find their way." T'Challa smiled down at her and turned away.

"You know, I could have been the Panther. If things had been a little different." Shuri stood up and watched T'Challa head for the shower. "And I just may challenge you in the tournament next year."

T'Challa turned in the doorway. "Just remember I have full confidence in you, sister. As does our mother. Remember that."

He disappeared through the door.

A SPEAKER posted on the nondescript office door crackled slightly. "May we help you, sir?" a female voice announced.

The tall man, wearing a brown trenchcoat and hat, never stopped smiling, even as he spoke softly into the speaker's microphone. "Tell Friedman that Ulysses Klaw is here, as agreed."

The camera focused on his face for a moment before the doors slowly swung open, leading into an anteroom. Klaw walked through and down the hallway to an office, where a toothpick-wielding man was lounging behind a large oak desk. He gazed out over the parking lot, his cowboy boots propped up on the windowsill.

"Klaw," the man said without turning around.

"Friedman," Klaw said, pulling a chair up to the desk. "You have something for me?"

Friedman swung around in his chair and looked Klaw up and down. "No small talk? No, 'How are you doing?' Just down to business, huh?"

"Travel across international borders isn't the easiest for me these days, as you well know," Klaw groused. "Let's just get to it and let me get back home."

The man opened the desk's top drawer, pulled out a manila folder, and slid it across the desk. Klaw caught it, pulled out a handful of photos, and spread them across the desk. Klaw picked up one of the photos, a black-and-white shot of T'Challa in his Black Panther armor on the streets of D.C., and held it up to the light.

"I figured you would jump at a chance to kill two birds with one stone," Friedman smirked.

Klaw studied the photo for a moment more

before looking back at the grinning Friedman. "Why do you care about Wakanda? I'm not saying I wouldn't love a chance to take a shot at him, but why does America care?"

"Uh-uh." Friedman waggled a finger at Klaw. "You know that's against the rules. I give you the target, you get the money, and then we go our separate ways."

Klaw leaned back in his chair. "I'm not saying this can't be done, but it won't be a one-person job, you know. I'll need some backup."

"The great Klaw can't get it done alone?" Friedman laughed. "Maybe I have the wrong cleaner for this job."

Klaw leaned forward, hands gripping the lip of the desk. "I'm the only person alive who can accomplish the task, as you well know since I'm sitting here. But I'm not stupid enough to take on the Black Panther and those damnable women alone. We'll need some specialized mercenaries, the kind that would be easier for you to recruit than me. Is this agreeable?"

Friedman shrugged. "Feel free to spend your fee however you like. I just need it done. However, there are some people I can put you in contact with. Give me a couple of days."

Klaw nodded, and stuffed the picture of T'Challa in his coat pocket. "The usual accounts?"

"Of course. Half up front, and the rest upon completion." For the first time, Friedman looked serious. "There are some heavy hitters in the private sector who would love to contract with you if you pull this off. Realistically, what are our chances of success?"

"Pretty good. I've got...experience in dealing with the Panthers." As Klaw raised his right hand and flexed his fingers, a small mechanical whir emanated from them.

"Make sure you leave something standing," Friedman said. "There's some valuable technology that my clients would like to retrieve during the confusion."

"No promises." Klaw smiled before disappearing out the door.

o———————o

T'CHALLA hated his throne.

No, he thought as he sat through the third supplicant of the day, hate was probably too strong a word. Apprehension was more like it. He was intensely uncomfortable in the onyx-colored, high-backed chair. He remembered being bounced on his father's knee in that very same throne; the intense feeling of shame he'd felt when he had to stand before it and admit that he'd broken the Spear of Sacred Wind; and the look of pride on T'Chaka's face when he'd told his father he had passed the first level of his training.

There were a lot of emotions wrapped up in this throne. When he was small, T'Challa would sit on a small chair just out of sight behind some draperies and listen to his father make rulings. He had loved hearing the royal timbre of his father's voice, and T'Chaka would always invite him up to sit in his throne when the judgments were done. T'Challa's small legs would swing back and forth as he waited to be large enough to be entrusted with the secrets of the kingdom.

This was his father's place, and it didn't feel right for *him* to be seated there. T'Challa made a mental note to ask about the mechanics of getting a new throne made, then refocused himself on the people around him.

Behind him, watching carefully over his shoulders, were Nakia and Okoye, who were back in rotation after the overseas shift. His regular palace guards stood watch at the doors, charged with escorting his subjects in and out of the throne room as he dispensed what wisdom he could.

Lucikly, this round was pretty easy: an argument between a couple over whether their child should be encouraged to join the Wakandan military or the science corps. (He suggested that there would be honor in either choice, but perhaps they should wait until the boy was out of diapers before committing him to a career. And, oh, marriage counseling might be a good idea.) A request from a farmer for the Hesuti Dam to release more water because of a mini-drought in the farmland to the east. (He'd promised to bring it to his agricultural minister's attention posthaste.) And, finally, a request from a promising

Wakandan science prodigy to study overseas at an Ivy League college.

T'Challa smiled to himself, remembering the uproar he'd caused when he informed his mother and the ruling council that he'd be completing his studies at Oxford, Harvard, and the Swiss Federal Institute of Technology before coming home. His mother almost blew her top, and Uncle S'Yan jokingly threatened to lead a coup if he insisted on leaving Wakanda for that amount of time.

That was one of the first times he'd used the weight of his future crown to get his way. He'd told them to make whatever security arrangements they needed to, but he was going and that was that. A few months later, "Luke Charles" enrolled as a college student triple-majoring in physics, modern economics, and astrobiology.

T'Challa loved his secret identity. For the first time, he wasn't special. No one treated him any differently than any other student on campus. He could eat junk food (it made him sick until he realized that moderation was the key), drink truly awful liquor (the first time he had American beer, the spit take was priceless), and date whomever he liked, regardless of skin color or social standing.

Of course, a couple of his sharper dates eventually wondered why every time they went out, there would be at least one or two African beauties standing on the periphery of the crowd or sitting in a booth a few feet away. Apparently leaving the *Dora Milaje* behind in Wakanda was a step too far, so they had enrolled in classes as well. Luckily, they all excelled, and when they all returned to Wakanda, he'd granted several of the *Dora Milaje* special dispensation to resign and use their educations in government and private-industry positions around his country.

T'Challa gave his blessing to the child for her overseas study, and won a promise from her to report back to him personally on how her studies were going. Once she was escorted out of the throne room, he yawned and looked down at his itinerary.

"Is that it for today, Uncle?"

"I believe so, my king." S'Yan smiled, watching his nephew shift uncomfortably about in the throne. "Not quite used to that seat yet, are you?"

T'Challa grinned. "Is it that obvious?"

"Only to those who know you, son." S'Yan shuffled some of the ever-present papers he carried with him instead of the touchpad T'Challa and the others preferred. "It didn't fit me all those years I was regent, but I figured you might want it once you became king."

"I did. Now I'm thinking of making a change. But that's a matter for another day. How far behind schedule are we?"

S'Yan scratched his head where gray strands of hair betrayed his true age. "I actually believe that you are ahead of schedule, your majesty. In fact, you have a whole 10 minutes you can spend doing whatever you want before we have to get you ready for the defense council meeting."

"A whole ten minutes." T'Challa sighed. "Whatever shall I do with my time?"

Okoye shifted almost imperceptibly, but enough that T'Challa noticed her rare movement. "Did you have a suggestion, Okoye?"

Okoye looked over at the wide-eyed Nakia, who was shaking her head—apparently trying to telepathically tell her sword-sister to stand down. But when Okoye walked around the throne and knelt before T'Challa, she followed.

"We have a petition, Beloved," Okoye whispered, her eyes downcast.

There was an audible gasp from S'Yan. "Wakandan is the only language allowed for petitions in the king's chambers, Okoye, even from the *Dora Milaje*," he warned.

"Beloved?"

T'Challa thought about it for a minute. "Uncle is right," he said in standard Wakandan. "If you have a petition, it can only be heard in Wakandan."

"Yes, my king," Nakia interrupted. She looked over at Okoye and shrugged. *"In for a penny,"* she whispered.

Okoye cleared her throat and looked up at T'Challa. "The *Dora Milaje* have defended the throne and the Black Panther for generations, but it now seems that the king no longer wants our protection. What is to become of us?"

T'Challa looked down at the two women

thoughtfully. "I quite enjoy conversing with you, Okoye. There is no pretense with you, no time wasted with verbal jousting. You cut straight to the heart of the matter." He stood up and began pacing back and forth across the platform.

"I won't bother denying it. That would dishonor both your intelligence-gathering capabilities and the close relationship the throne has with the *Dora Milaje*. It's true, I have been considering other responsibilities for the *Dora Milaje*."

T'Challa raised his hand to stop the protests beginning from the two women. "This is no fault of yours—and in fact, I have entered commendations for the both of you in the annals of your ancestors. But there are some things that I will not do as my father did, and this is one of them. As we open our borders to the world, we must also put aside some of the treasured ways of our forefathers."

T'Challa took a breath. "I have seen no need for a protective cadre dedicated solely to the throne so far, and so have been considering tasking the *Dora Milaje* to different responsibilities—intelligence gathering for the military, perhaps, or as the basis for a new clandestine service for the council. Your service to the throne would come to an end, and instead you would dedicate yourselves to our country."

"You can't," Nakia cried. Okoye grabbed her her sword-sister's hands and squeezed. T'Challa looked on impassively as the two gathered themselves.

Downcast, Nakia stared down at her feet. "You

would make us into spies? Skulking about the alleys of our enemies, listening at keyholes?"

"You would be serving in an area of need," T'Challa said. "It is wasteful for so many to be dedicated to the protection of just one, even if that one is the king of Wakanda. This is more responsibility and more prestige for your order, Nakia."

The two women fell silent as they contemplated their king's words.

"Is this decision final?" Okoye asked.

"Is there a reason it shouldn't be?" T'Challa responded.

"My king, I beg of you, give us a chance to prove our worth to you," Okoye said. "The Black Panther has been the focal point of the lives of the *Dora Milaje* for generations, and I am loath to be the last of my line."

"I am sure," Nakia added, "that we are indispensable to the throne, and we are willing to prove it to you, your majesty."

"How?"

Nakia looked at Okoye. "As the occasion arises, my king," she finally said.

"Uncle, what do you think?"

S'Yan looked thoughtful. "I consider the *Dora Milaje* an invaluable asset to the throne, your majesty. Their order brings stability to a once fractured land, and as a fighting force there are few that can reckon with their training. Their loyalty is irreproachable, and their names are whispered in fear by our enemies around the world. That is not something to give up lightly."

T'Challa sat back in his throne and looked out at the kneeling women. They were both beautiful. That thought rose unbidden in his head and he pushed it aside. There was truly only one solution.

"My judgment is this: The *Dora Milaje* have served the throne for years and deserve a hand in shaping their future. Before assigning them new duties, I will observe, record, and judge their capabilities in their current protective functions, and will render a decision upon making up my mind. In the meantime, I would suggest that Princess Shuri be given all due courtesy in her training as she prepares herself for her royal duties. Is that fair, Adored Ones?"

"Quite fair, your majesty," Okoye said. She and Nakia resumed their places at the king's side, their impassive masks falling back in place.

S'Yan watched the two women resume their posts before consulting the schedule in front of him. "Well, that was exciting," he sighed. "And now you need to head to the defense council, your majesty. Can I grab you something to eat or drink before you go?"

T'Challa walked down the steps, the *Dora Milaje* following a few strides behind. "No, I think I'll be fine until lunch." He patted his uncle on the shoulder as he passed. "We'll grab something later."

S'YAN waited until T'Challa and the women were almost out of eyesight before whispering to himself, "Don't give up on him yet, girls. He's stubborn, but he's fair. Do your thing, and he'll see your worth."

As regent between the time of his brother's death and T'Challa's crowning, S'Yan had enjoyed the loyalty of the *Dora Milaje*. Together, they had brought the body of his brother back home and kept Wakanda from falling into disarray after the assassination. Only a fool would give away such loyalty, he thought as he walked out.

But some young men are known to be fools. The thought made him smile. *That's why they have elders around to advise them.* He hummed to himself as he pulled the doors to the empty throne room closed behind him.

T'Challa was a genius, and along with that came impetuousness and overconfidence—and sometimes arrogance and haughtiness—all signs of proper breeding for royalty. But T'Challa was no fool.

He won't throw away a valuable resource like the Dora Milaje on a whim, S'Yan thought as he turned to enter the Hall of Kings. Down this corridor were paintings of all the rulers of Wakanda, including his brother and his father. He gazed up at his brother's visage. *For someone so studious,* he reflected, *T'Challa has made some rash moves before. The tournament proved that...*

CHAPTER SIX

RAMONDA barely remembered running out onto the royal balcony overlooking the tournament arena. All her concentration was focused inward, trying to control the panic that threatened to overwhelm her. As she stared down at the thousands gathered underneath the enormous Panther statue, half of her soul beamed with overwhelming pride while the other half felt frozen with mind-numbing fear.

Two *Dora Milaje* breathlessly joined her on the balcony. "Your majesty, there is no sign of him," one reported. "We are sweeping the crowd now with scanners, and we have activated his personal trackers. We're mobilizing the palace guard as well, and I expect to have his location soon."

Ramonda waved them off. She continued desperately to search each face below, looking for her son. But with the thousands of citizens crowding up against the arena ring, she knew it was a futile effort. *They won't find him in time,* she despaired silently. *He's not ready. I'm not ready. I knew—I knew I should have postponed the tournament this year. T'Challa's been too quiet, too quiet by half.*

As Queen Mother, Ramonda had shared power

with S'Yan for years. While not anointed by the Panther God, the regent had kept peace in Wakanda as they waited for T'Challa to mature. Ramonda had grown to enjoy the long evening talks with her son as he tinkered with his gadgets and talked about scientific principles that she barely understood. But he was safe—and after what had happened to T'Chaka, she appreciated that most of all.

But as his voice deepened and his muscles hardened, their discussions took a disturbing turn. T'Challa began discussing matters of state in between his experiments, probing her thoughts about how S'Yan was handling them. For years, she deflected, hoping that her son's keen love of science would dampen thoughts of ruling for a few decades more. But it was futile. By the time he was 12, she could see the impatience in his eyes as they stood together on the balcony watching the tournament below.

"Next year I will take my turn in the ring," T'Challa had declared that day. She looked over at him, but masked her fear behind what she hoped was a motherly smile.

"Perhaps," she tenderly stroked his cheek.

"I *am* ready, mother." The fire burning in his eyes scared her a little. "I have passed the trials. What more do I need?"

"Have you been given the dream?"

T'Challa deflated like a flower wilting in the heat. Her poor baby. "No, Mother."

"Then you are not ready. When the Panther

God wants you to step forward, she will tell you. Until then, you will have to wait."

She could see his fists clenching and the veins throbbing in his forehead. "How long, Mother? How long?"

She pulled him into a motherly hug, fighting his natural teenage inclination to pull away. "Soon, my boy—soon. The Panther God knows you are here. She will tell you when you're ready. Until then, live what life you can, T'Challa."

She held him close for a moment more, and then let him go. God, he looked just like his father, right down to the shifting of his weight and the flaring of his nostrils. "Every night, I wished I had known your father when he was young and carefree, before the weight of the crown. I see much of him in you, T'Challa—I do. Do not rush to complete the circle just yet."

T'Challa gave her a little smile and went back to the balcony to get a better look. "Uncle S'Yan will win again this year," he declared as if she hadn't said a word. "He's the one I will have to face, and defeat, to gain the crown."

"Not this year," Ramonda joined him, looking down at the crowd below. "Not this year."

She and T'Challa had had that same conversation almost every year until he left for college. But since his return, he hadn't asked about fighting in the tournament, instead cheering on S'Yan as he held the crown in trust as the regent for another year.

Instead of glaring down from the balcony as he did as a child, T'Challa laughed and joked with Shuri while she provided a running commentary of all of the defeated contenders who fell at S'Yan's feet.

He had even started training with Shuri, who had declared as a precocious little girl that she would fight in the tournament someday. T'Challa humored her for years, sparring frequently with his little sister. Then, one day, Shuri slipped through his defenses and, with a mighty yell, planted him on the floor with a roundhouse kick. Without a word, T'Challa picked himself up off the floor and delivered her to the royal family's trainer, Zuri, who began her instruction in earnest alongside her brother.

Soft footfalls and a hand on her shoulder shook Ramonda from her reverie. It was Shuri—but instead of wearing her usual royal attire, she was dressed in skintight black workout gear, carrying a black ski mask. Determination shone in her eyes as she squared off in front of her mother.

"Queen Ramonda, I am entering the tournament this year as the representative of the ruling family, since we have not had one in several years. Do I have your blessing?" Shuri declared.

Ramonda looked at her in shock. "No, you do not. You are barely of age, girl. And I will *not* have both of my children putting themselves in mortal danger at the same time."

"Both of your children?" Shuri looked around the balcony in horror. "Where is T'Challa?"

"Down there, I suppose," Ramonda waved her hand toward the crowd before slumping down in her chair.

Shuri howled in despair and sprinted off the balcony. "He didn't enter the tournament—that means he didn't want to be king. He can't do this now! It was supposed to be *my* time!"

Ramonda put her head in her hands as she heard the mouth of the giant Panther statue creak open. S'Yan, dressed in the dark Panther habit, appeared in the opening, then effortlessly flipped down out of the mouth and into the ring. A deafening cheer rose up from the crowd, and she barely withheld a wail from escaping her mouth. No matter what happened, she knew her children would never be the same after this day.

T'Chaka, give me strength, she prayed.

SHURI sprinted out the front of the palace into the cheering mass that covered the spectator area of the open-air arena. All around her, bodies pressed together into one joyous throng, yelling and cheering as the Black Panther dropped down from the huge Panther totem into the middle of the ring.

"PANTHER! PANTHER! PANTHER!"

The chant from the stands became even louder as S'Yan raised his powerful arms into the air and acknowledged the crowd's reverence. It was almost deafening to Shuri's ears. She pushed and shoved her way toward the ring, but was only making slight headway when the first challenger appeared on a huge screen hanging above. This man was dressed like her, in a black singlet and mask that obscured his features from the crowd and accompanying cameras.

Shuri had asked T'Challa years ago why the challengers had to wear identical clothes and disguise their faces. Her brother laughed and said she could figure it out for herself. So she did. With the disguises, anyone could vie for the throne and not face public ridicule for failure. And since the Panther would have no idea whom he was facing, he could not attempt to throw the match for a particular individual—whether son or daughter, commoner or royalty.

Shuri shoved her way toward the holding pen for potential challengers. From her vantage point, she could just barely see the inside of the ring. *Everyone in Wakanda must have shown up this year,* she thought.

In fact, people traveled to the Golden City from throughout Wakanda every year for the tournament, both to compete and to watch. Over the decades, it had become one of the largest outdoor festivals on the Wakandan calendar. When there was a king, it was almost a rite of passage for Wakanda's youth to pit themselves in friendly matches against the crown. But with the kingship vacant and a regent in place, the matches took on a more serious tone. Now there was an actual throne to be won.

Shuri wasn't worried, however. She'd been training since childhood for this moment.

Zuri had been a demanding taskmaster from that first day T'Challa delivered her into his hands. A mountain of a man who growled constantly, he pushed her beyond her limits in weapons training and personal combat, never allowing her to slack off. Despite his heft, he was surprisingly quick. If she dodged his first spear thrust, he was there with a counterstrike that bloodied her lip or left a jagged scar down her calf—until she learned to block him every single time.

There were no dummy weapons in Zuri's arsenal. Everything was real for him—from the iron tip of his spear as it ripped through her skin, to the arrows they shot at each other to learn trajectory and aim, to the bullets in his gun as he fired at her to teach her avoidance techniques. And he didn't like lip. He sweated with her, perspiration dripping from his graying dreadlocks. Once, when she complained about being tired, he made her run from dawn to dusk every day up the side of a mountain for three months. When she asked to sit down, he built a bed of red hot coals and invited her to take her seat at any time. If she wasn't breathing quietly enough for him, or wasn't holding still enough, he would make her meditate in a pit of scorpions until she learned to be at one with her surroundings without disturbing her companions.

After a particularly brutal day in the gym, she'd

asked Zuri whether he was as tough on T'Challa, or whether his hate was saved particularly for her. For the first time in years, she heard him chuckle. His laughter grew until tears were streaming down the man's scarred face. Finally, Zuri drew a long breath and wiped his craggy eyes.

"What is it with this family?" Zuri chuckled. "You'll be glad to know that you held out longer than T'Challa and T'Chaka, who both asked a version of that question during their training. But they asked earlier than you, Princess."

Shuri didn't like to hear him laughing. It was… wrong, in some way. "You trained my father?"

"And your uncle." Zuri propped himself up against his ever-present spear, and got himself under control. "We all have our destinies, young lady. My family's destiny is to stand between pretenders to the throne and the real Black Panther. *That* is why I'm so tough with you. To see if you're worthy."

Shuri stared him in the eyes, wondering what he saw when he looked at her. "And?"

Without warning, Zuri thrust his spear at her face. Shuri dodged right and immediately dropped down into a crouch, hearing the wood of the spear whistle only millimeters over her head. She leaped at Zuri, hoping to land a blow while he was extended, but was surprised by a kick to the side of her head. Rolling with the impact, she dodged a couple more strikes until she could backpedal out of his reach.

Zuri kept advancing on her, using his spear to

parry her kicks and back her into a corner. Finally, she had nowhere to go. Zuri advanced slowly until his spearpoint was directly aimed at her eye.

"You'll do…someday." He smiled, spun his spear around, and headed toward the door, leaving her panting in the corner.

She redoubled her training after that, and even Zuri finally admitted that she'd come a long way. They never let her train with T'Challa, however, so she couldn't compare herself to him. But she felt she was ready.

Even if her mother had refused to give her blessing, Shuri had planned to compete in the tournament. She had told no one, not even Zuri, whom she had become fond of during her years of training. He had probably figured it out, anyway, but Shuri was sure that he wouldn't rat her out to either her mother or T'Challa. At least, she thought she was sure. Then she'd found out T'Challa was not where he was supposed to be.

Damn it, I need to make it through this crowd. What if someone else beats Uncle before I get there?

That seemed unlikely as the first contestant fell face first on the mat, knocked unconscious by a quick heel strike from the Panther. Shuri heard the crowd groan. Medics pulled the man out by his ankles as a second masked man clambered into the ring—and was dispatched just as quickly by two lightning-fast jabs to the face.

The crowd roared as the Panther bounced

back on his heels like a boxer, waiting for the next contestant. Shuri pushed her way into the holding pen and looked around. There were only three aspirants left: a slender, graceful-looking man, a massive giant of a man, and herself. The three looked at each other warily until the slender man bowed and silently indicated that the giant should go next.

Shuri watched the giant walk confidently up the stairs to the ring. When he reached the ring, instead of walking through the ropes, the man swung one of his massive legs over the top, easily stepping over and into the ring. A hush came across the crowd as the Panther sized up this giant. The only sound came from a pair of ringside announcers, who had been narrating the fights to the surrounding crowds as if this were a championship boxing match.

"This big son-of-a-biscuit-eater must be a miner, with arms like that, K'Tyah," the announcer said excitedly.

"Yes, M'Shula, he truly is a big one," the analyst agreed. "But I've seen bigger, and the Panther has taken them all."

The giant stretched his muscles as he walked toward the Panther, the cracking of his knuckles reverberating around the arena.

"I don't know—he's one of the biggest I've ever seen. Look at those tree trunks he calls arms! The Panther looks absolutely tiny in there with him." M'Shula seemed worried. "We've not had a Panther that size since The Wall died."

"And we may not again, my friend. Just watch. I bet the Panther's superior speed will chop him down to size."

The lumbering giant took a swing at the Panther, who danced lithely out of the way. Another swing, another miss, and the Panther slipped under the miner's defenses and slammed a fist under his rib cage, aiming for the liver and a quick defeat.

The miner just laughed and flexed his pectorals at the Panther. "That's it?"

A quick uppercut rocked back the big man's head, but only for a second. With speed belying his enormous bulk, the miner grabbed the Panther and lifted him into the air. A meaty hand clamped onto the regent's head and shook him like a rag doll.

"A knockout might not be enough to take the crown." The miner's voice was like gravel, low and deep. "I might have to kill you to stake my claim."

With that, the miner picked up the Panther and slammed him headfirst into the mat. The crowd, stunned silent at first, went wild, sensing that there was a real opportunity for them to see a new king crowned for the first time in decades.

"No, no—this can't be happening," Shuri moaned behind her mask. "Not when I'm so close."

Again, the miner picked up S'Yan by his head and slammed him down, making the regent gasp. "I can't believe my father lost to your brother," the miner said. "Maybe he had a little more fight than you."

"I'll show you fight," S'Yan replied, aiming a

strong kick to the miner's groin. With an *oof,* the giant released S'Yan's head, and the regent used his legs to leverage the huge man up and over. The man's eyes closed, and he made a gurgling sound, flailing his arms impotently as he flew backward. He landed on the floor with a tremendous thud.

The Panther rose with a slight groan and began working over the large man, snapping quick jabs at his head and quick but powerful kicks at his chin. The big man, obviously dazed, swayed back and forth; he spat blood as the Panther rocked him with two-handed blows to the face. A woman ran up to the side of the ring, waving a white cloth frantically at the Panther.

"Mercy, my lord—mercy for my boy!" the aged woman sobbed.

The Panther looked down at the woman and nodded slightly. Stepping forward, he grabbed the large man and, with surprising strength, lifted him off the ground and held him above his head in triumph. Then, with unerring aim, the Panther tossed him back into the holding pen. The man missed the slim contender but landed directly on Shuri, pinning her to the ground.

"Get off of me!" Shuri struggled to move the massive man, making little headway. As she pushed, she could see the slender man hop lithely into the ring. But from her vantage point, she couldn't see what was going on in the ring.

"He's...bowing? Hmmm, this next contestant

sure is cocky, M'Shula," the announcer intoned. "A better strategy might be to press the regent now, when you know he's been stunned a little bit by the previous contestant."

"I guess he doesn't want anyone to question his victory, K'Tyah."

"As if," the announcer snorted. "If the big guy couldn't get it done, what chance does this shrimp have? Anyway, everyone gets a chance, and I'd bet just being in the ring is a thrill this young man will talk about for the rest of his life."

Move it, move it, move it, Shuri told herself. She pushed as hard as she could, desperate to get free of the still-dazed miner before she lost her turn. The man's sobbing mother tried to help her, but no one else in the arena was paying them any attention. Everyone was engrossed in what was happening in the ring.

"I don't believe this, M'Shula," the announcer said. "This young man is matching the Panther move for move. I've not seen anyone block that overhand thrust in years!"

"Now this is a fight, K'Tyah," the other man intoned. "This is what we came here to see, a real challenge—and perhaps, just perhaps, a new king."

Shuri was pulling at her leg, trying to free her ankle from underneath the slow-moving man, when she felt the man's weight unexpectedly vanish. A rough hand pulled her upright, and she could feel hot breath on her neck.

"It's not your time, Princess." Zuri stared into her eyes.

Shuri jerked her mentor's hand away. "Who are you to tell me that? I am just as worthy as anyone here today."

"Look, girl—look." Zuri forced her around so she could see the two men grappling in the ring. Their leaps and thrusts looked like some sort of grotesque ballet. "Do you see what I see, Princess?"

Shuri watched the two men closely. Their moves were coming at almost blinding speed now. Her eyes widened in shock as she realized movements, their bodies and even their fighting styles were almost identical. Every leg sweep was countered with just the right leap. If one punched left, the other dodged right. They were fighting as if they'd had the exact same training...

The masked man feinted left. When the Panther moved to block, he launched in an unexpected jab to the Panther's solar plexus, startling the older man.

"That's not how you're supposed to do that," Shuri said, disappointment at her missed opportunity growing in her mind.

"Yes—I know that, and you know that. S'Yan also knows that, and that's why he fell for it." Zuri puffed himself up with pride.

The masked man rained down blows on the regent's head, never letting up for a second as he backed the older man into a corner. Finally, he launched a haymaker that dropped the Panther to his knees. S'Yan tried to stand, but he only got to one knee before he collapsed to the ground.

"The match is over! The match is over!" screamed M'Shula. He and K'Tyah rushed into the ring as the young man threw up his arms in victory. "We have a new king!"

The crowd screamed and stomped as they charged into the ring in jubilation and lifted the masked man on their shoulders.

"PANTHER! PANTHER!" The jubilant crowd mobbed the young man until four surprised *Dora Milaje* rushed the ring and formed a protective circle around their new liege, glaring menacingly at anyone who tried to come too close.

At the side of the ring, almost forgotten, S'Yan dragged himself upright using the ropes. He slowly removed his Panther mask, revealing puffy eyes and a swollen jaw. He looked down at Shuri, who took one step toward him—but halted when she saw the shamed look on her uncle's face as he dropped the Panther mask to the ground. There was nothing either one of them could say. Their family had never lost a tournament, an unbroken line of succession that stretched back years. Now S'Yan's name would go down in history as the one regent who couldn't preserve the throne for its rightful holder.

Then Shuri looked closer at the masked man. This guy's build was awfully familiar, and some of his moves were straight from the training she and T'Challa both got from W'Kabi.

S'Yan walked slowly toward the masked man. The circling *Dora Milaje* parted to let him near, then watched silently as the regent dropped to one knee. M'Shula, watching the female guards' spears warily, crept closer with his microphone and thrust it over S'Yan's downcast head.

"Congratulations on a well-fought match, your majesty." The man withered under the fierce glare of the *Dora Milaje*, but carried on. "If you would please remove your mask…"

The new king pulled off his mask and grinned down at Shuri, wiping sweat from his brow.

"Ladies and gentlemen, the new Black Panther is T'Challa, son of T'Chaka!"

"T'Challa?" S'Yan looked up in shock as Shuri scrambled toward the ring, Zuri right behind her. T'Challa, hands still slick with sweat, reached down to pull his uncle to his feet.

"Are you okay, Uncle?"

"Fine, now that I know it was you!" S'Yan said gratefully. He lifted his nephew up in a friendly bear hug, before remembering himself. The *Dora Milaje* surrounding them growled in warning at his overfamiliarity with the new king.

"My apologies, your highness. May the Panther God bless your rule." S'Yan bowed deeply, and then reached out and raised T'Challa's arm into the air in triumph. The crowd began to chant again.

The two men circled around the ring, acknowledging the crowd on all sides. When they stopped before the royal balcony, T'Challa looked up into his mother's eyes and gave her a small nod. A tearful Ramonda put her hand over her mouth and rushed out of sight.

T'Challa frowned slightly, but his attention was drawn away from the balcony by Shuri, who stalked up in a huff. "I was robbed! By my own brother!" The *Dora Milaje* snarled a warning at her.

S'Yan put his hand on his niece's shoulder. "T'Challa had nothing to do with it, Princess. The Panther God willed events to happen as they did, and we all must accept her judgment. T'Challa is the new king."

Shuri snorted, earning her a harsh stare from Zuri. "Bow now, Princess," he growled. "Show your king the respect you would demand in his place if *you* had been anointed by our god."

Shuri glared at the old man, then back at T'Challa, who was looking at her serenely, his face a sea of calm. "Please, Princess," Zuri whispered, falling to one knee. "Do not betray your training and shame me."

Shuri struggled for a moment, her pride warring with her strong love for her brother. In the end, there was no choice. She walked up to her brother, took his hand, and kissed it. Then, smiling, she dropped to one knee in front of him. Seeing their princess bow, the rest of the crowd grew silent. Following her lead, they genuflected to the new Black Panther.

Shuri would remember the next moment for the

rest of her life. Later, she would swear it was a trick of the light. But when she sneaked a look up at her brother, she could have sworn his face was changing, becoming more angular, his eyes narrowing slightly. When she looked in those eyes, she saw something moving behind his pupils—a shimmering, as if something was suddenly sharing the space with her brother.

She caught her breath and looked back down. There was only one thing to do, she realized. Even so, it caught her by surprise when she heard herself chant "T'Challa!"

She called again. "T'Challa! T'Challa!" Even without looking, she could feel the smile from Zuri as he picked up the chant. S'Yan and the *Dora Milaje* were next, and before long the entire crowd was cheering and stomping as they celebrated the rise of their new Black Panther.

"T'CHALLA! T'CHALLA! T'CHALLA!"

The new king smiled.

RAMONDA rushed to her quarters, pushing her way through the crowd heading out to the arena at word of a new king. She slammed her door before the tears began falling down her cheeks. Falling on her bed, she curled up in a ball and sobbed her heart out, cursing the fates that had made her son the king.

She stayed that way for only a minute, knowing she still had royal duties to perform. Sniffling quietly, she walked over and draped on her dressing gown.

Sitting in front of a mirror, Ramonda began to repair her tear-stained makeup.

One of her attendants opened her door, arms laden with linen. K'Tiya, she thought. This one was K'Tiya, a girl from the Plains who loved romance novels and dreamed of a life of adventure, including an unhealthy fascination with skydiving. The green headwrap she wore that day was pretty, Ramonda thought. Her mind returned, unbidden, to her time as a young woman trying on clothing for her first date with a handsome man whom she would only find out later was a king.

"My queen?" The girl started upon seeing Ramonda in her rooms. "Why are you here? Did you not hear? Your son..."

Ramonda, her royal mask back in place, looked haughtily at the girl, who shrunk involuntarily. "Won. Yes, I know. It was inevitable that he would take his father's throne one day."

Placing the linen on the bed, K'Tiya rushed over to help her mistress, finger-combing the older woman's graying braids into a semblance of order. Looking at Ramonda in the mirror, the girl could not miss her red, puffy eyes.

"Why are you sad, my queen? Your son has ascended to the rank of Black Panther. He is now king..."

Ramonda smiled. Youth had the luxury of hope. She knew better. "Making him a bigger target," she finished for the girl.

CHAPTER SEVEN

SOME said the Hanging Gardens of the royal palace of Niganda represented the pinnacle of African architecture, a beauty rivaling the biblical Babylonian gardens of Nebuchadnezzar. From his seat in the nearby bazaar, Georges Batroc could see monkeys playing in the lush, swaying trees that lined marble staircases, and succulent berries hanging from vines that climbed the ornate white columns. Gurgling water bubbled up and trickled down from manmade streams and waterfalls. If he squinted, he could make out small rabbits and other harmless creatures frolicking through flowering bushes and dashing across fields of immaculately groomed grass.

He hated every inch of it.

The mercenary was traveling under papers declaring him to be Stephen Rodgers, owner of a Brooklyn lingerie shop—a private joke he hoped his target would hear about one day. He sipped his cup of absurdly strong Nigandian coffee and watched the palace. A cute barista with immaculately braided hair had suggested the blend, warning him with a grin that most white men couldn't stomach it. He'd never backed down from a challenge, so he'd given the girl a wink and ordered the strongest blend she could make, laying on his flirtiest French accent.

With a sultry smile, she sashayed her way over to his outdoor table and watched him take his first taste with interest. Her eyebrows quirked as he savored the beverage. He suggested that a second one would be appreciated, but only if she joined him. The barista, twirling a braid through her fingers, begged off but hinted that her schedule was wide open after closing time.

Batroc saluted her with his cup and a twirl of his mustache as he watched her return to the counter. His eyes then returned to the palace. He watched the entrance from behind designer sunglasses, waiting for the proper time for his rendezvous with Klaw.

A few blocks from the palace, children dressed in rags darted from the shadows, dodging armed police patrols to beg for coins or bits of bread from tourists. The stink of desperation filled the air, no matter how hard the Nigandans tried to sanitize the palace district. The smell of garbage filled back alleys, mixing with the hopeless sweat of women offering up their bodies to make ends meet. Bedraggled men dragged themselves home from another day of work, their eyes dead and hopeless.

Batroc—a hard-bitten, world-renowned mercenary and master of the French martial art Savate—wasn't bothered by the sheer opulence of the palace. In fact, once his hidden Swiss bank accounts hit $200 million and could be invested at a reasonable rate of return, a small version of those gardens would look *magnifique* at his Caribbean mansion, which was already under construction. He had no compunction about lying, cheating, stealing, or killing to reach that goal—and if someone asked him to do something unspeakable, his only question would be the amount of his fee.

But even with all of that, Batroc felt he still had honor. And it was dishonorable to allow one's subjects to live like this, especially in the shadow of such extravagant beauty.

A scrawny man crawled up to his table, open wounds oozing on his arms and torso, and begged for a coin, his bloodshot eyes desperate and hungry. Batroc gently pushed the man away with his boots, shaking his head no. He had seen men and women like this before, in similar places around the world. He guessed it would be about a decade before these people would storm the castle, destroy the gardens, and kill every living being inside for forcing them to live in such squalor. But the spark of *La Révolution* wasn't quite there yet. He placed a coded reminder in his smartphone to start making covert contacts with Nigandian dissidents five years down the road. There was always work for men like him.

But for now, M'Butu—the august emperor and president-for-life of Niganda—still held an iron grip on his people. And since Klaw had indicated that the royal coffers would be opened for this misadventure, Batroc would swallow his distaste and collect his check.

It would be too bad about those gardens, though.

A small beep from his smartphone startled him out of his thoughts. He quickly typed a response and pocketed his phone, securing it to ensure that none of the hundreds of roaming child pickpockets could take advantage. Wandering back up to the counter, he tossed a wink at the barista and threw a couple of bills and a business card into her tip jar. The phone number on the card led to an answering machine in Algiers, but he'd check the messages later, just in case she felt like getting lucky tonight. Batroc strolled out into the crowd, whistling as he meandered out into the grand bazaar.

To the untrained eye, Batroc knew he projected the air of an uncaring, pampered dilettante—perhaps a muscular young French lord whiling away his days, waiting for his father to die so he could waste the inheritance. Perhaps it was the perfectly tanned skin, the pencil-thin, waxed-and-twirled moustache, or the thick French accent.

A fellow merc had once called him comical, an ethnic stereotype that confirmed everything Americans believed about the "frogs" who lifted their skirts for the Nazis back in the so-called "Big One." Less than a minute later, Batroc had pried one of the man's teeth from the sole of his boot. He was forced to borrow pliers to pull it out from between his treads, and in what he viewed as a boundless act of generosity, he threw it down next to the American on the bar floor. At least he'd be able to get a dentist to re-implant it. The other teeth—the ones Batroc had kicked down his throat—would have to wait until they passed through his bodily systems.

But these people, these Nigandans—they knew a predator when they saw one. So they gave him a wide berth as he strolled toward the city's main avenue and the white limousine waiting for him. Batroc climbed in, and the car eased out into the palace-bound traffic.

"Is everyone in place?" Klaw looked up from his tablet, adjusting his tie and fluffing his jacket collar, eyeing his reflection in the car's window.

Batroc shrugged. "I have seen cars come and go from the palace, so I must assume that all is ready. I did mark our glowing friend's entrance, however. So at least he is on site."

Klaw dipped a comb into a glass of water and ran it through his hair, slicking it back. Batroc watched with amusement as the assassin primped, placing a rose on his lapel and picking up a leather attaché case.

"M'Butu is very much into appearances," Klaw growled.

"I have said nothing," Batroc replied as their car maneuvered through the palace's extensive security.

A sweaty M'Butu was waiting for them in an enormous courtyard, surrounded by machine-gun-toting lackeys and sycophants masquerading as palace guards. The flatulent Nigandan king had recently retired his undeserved military uniform and taken to wearing what Batroc assumed was a traditional Nigandan robe. To him, the long, flowing garment looked like a multicolored muumuu designed to hide the corpulent belly M'Butu had developed dining on delicacies while his subjects starved. Wiping beads of sweat from his forehead, the king waved Klaw and Batroc over to a shaded portico inside the palace, where it was blessedly cool and comfortable.

Waiting for them was a servant girl balancing a tray of artesian water, grapes, and dates. M'Butu slapped the girl on her rear, sending her scurrying toward the two men.

"My friends, welcome, welcome," M'Butu exclaimed, his beady eyes going from one to the other. "May I offer you some water or delicacies from my gardens before we conduct our business?"

The huge man farted and reached over to pinch the small girl's buttocks as he picked grapes off the tray, causing her to flinch slightly. M'Butu frowned and was about to speak when Batroc, seeing the terrified look on the girl's face, waved her over for a bottle of water to sip on later. Giving him a grateful look, the girl genuflected before M'Butu before slipping out a nearby door.

"Mjaki!" A tuxedoed waiter appeared at the king's side as if by magic. "Remind me to punish the servant girl tonight for her insolence." The waiter nodded and vanished down a hallway.

"This way, my friends." M'Butu waved them toward the interior of his palace, spitting grape seeds on the tile as he strolled. "I have one piece of government business I must complete before we talk."

The king led them to his office, which was decorated like a hunting lodge. Animal heads adorned the walls—along with the bloody whips, hooked spears, and other weapons that likely had been used to kill many of the creatures. In the center of the room, kneeling at gunpoint before two cruel-looking guards, a young man wearing a T-shirt and jeans watched M'Butu's approach with a combination of horror and disgust.

M'Butu walked over to the wall, pulled down a bloody cane, and whipped it through the air. "Is this my 3 o'clock?"

The guards nodded. Without saying a word, M'Butu suddenly began beating the young man across the back, drawing bloodcurdling screams with every strike.

"I understand you felt the need to tweet about life here in *glorious Niganda*." M'Butu struck with each word. The young man tried to dodge some of the blows, but a guard slammed the back of his head with the butt of his rifle. This forced him to curl up his hands for protection, leaving his back exposed.

M'Butu was unrelenting, whipping the young man until he was prone on the floor, blood gushing out of his furrowed back. Winded, M'Butu waved for the two guards to lift the crying teen off the floor and hold him. He placed his hand under the boy's chin and slapped him repeatedly until his head lagged to one side.

"If you have any further criticisms, you can reach me during my office hours, which are..." M'Butu prompted. The guards shook the man until he opened his swollen eyes.

"N-n-nine to fi-fi-five, sir," he mumbled.

M'Butu glared at him for a moment, then nodded to the guards, who let the man flop to the floor. Wiping the blood from the staff with a handkerchief, M'Butu placed it back on the wall and retired to his desk.

"So, gentlemen, shall we talk business?"

Klaw and Batroc exchanged glances. They carefully stepped around the still-sobbing young man to sit in chairs before M'Butu's ornate desk. Batroc breathed through his mouth to avoid the stench from the bleeding young man, who had apparently lost control of his bowels.

"Out of curiosity, what was that about?" Batroc gave a slight nod toward the man.

"Just discussing politics with a local journalist," M'Butu said breezily. "Don't worry, we can talk in front of him. He knows now how to keep secrets, don't you, boy?"

The sobbing intensified. Batroc knew without looking that the man was trying to nod.

"To work, then," Klaw said. "I take it everything is ready?"

M'Butu reached into his desk and pulled

out a manila folder filled with black-and-white photographs. He tossed it to Batroc, who began flipping through the photos.

"Everyone you asked for has arrived, and the special accommodations for your Russian friend are just about complete." M'Butu leaned back. "Incidentally, the 'foreign aid' I was promised from your American friends came through today. I am thinking of having another statue of myself placed in the Capitol Building."

Batroc snorted. "I'm sure your citizens will appreciate that. Who needs food when you have art?"

M'Butu narrowed his eyes. "Curb your mercenary's mouth, Klaw, before I forget you are guests here."

"Gentlemen, let's stay on topic," Klaw inserted himself back into the conversation before it got too tense. "If everyone is here, then we're ready to launch. Batroc, would you please…"

Wordlessly, the French mercenary rose; carefully avoiding the still-prone man on the floor, he walked toward the door. With a nod, M'Butu sent one of his guards to guide Batroc to the lower levels. Once the room was clear, Klaw leaned forward to stare into the Nigandan king's eyes.

"I need to know that your men are ready," Klaw said.

M'Butu slammed his hand down on the desk. "The Nigandan army is more than prepared to topple the Wakandans! Our righteous fury cannot be denied. The Wakandans have insulted our fathers, and our fathers' fathers and their fathers. This can no longer be borne!"

Klaw's eyes glazed over as he watched the man work himself into a frenzy. The speech ceased to be interesting around the third or fourth declaration that Wakanda had stolen the Nigandans' birthright.

"That Vibranium mound is mine," M'Butu snarled. "The Wakandans stole the land from my people ages ago in a cowardly sneak attack. Now they force my brave Nigandans to live off their scraps, as if we are their pet dogs."

M'Butu walked over to a map of Africa on the wall, where Wakanda's border with his country had been erased, merging the two into one enormous nation. M'Butu traced his hand around the border. "My men will avenge this insult once and for all, and lead your glorious attack to victory!"

"Hmmm, yes, I'm sure they have the best of intentions," Klaw said neutrally. "I hope your general will be comfortable taking orders from my field commander."

M'Butu chuckled. "From that mouthy Frenchman? Of course, he won't. But he doesn't want to end up here, does he?" He waved toward the crying young man still huddled on the floor.

Klaw smiled. "Good enough."

"But I am curious about one thing." M'Butu reclined back and looked at Klaw. "I'll get Wakanda... for my people, of course. Your mercenaries will get their generous payments. Our foreign friends will get their commerce streams and new converts. But you? What are you getting out of this?"

Klaw smiled. "Let's just say...satisfaction."

BATROC leaned against a shaded wall in the dusty courtyard, shaking his head as he watched a rickety military Jeep creak into view along one of the backroads leading into the palace. The back of the vehicle was only inches off the ground from the weight of its rear passenger. Batroc looked down at the ground to hide his grin as the massive Rhino struggled to pry himself out of the Jeep.

The vehicle groaned in relief as the gray-armored man got both feet on the ground and padded toward Batroc. One of the strongest people in the world, the Rhino got his name from his animal-like armor with the huge horn protruding from the top.

Batroc had known the previous owner of the armor, a thick-headed Eastern bloc thug, who was as dumb as he was strong. However, he was dependable, once you got his attention. This man, one of a new younger breed trying on their elders' identities like a father's tie—he was an unknown.

But if he were anything like the others of this "new breed," Batroc suspected this new Rhino would be unnecessarily vicious, prone to disobeying orders, and arrogantly immature. Plus, unlike Batroc, he'd be stupid about his money—and therefore forced to work until someone figured out how to get him out of that armor and into a maximum security prison.

But until then, someone who could walk through a missile barrage without blinking would come in handy.

"Rhino," he said in greeting.

"Batroc," the Rhino said dismissively, glaring through his armor's visor with cruel gray eyes. Batroc could hear a faint Russian accent in the man's voice, although he had obviously worked hard to mute it through English lessons.

Batroc had never bothered. His native accent was beautiful. He would never change it.

Looking up at the Rhino's horn, he saw something. Batroc reached up and plucked a tuft of hair from one of the armor's crevasses and held it up questioningly.

"Part of my payment," Rhino sneered. "M'Butu has a private stock of black rhinos on his personal preserve. I had a…standoff with one. I won."

"Great. One less black rhino in the world. They're an endangered species, you know." The stupidity with this one was almost as strong as his predecessor, Batroc thought.

"I didn't think you were such an animal lover, Frenchie," Rhino scoffed.

"We are guests in this country. It's just good manners," Batroc explained.

Rhino snorted and stalked off. Batroc grinned and walked over to Klaw, who had been watching the exchange from the shadows.

"Why does the muscle in these operations always have to be so stupid?" Batroc groused.

"Bringing him along was a good call," Klaw said, clapping Batroc on the back. "That armor has faced off against some of the heaviest hitters in our world. God help us when the operator actually develops a brain."

"And the young one?" Batroc shaded his eyes from the evening African sun as he scanned the skies. "He took Valinor out, but he should have returned by now."

"I'm sure he's still acclimating himself and his horse to this climate," Klaw assured him. "He'll be ready when the time comes."

Batroc looked over at Klaw with a bit of worry. "I don't know where you found him, but I am uncomfortable about including the churchman in this operation," he admitted. "I find the religious ones are always susceptible to temptation."

"You don't have to worry about this one. He has…shall we say…higher orders that he's following." Klaw heard large wings beating in the air. "And here he is."

They looked up to see a black shape curve through the air, flying out of the sun and over the palace. Batroc couldn't make out the figure until it dropped to the ground and started trotting toward them.

A huge black horse whinnied and reared back on

its hind legs, kicking up dust toward the two men. Two massive black wings spread out from the horse's body, flapping furiously as the excited steed settled itself back on the ground. Astride its saddled back sat a man wearing an ornamented black-and-yellow helmet and a red cape, with a large black broadsword strapped to his waist.

"He's got a thing about King Arthur," Klaw whispered quietly to Batroc. "Says he's a descendent of Lancelot."

"Gentlemen." The Black Knight greeted them with a mock salute before jumping down off his horse. Gathering up the reins, he walked the animal over to Klaw and Batroc. The horse folded its wings on its sides and shook its head.

"Sir Knight." Klaw nodded.

"It is a glorious day in our Lord's creation, is it not?" said the knight, removing his helmet and running his hands through his sweaty black hair. Without the headgear, Batroc could see just how young the handsome crusader was, but was taken aback by the zeal in his blue eyes. Those eyes would make even a French woman go weak in the knees, Batroc thought dispassionately, but this one would probably scourge himself with whips if a woman got too close.

"Yes, it is a glorious day," Batroc replied cautiously. "Sir Knight, Klaw and I were just discussing the religious implications of our mission here. Would you have any thoughts on this?"

"God blesses our mission, Batroc," the knight

said calmly. "Just as in days of yore, it is incumbent upon us to bring civilization and knowledge of the Lord to these uncultured lands. The Wakandans are animal-worshiping pagans. All of that technology and advancement, and they still pray to a panther god like jungle heathens despite all of the hard work missionaries put into saving their souls. Their people must be starving to hear the real word from a man of the cloth."

"And I assume the missionaries were cooked in vats and sacrificed to their heathen gods," Batroc said sarcastically. "Or just didn't convert the poor jungle savages fast enough."

The knight looked at him blandly. "The last missionary sent into Wakanda never returned," he said.

"There are rumors he married a local woman and now runs a vegetable stand in their capital city," Klaw whispered.

"We've tried the book. Now we try the sword." The knight drew his broadsword from its scabbard. The blade glinted strangely in the evening light as he slashed it through the air. "With this unbreakable Ebony Blade, there is nothing that can stand in my Lord's way. 'You are my hammer and weapon of war: With you I break nations in pieces; with you I destroy kingdoms.'"

Klaw snapped his fingers. "Jeremiah 51:20. A favorite among warriors."

The Black Knight nodded his head. "Very good, Mr. Klaue. Perchance are you a believer?"

"My mother took me to Sunday school without fail," Klaw replied with a smile.

"God bless her. Gentleman, I must see to my horse and conduct evening prayers for King M'Butu. He has seemed receptive to my entreaties to work with his staff." The young man bowed and walked away, leading his horse toward the castle.

"I would have loved—loved—to have heard him try to convert M'Butu," Batroc laughed once the young man was out of earshot.

"It's not as hard as you might think," Klaw said thoughtfully. "Promise someone a country, plus a few million dollars in a Swiss account, to get his people to pay lip service to a religion, and miracles can happen."

With that, Klaw nodded toward a stone bunker at the far edge of the compound. "Anyway, what's the status on the rest of the team?"

"Go see for yourself," Batroc shrugged. "He wants to chat."

The brownish bunker was stark and utilitarian, nothing more than a solid square box with a narrow slit for a window. It only had two splashes of color: First was the universally recognized yellow-and-black radiation warning symbol painted in several places around it; the second was a sickly greenish glow emanating from the window, signifying the unique presence of the man inside.

Even hardbitten men like Klaw and Batroc stepped carefully around Igor Stancheck, the

Radioactive Man, whose powers could burn a man to a crisp or condemn the unlucky to lingering deaths in cancer-riddled bodies.

"How's it going in there, Igor?" Klaw called, while keeping a respectable distance from the window. "Did you need something?"

Batroc could see the green glare shift, altering the shadows inside the bunker, as Stancheck approached the slot and peered out. Batroc placed his hand over his crotch and took a couple of steps back, just to be safe.

"The toilet in here is backing up again." Stancheck's green, glowing eyes peered through the window, looking around. "It stinks to high heaven, comrade. I need a plumber, posthaste."

Klaw reached over to a nearby crate and picked up a Geiger counter, which began to beep madly as he waved it toward the window. "We can't send someone in now—the radiation levels are way too high. You'll have to tough it out for a few more days, my friend."

"Come on, man," Stancheck pleaded. "M'Butu's got to have a tech to spare somewhere around here. I'm going crazy in here, Klaw."

"I'll see what I can scrounge up," Klaw promised, backing away from the door. "Until then, keep working on the radiation signature of that rock I gave you. Our plan won't work without it."

"Yeah, yeah." Klaw barely heard the grumbled response as he and Batroc headed back toward the castle gardens. Once out of earshot, the mercenary pulled Klaw to the side.

"You know the Nigandans that M'Butu is letting us 'borrow' won't be of any use to us once the crap hits the fan, right?" Batroc said. "That leaves us with the brute and the glowbug."

Klaw eyed him silently for a moment. "And?"

"I do my research. This Panther, he and his lady bodyguards are no pushovers. In fact, they are supposed to be some of the best warriors in the world. And that's not counting his country's defenses and so-called secret police, the doggies of war or something like that.

"I have complete faith in your abilities, Klaw," Batroc continued, a slight frown on his face. "My skills are prodigious as well. But we will be badly outnumbered, and I can't spend my money if I am in a Wakandan prison. What chance do we realistically have against the Panther?"

Klaw hesitated, and Batroc understood the man's internal struggle. While the two of them had worked together for years, they weren't exactly friends. And in their line of work, information was power—and only grudgingly shared.

But there was something personal in this mission for Klaw, and that shifted the balance of power between them somewhat. Klaw desperately wanted T'Challa dead. And to do that, he was going to have to make some exceptions.

"Our chances?" The Belgian assassin looked

around to ensure no one else was listening, before leaning forward and whispering. "I'd say they were pretty good, considering I've already killed one Black Panther."

Batroc took a step back in shock. Everyone in the mercenary/assassin community knew about the Bilderberg job, if only because the Wakandans had been scouring the world for the perpetrators for more than a decade. The death of a king by an assassin's bullet was something special. But no one had ever identified the assassin who had pulled it off.

"That hit was *you?*" Batroc could not keep the amazement out of his voice.

"I almost killed the son then, too. He hurt me, but he made the mistake of not killing me." Klaw paused. "They will all regret that mercy."

KLAW grabbed Batroc by the arm and dragged him into the palace, searching for an empty room. Finding an abandoned office, Klaw pulled out a small electronic box and plugged it into a port in his metal hand. Batroc heard a soft hissing and popping sound, and pulled out his cellphone only to find that it was dead.

"Miniature electromagnetic pulse, which fries unshielded electronics and ensures privacy from snooping devices," Klaw explained.

"I will add the phone to my list of expenses," Batroc said. "But continue."

Klaw took a breath and expelled it. Despite himself, he admired the French mercenary more than he should. Assassins didn't have friends—certainly not mercenaries, who were known to switch sides in the middle of a fight for the right paycheck. And Batroc was totally immoral and untrustworthy. He could only be expected to be loyal as long as the money lasted.

But Klaw had carried this familial burden alone for decades. He was weary. And while sharing unnecessary information was dangerous for people like them, someone should know what Wakanda had done to his ancestors.

"This isn't a coup," he sighed. "This is a blood feud. My family has a...history with the Panther clan of Wakanda."

Batroc stepped back, slowly edging his way toward the door. "This is personal? Mon ami, when it gets personal is when it gets bloody. And unnecessary blood is bad for business."

Klaw grabbed him by the arm, eyes desperate. "I need you for this," he hissed. "Like you said, the rest of the team is either crazy or just plain incompetent."

Batroc looked unsure. "I charge extra for the personal jobs. And I'm going to need to know everything." He poked Klaw in the chest. "Everything. If I'm going to die for someone else's honor, I want to know what I am fighting for."

Klaw let go of his arm, then walked over and sat on top of the desk. His eyes strayed up to the ceiling as he immersed himself in the memory. "I'll tell you everything, I promise. But for you to understand, I have to give you a little history."

Klaw walked over to the wall, which held a massive painting of M'Butu on top of a tank, leading troops across a bloody plain. He studied it for a while before turning back to face Batroc.

"Contrary to the delusion the leader of this country peddles, Wakanda has never invaded another country. They certainly didn't steal their greatest resource, something they call the Great Mound. Instead, Niganda has repeatedly been rebuffed in its attempts to invade Wakanda and take possession of the Vibranium underneath the Great Mound." Klaw hesitated. "You know what Vibranium is, correct?"

Batroc nodded. "Rare metal, absorbs and dissipates any blunt force or energy impact. The most valuable single natural resource on the planet."

"And Wakanda is sitting on top of *all* of it," Klaw continued. "Which has put them in the crosshairs for the country's entire existence. The Nigandans have repeatedly tried to conquer Wakanda, and repeatedly they've been thrown back beyond the borders with nothing to show for it. Nothing but dead warriors—and stories about a fearsome were-cat with magic powers.

"At least that's what my great-great-great-grandfather was told by his Nigandan slaves as his"—Klaw put air quotes around the next word—"exploratory force neared the Wakandan border.

"The first Ulysses Klaue, the man I'm named after, was one of the founders of South Africa. He had heard stories about the fabled land of Wakanda and its fearsome king. More importantly, he'd heard about the massive wealth the land supposedly contained, and he wanted his fair share before someone else got there."

"So he just decided to take it?" Batroc looked confused.

"Yes," Klaw sighed, with a faraway expression on his face. "Remember, this was the 19th century. Back when a man could be a man, and seize his own destiny.

"So my ancestor bought some extra slaves and marched them toward Wakanda with the finest weapons the Belgium government could provide. I've found letters from some of the men who went with him. They say the blacks were nervous as they got close to Wakanda, despite having been capable fighters in South Africa and other campaigns across the continent. Finally, my ancestor's men had to shoot over half of them because they simply refused to go any farther."

He looked over at Batroc, searching his face for any emotion or judgment. Finding none, he continued.

"Well, according to the stories we've been told, the white men and what few slaves were left made it to the edge of Wakanda. I think about what they saw sometimes. A virgin land where no European had set foot before that day. Vibranium and gold everywhere, and nothing but a bunch of spear-chucking, bare-chested Africans between them and the booty."

Klaw sighed. "I'm sure they told themselves that a barrage from the cannon they had lugged across half the continent would settle the Wakandans' hash. If not, they had Gatling guns, grenades, and other weapons no African had ever seen before. Or so they thought.

"The survivors said the Black Panther appeared out of nowhere in front of them, staring at them from across a plain. Even back then, he wore that stupid cat mask, but this one also had some kind of cape flapping in the wind, a loincloth, and a spear, like some damn primitive caveman.

"Now, Ulysses Klaue had more than 50 well-armed men, so I'm sure a lone jungle kook in a cape didn't faze him at all. He ordered his men to take aim. Then he shouted for the Panther to surrender, and send out the women and children to be held as hostages.

"The survivors said the Panther never moved, but behind him some kind of…mechanical totem rose up from the ground. To this day, we have no idea what that thing was, but the Panther was supremely confident in the safety it gave him and his people.

"They said he spoke, and even though they were all the way across a grassy field, every single man heard him clearly: 'Leave now, and I will let you live. Attack, and only one of you will be left standing to tell the story.'

"Even back then, no one—and I mean no one—threatened a Klaue and got away with it. I'm sure the men had a good laugh as Klaue ordered them to cut the Panther down. What happened next we've never been able to explain." Klaw rubbed his head in exasperation.

"Every single gun misfired, like someone had placed charges inside. Men screamed and flung down burning weapons, tearing off pieces of burnt skin that had fused to the hot metal of the rifles. One unfortunate bugger's clothes caught fire, and he burned alive before they could get the flames out. Another man's grenades ignited, blowing off his hands before he could fling the grenades away.

"The whole time, the Panther never moved. He just stared as they fumbled about in distress.

"My great-great-great-grandfather shouted at his men to form ranks again, but it was useless. The whole time they had been in Africa, no one had put up true resistance to them, and it seemed they'd gone soft. At least that's what Ulysses is reported to have screamed at them, as he ordered the survivors to man one of the Gatling guns and blast the bastard. But no one would listen, afraid of more misfires.

"Even over the moan of the maimed, they could hear the whispered warning from the Panther. 'Last chance to leave with your wounded.'

"Klaue refused to admit defeat and manned the gun himself. The last thing they heard him say was a challenge: 'Can your ju-ju handle 700 rounds a minute?' The Panther, they say, never moved an inch. 'Die, you black—'

"The explosion threw bits of my grandfather all across the plains. The Panther apparently showed the rest of them mercy and allowed them to scour the ground for his remains after he forced them to dig graves for the slaves they had killed. Now weaponless, the Panther marched them to the coast and told them never to return upon penalty of death.

"When they got back to South Africa, they presented my pregnant great-great-greatgrandmother with the largest piece they could find of her husband, which was his boot. Upon her husband's body, Adalheida Klaue swore that her descendants would never forget or forgive."

Klaw looked up at Batroc, eyes shining with hatred. "And we haven't. The Panther killed my great-great-great-grandfather in an unfair fight. It was only appropriate that his descendants die in just as ignoble a way, and for it to be at my hands was perfection personified."

Mesmerized, Batroc realized that he had been holding his breath. "But you still haven't explained how you did it," he pointed out. "Wakandan security and technology is supposedly only rivaled by Latveria and Symkaria. There should have been no way you could penetrate their defensive perimeter, even at the Bilderberg."

Klaw just smiled.

CHAPTER EIGHT

SHURI padded silently down the Hall of Kings, sweat dripping from her leopard-print workout gear and the drenched braids tied up behind her head. The palace servants had already fled from the raised voices echoing off the arched ceilings, leaving her alone as she crept past T'Challa's office and the large painting of T'Chaka. The voices grew louder as she drew near her mother's suite, the eyes of her ancestors seeming to disapprove of her presence as she glided soundlessly down the unfamiliar halls. Any argument she could hear from the downstairs gymnasium was one worth finding out about, especially if it concerned her.

Sneaking around really wasn't necessary, she knew. As crown princess, Shuri had her own office space in the same section of the palace, but she rarely used it. She preferred to work in her private suite with its warm brown panels and wall-length bookshelves. She loved her electronic readers, but preferred the heft, weight, and smell of a real book when relaxing alone. And, of course, the large paneled windows overlooking the topiary she had begged for as a child. Her mother had rebuffed her for years, not understanding her juvenile fascination with ornately trimmed bushes in the shapes of griffins, dragons, and unicorns. She'd negotiated, sulked, screamed, and finally flat-out pleaded for months with no success, her mother insisting it was unnecessary, extravagant, and unseemly. Why, she said patiently, would anyone install imaginary leafy beasts in a palace where the children could see live animals like elephants and giraffes anytime they wanted?

Only when T'Challa added his voice to the pleas had the Queen Mother grudging relented. Ramonda had ordered the shrubbery planted and trimmed, with the majority of it easily visible from Shuri's bedroom. Even now, Shuri smiled at the memory of T'Challa's teenaged grin as she bounced up and down excitedly, cheering their victory over their mother. It had been years before she realized that her mother hadn't planted the topiary because her daughter wanted it, but because her stepson wanted it for his sister. Sometimes, when looking out at her favorite scene—a spiky green dragon with a flared tail and curly horns rearing up, menacing a smaller winged unicorn—that thought made her sad.

Shuri's eyes and ears were much sharper than most people knew. Few outside the castle realized she was undergoing the same training T'Challa had endured, and even those who did know underestimated how much her senses had been enhanced. Consequently, she heard much of what the palace servants whispered, despite their attempts to stifle conversations upon her entrance into halls and offices. She heard the sneers they thought they were masking from her, the questioning of her value to the royal family. She knew they, along with many of her countrymen, only considered her a "spare"—and a substandard one at that.

Lately, although her mother had yet to broach the topic with her, the questions had turned to which African prince or millionaire she'd be matched with to birth more spares for the line of succession. Luckily for her, T'Challa had yet to choose a queen, so most of the rumormongers devoted their attention to speculating about every woman her brother gazed at when they attended the hundreds of balls, charity events, and conferences the royal schedule demanded. They often laughed—privately, of course—at how quickly the puffed-up, pampered princesses and heiresses shrunk back at the glares of the statuesque and well-armed *Dora Milaje* at his side. T'Challa had once confided during one of their morning workout sessions that he had caught Nakia subtly adjusting her high heels and "accidentally" flashing a wickedly long blade strapped at her thigh beneath her floor-length velvet evening gown at one moon-eyed suitor who hadn't gotten the message.

No, T'Challa wasn't likely to be married anytime soon. Shuri knew the attention would soon turn to her, now that she was legally "of age" and eligible to be betrothed. But she wanted what T'Challa had had: years of freedom in overseas lands where no one knew her or cared about what clothes she wore, what clubs she frequented, or whom she kissed. While she lacked her brother's incredible intellect—it grated on her how hard she had to work to grasp the challenging scientific concepts that T'Challa seemed to absorb easily—Shuri knew she could ace the entrance exams of the finest institutions in the world without breaking a mental sweat. The question was: Would her mother give her that chance?

Shuri made a mental note to approach T'Challa about the idea when he returned later in the day from his inspection tour of the Great Mound. Getting her brother on board would make convincing their mother a lot easier. T'Challa had been weirdly protective of her since ascending to the throne, but Shuri was confident that she'd be able to convince him of the merit of her getting more experience in the outside world—especially since she anticipated being given expanded duties soon as crown princess.

But the first hurdle was finding out what had Mother so aggravated, she thought as she crept up to the wood-paneled door. The usually even-tempered woman had raised her voice loud enough that it could be heard outside her office. No one had dared to inspire that level of fury from the Queen Mother, not even Shuri—at least not since the king's death.

"It was your fault they were there in the first place, Ramonda!" a female voice shouted. "You wanted freedom. I warned you again and again about the evils of the outside world, but you forced Beloved's hand, and we all paid the price."

"You need to watch your tone with me, General," Shuri heard her mother hiss. "You go too far. I am still the Queen Mother, and your allegiance is still to me. Do you understand?"

"My allegiance is to the king, who is the son of my best friend, the queen," the voice replied haughtily. "Do not punish my sisters because of my past failures—if not for your son's sake, then for his father's, who only wanted what was best for *his* beloved."

"How dare…" Shuri heard her mother stop, and footsteps approach the door.

Shuri quietly slid away from the door, hoping she would be able to get a glimpse of the person willing to talk to her mother in such a disrespectful way, even in private.

The room had gone silent. Hesitantly she creeped closer and leaned forward against the ornately carved double doors for a peep through the cracks. Suddenly they swung open, almost toppling her into the room.

Standing there, glaring through her remaining eye, was Amare.

If not for the cloudy glass eye and distinctive jagged scar across her face, Shuri felt as if she would never have recognized the *Dora Milaje's* general. Instead of the traditional light armor, Amare wore a sleeveless black dress that hung off her powerful shoulders and accentuated the multicolored wrap wound tightly around her head. A stark-white cape was clasped around her neck, held on by a jade panther amulet with glittering diamond eyes. Shuri admired the woman's willingness to wear such revealing clothes despite the milky white, jagged scars and missing flesh that marred her arms and legs. Amare could be easily mistaken for a visiting dignitary.

As Amare stepped forward, Shuri could make out the faint whir of the electronics in the woman's prosthetic leg, which was capped off with a stylish black high-heeled boot. Absurdly, Shuri wondered for a quick second how much work the woman had put into relearning not only how to walk, but also how to fight in heels.

"Princess." Amare gathered up her cape around her body, shielding her scars from Shuri's probing view. She spoke in a gruff, clipped tone, as if she were holding back strong emotions. "Okoye and Nakia will meet you later this evening in the gymnasium to map out a regimen of training for you that will satisfy both your and their needs. They are my most prized students, and they will serve you well."

Shuri nodded hesitantly and looked over at her mother. Ramonda was seated behind her desk with a stony look on her face. "That will be…satisfactory, General."

Amare turned back toward the desk and nodded, avoiding making eye contact with the queen. "By your leave, my queen."

"Dismissed." Ramonda flicked her hand toward the woman, who stalked off down the hallway. When the click of Amare's heels was not as loud in her ears, Shuri closed the double doors and flowed over to her mother, who had leaned back in her chair with her hands covering her eyes.

Shuri leaned over and hugged her clearly distraught mother, rocking back and forth slightly. For a moment, Shuri felt her mother relax in her embrace—but then the older woman tensed up again. Disappointed, Shuri let her go and sat on the desk.

"Mother, is something wrong?"

RAMONDA wiped her eyes gently, then cleared her throat. "First, young lady, get your sweaty rear end off my desk."

Shuri hopped down, pulling around a chair to stay within hugging distance of her mother. *Hope springs eternal,* Ramonda thought darkly.

"Second, it's simply gauche to eavesdrop on private conversations, even for a princess with enhanced hearing. My past with General Amare has nothing to do with you, and I expect you to keep whatever you heard in confidence."

"Of course, Mother. But what was that all about? What past?"

Ramonda rocked forward to prop her head on her hands on her desk. "Really, daughter, I am in no mood to go through this with you," she sighed. "Perhaps some other time."

Ramonda jumped when Shuri slapped her palm down on the desk. "No, Mother—now. Decisions are being made about my life without me, and I won't have it. Tell me what's going on and why General Amare is so angry with you. You're talking about putting me in the hands of a woman who may hold some mysterious grudge against my mother, without giving me any ammunition to defend myself. I have not fought you on any major decision lately, but I promise you, I will not willingly walk myself into what could be a trap just because you're 'not in the mood.'"

Ramonda's eyes flashed for a second at Shuri's defiance, but then softened. "You're so much like my mother," Ramonda whispered, almost to herself. "I see T'Chaka when I look at your brother, but I see my beloved mother in your eyes. Even as a baby, you looked just like her. You even have her voice, and her frustrating stubbornness. She never listened to anyone, either."

Ramonda stood with a huff and walked over to a glass-topped bar in the corner. She poured two small brandies into tumblers, tucked the decanter under her arm, and glided over to a white leather couch ensconced in a quiet corner of her office. Shuri followed with hesitation as her mother plopped down on the couch. Shuri folded her legs up next to her on a pillow, and watched her mother take a small sip from one of the brandies.

Ramonda nodded toward the second glass. "If you're old enough to hear this, you're old enough to drink with your mother. And I'll need this and more if I'm going to tell you the full story."

"The full story?" Shuri picked up her brandy and ran one of her nails around the rim. "What full story?"

Ramonda smiled sadly. "The story of how your father died. Though young, T'Challa was there. You hadn't been born yet, so I've never felt the need to dredge up that day beyond the official accounts. But you're right: You deserve to know, since the repercussions of that day are still affecting us now."

"Mom." Ramonda quirked her eyebrow at that. Her children usually addressed her with the less familiar "mother." "Whatever it is, you can tell me. I won't judge."

Ramonda half-laughed into her brandy. "You would be the first, then, baby. You see, it was my fault that your father decided to go to the Bilderberg Conference in the first place. I convinced him to take that meeting, despite the warnings of his brother, the *Dora Milaje*, the war cabinet, and the ruling council. And they've never let me forget."

Ramonda looked down into her glass, avoiding Shuri's eyes. "Every Wakandan child is taught that King T'Chaka was felled by an assassin's bullet while negotiating trade deals. 'Sacrificing himself by throwing himself in front of his family, T'Chaka saved the royal lineage by taking what would have been a fatal shot for the pregnant queen.'"

Shuri picked up from there, reciting the well-worn, rote lines they taught about her father. "'The cowardly assassin struck down the two members of the *Dora Milaje* with a grenade while they were fighting valiantly to get the king and his family to safety. All was lost until Prince T'Challa, who was still a youth, got his hands on one of the assassin's weapons and struck back, wounding the assassin and forcing him to flee for his life. But by the time backup arrived, the king had perished…cradled in his love's arms, with the young prince at his side. The boy's childhood was over.'"

Shuri wrinkled her nose at her brandy before taking a tiny sip. "As you say, Mother, everyone knows that story. An unknown assassin shot my father and escaped after being winged by T'Challa. What else is there to know?"

Ramonda exhaled. "What else? Everything. You see, that's not exactly what happened.

Ramonda sighed, lost in her memories as she unconsciously rubbed her now flat stomach. "I was so tired during my pregnancy. Your father was so kind to me…he knew I was lonely for hearth and home. My hormones were running wild, and he found me in tears at night sometimes, inconsolable and homesick."

Ramonda looked at Shuri, sadness in her eyes. "Wakanda is a paradise on Earth. Truly, there is nowhere else comparable to the Golden City— but it just wasn't *home* to me back then. However, foreigners had to choose permanent residency if they wanted to live in Wakanda, and that applied to the future queen as well. T'Chaka understood my sorrow, but there was little he could do to change the law. And then we got an invitation from the Bilderberg Conference.

"W'Kabi had just been named security chief and was chafing to show how crucial his counsel was to the king. So he and S'Yan, T'Chaka's two closest advisors, argued that it was foolish for the king to attend the conference, given the kingdom's stance on keeping Wakanda isolated. What, they argued, could the West offer us in exchange for Vibranium or our technological advances? A better hydrogen bomb? More caviar? There was nothing the kingdom needed from greedy capitalists.

"But I argued that it was time for Wakanda to join modern society—to do more than just protect its own sons and daughters. The world needed Wakandan science and technology to improve mankind's lot. We had the potential to influence lesser countries to forsake the evils of the past, like apartheid and Jim Crow, if we'd only try.

"S'Yan told me later that I gave the most impassioned speech he'd ever seen in chambers. T'Chaka was certainly impressed, even though it was never clear which way the rest of the council would have voted on my suggestion to open the borders.

"They all agreed to leave our attendance at the Bilderberg Conference to the king's discretion. With my influence, he agreed to go. Did I have an ulterior motive? To open the borders as a way to openly travel back to South Africa and raise up my people from a life they didn't deserve? Maybe—but I truly thought I was arguing for the greater good, for both Wakanda and the world. Unfortunately, not everyone wanted T'Chaka striding across the world stage."

KLAW stared grimly into Batroc's eyes, his hatred for the Panther clearly visible. The sound of metal on metal reverberated through the office as the Black Knight sparred with the Rhino, who chuckled as he deflected the young knight's thrusts and parries. Nigandan troops gathered around the pair in a ring, shouting encouragement or curses, depending on the bet they had made.

Klaw ignored all of this, intent on his story.

"I would have killed T'Chaka for free, but the fact I was getting $10 million for his royal head only made it sweeter. This job was going to make my reputation internationally, especially since global economic conferences attracted many potential employers for an assassin.

"But no one knew what to expect once Wakanda was invited to the big-boy table. And the Panther himself would be no pushover. Back then, though, I was young and eager to make my name, you know? There weren't as many powered people around, but the team I assembled was top-notch. With a month to plan, I thought we put together a reasonably actionable strategy, considering what we were dealing with. The Bilderberg Conference's security was always tight, but it was nothing we couldn't handle. The biggest concern, however, was would we get the green light?"

Klaw pulled out a pair of sunglasses and began shining them on his khaki shirt. "Remember, the powers that be wanted Wakandan resources and technology. Untouched petroleum deposits, medical breakthroughs unknown to the Western world, and don't forget the Vibranium—the rarest, most valuable mineral on Earth. If T'Chaka agreed to open the borders, then they wanted him left in power so they wouldn't have to restart negotiations with a whole new government. Only if that arrogant potentate threw the business offers back in their faces was I to act—and I would even get a bonus if I eliminated the entire line: father, mother, and son."

Klaw smiled. "I wasn't worried. The Black Panther I had researched for the past month was never going to take their offers."

FIFTEEN YEARS AGO

T'CHAKA strode down the hallway, trailed by the *Dora Milaje* and his business-suited personal economists. The king brushed some lint from his royal boubou as he walked into the main conference room, the wide black sleeves of his velvety green robe quietly rustling with every move. As he made his way to the head of the table, T'Chaka looked around at the white men gathered in the room and quietly computed in his head the combined gross national product of each country or corporation represented there that morning. If they pooled their resources, T'Chaka thought, they could end world hunger within six months, eradicate malaria in another three, and eliminate homelessness completely within the decade. But that wasn't on the agenda for these gentlemen, who saw Wakanda as nothing but a way to increase their own personal profit margins.

T'Chaka took his seat and declined the offer of alcohol from a secretary. A Roxxon Corp. representative cleared his throat.

"Your majesty, we at Roxxon don't believe in wasting the time of august persons such as yourself." The weasel-faced man smiled a sickly insincere smile across the table. "Here's our offer, and I speak for all of the varied interests at this table: We'll pay whatever price you set for your goods. You won't get a better deal than that anywhere."

T'Chaka strummed his fingers on the glass-topped table, careful not to press his fingers down on the slick surface. He pretended to consider the offer. He could feel Amare shift her weight behind him as she triggered the customary jamming signals the *Dora Milaje* used when the king was abroad. When T'Chaka walked out the door, these men would have no recording of his voice, no photographs of his face, and no fingerprints for their corporate spies to use in future mischief.

T'Chaka stood, towering over the table. "Here is

my answer: Wakanda's riches are not for sale," he said calmly. "Until the spiritual advancement of the West catches up with its technological prowess, it would be irresponsible to share our scientific advancements with you. It would be like handing a child a loaded gun and hoping for the best. We will not be party to your destruction."

"Are you calling everyone here irresponsible children?" The Roxxon representative glared around the table at his compatriots, whose mouths gaped at the Wakandan's arrogance.

"No," T'Chaka began walking toward the door, the *Dora Milaje* at his heels. "More like sullen teenagers who believe themselves more mature than their behavior warrants. The fact that every conversation here is framed in terms of power and profit says it all, and confirms my worst fears about your society."

The king stopped at the door, angrily looking back at the stunned men. "You could have made half of our breakthroughs yourselves, but there's too much money to be made in misery." He shook his head at their stupidity. "Why not invest some of your wealth in educating your children, instead of building new and more powerful weapons you hope never to have to use? Why not build roads and bridges and hospitals, instead of million-dollar football stadiums with taxpayer money?

"I can tell you why: Your society's sick fixation with money has overridden your good sense to the point of obsession. Why cure a disease when you can force people to pay for medicine? Why provide cheap energy when you can continue to pump a limited resource that damages the—"

"We get the point, T'Chaka. We don't need a lecture from you." The red-faced Roxxon representative's interruption brought the *Dora Milaje* up short at the insult. T'Chaka shook his head slightly, stopping Amare—who had already slid a throwing knife out of her sleeve and was eyeing the weasel-faced man.

Oblivious to this, the man began to chuckle at T'Chaka. "I've never met a socialist with a crown on his head before, but I guess there's a first time for everything. Perhaps your people would do better with more…enlightened leadership, like the South Africans and the Nigandans?""

T'Chaka took a step forward and smiled dangerously down at the little man. Light glinted off the king's sharpened teeth. The man went pale under his gaze.

"Every breath you take from this moment on is a gift I have granted you," T'Chaka said quietly. "Any man or woman who talked that way to me in my homeland would be discussing their misstep with their ancestors by now, but I will forgive your mistake this once because of your childlike ignorance."

A man reclining at the edge of the table snapped his fingers. Two Nordic bodyguards rushed into the room from an adjoining anteroom, rifles held high and aimed at the Wakandans.

"Calm down, T'Chaka," he drawled smugly.

"You don't have the advantage here."

T'Chaka crossed his arms calmly. "I don't?"

As he spoke, Amare flung her knife with blinding speed, pinning the hand of the first gunman to the wall. He howled as blood spurted across his fallen rifle. At the same time, Bapoto produced a microfilament whip and cracked it across the room. The tail of the whip wrapped around the second man's rifle barrel; with a strong tug, Bapoto jerked the weapon from the man's hand and threw it across the room. One of T'Chaka's economists caught it and aimed it back at the men around the table with one smooth motion.

T'Chaka never moved.

"Who gave you permission to use my first name? You don't even *think* about me without using my earned title," the king snarled. "I understand your frustration in dealing with a black man who can't be bought with a truck full of guns, a planeload of blondes, or a Swiss bank account. But hold on to what little class you have."

A small yellow puddle pooled at the Roxxon representative's feet. "Your majesty," he stammered, "I truly apologize."

T'Chaka looked disgustedly across the room. He had wasted enough time with these men. "This meeting is over. Do not contact me again."

He turned his back and strode out the doorway, followed by his economists. The last one threw his purloined rifle down in the doorway, but pocketed the clip.

The two *Dora Milaje* silently gathered up their weapons, Bapoto coiling her whip back around her waist. Amare jerked her knife out of the guard's hand, causing him to whimper in pain again. The two women backed their way out of the room, never taking their eyes off the men gathered at the table in case one wanted to try for some last-second retaliation.

Once they had closed the door, the businessmen all exhaled as one and began to chatter amongst themselves.

"Smithers, you're pathetic," said the man who had summoned the guards. "Clean yourself up, then give our friend a call and tell him the operation is a go."

Smithers, the Roxxon executive, ran out of the room, leaving a trail of urine behind him. He swore that T'Chaka—King T'Chaka, his mind involuntary corrected—would pay for this humiliation.

I WASN'T told anything about what happened in the meeting until the inquest weeks later," Ramonda said, taking a strong pull from her brandy. "All I knew was that T'Chaka was in a foul mood when he returned to the suite. As always, though, he tried to hide it from me and T'Challa."

WHY DO we have to leave immediately, Daddy?" T'Challa whined, grabbing onto his father's leg and looking up pleadingly. "You said we could go skiing after your meeting. You promised!"

T'Chaka laughed and walked over to Ramonda, dragging the young T'Challa clinging to his leg along with every step. He folded his wife in his arms, inhaling her spicy scent, and felt a small kick from her belly against his leg. Prying T'Challa free, he knelt and kissed his wife's stomach.

"So you think we should go skiing as well?" he said to his unborn daughter, drawing a giggle from Ramonda. "This is why we have to leave. Our children grow more insolent with each breath of European air."

ONCE it became clear no deal was to be made, my job kicked in," Klaw said.

THE FIRST shot struck the glass window near T'Chaka's head. Two others quickly followed, thudding against the window like hammer strikes.

I KNEW the window was bulletproof, but that didn't worry me," Klaw said. "The armor-piercing rounds would blow right through that, once the outside shooter could pinpoint T'Chaka's location. What I didn't know was that earlier, the king's security team had laid a see-through microlayer of Vibranium weave across the glass. It absorbed the energy from the shots and stopped them cold.

"We only had seconds before we lost the window of opportunity completely, so to speak. Time for Plan B."

YOUR father threw me to the ground the second he heard the bullet." Ramonda wiped away her tears, the painful memories welling up to the forefront. "Amare tackled your brother, and yelled for Bapoto to get their gear from the cases near the front door. Bapoto hesitated for one second, and then took off at top speed toward the door. But by then it was too late."

THE EXPLOSION threw Bapoto across the room and into a wall-length mirror. Ramonda heard a sickening crack, and tried to peer around T'Chaka's encircling arms. "Keep down," the king hissed, but Ramonda could see the blood gushing from a scar on top of the young *Dora Milaje*'s head, and a jagged wooden fragment jutting from her throat. Half of her face had been burned in the explosion, and her eyes were wide and unmoving. "Bapoto!" Ramonda screamed.

T'Chaka looked over at the newly formed crater in the room as a gun slowly emerged from the smoke.

KLAW shrugged.

"I had been waiting underneath the floorboards of the room for a week. When you're getting $10 million for a hit, a week in a refrigerated sleeping bag to throw off heat sensors is small potatoes. As for T'Chaka's vaunted nose, an extra $20 for the cleaners to ensure a daily application of wood polish—lemon scented, I believe— was enough to mask my scent from the Panther."

"I was lucky right off the bat with the death of the first girl. The point of a distraction like the shaped charges is to create as much chaos as possible and gain an edge over a dangerous opponent." Klaw smiled. "When that piece of debris took out one of his beloved 'Adored Ones,' it really distracted the Panther."

KLAW stood up and took a second to survey the landscape for his targets. Someone—most likely several someones—was pounding on the door, trying desperately to get into the room. T'Chaka, still wearing his royal robes, looked on in shock as he cradled his pregnant wife, trying to put his body between her and the assassin. The remaining female bodyguard was trying to push the crown prince behind a sofa as she fumbled with a weapon, her useless right hand dangling down. Wood fragments had punctured her body in several places, including her right hand and her leg, which now was gushing blood.

I THOUGHT it would be a turkey shoot at that point," Klaw admitted. "I had two guns, and I had the momentum. But greater men than I have underestimated the Panther, and few have lived to tell about it."

A SLOW growl grew in T'Chaka's throat. Ramonda would later swear she saw his eyes flash green as he turned to tenderly cup her chin one final time. In the time it took for the assassin to swing his Uzis toward them, T'Chaka was up and leaping across the room at the pale-faced man, metal claws flashing.

"My king! *No!*" Amare shouted, uselessly.

HE WAS so fast," Klaw said admiringly. "Even with the explosion, his vulnerable wife, one dead bodyguard, and a crippled second one, he was able to suss out the situation and press the attack with speed and grace. You have to admire that kind of training. I don't even know where the claws came from—inside his robes, maybe?

"Anyway, he slashed my face"—Klaw traced the milky white scars across his cheeks and through his left eye—"here and here. I was about to lose an eye and my life. That cocky son-of-a-bitch even blocked my Uzi, sending it across the room. But the other one was right in position."

I FELT the bullets enter your father's body," Ramonda whispered in horror. "There's no other way to explain it. The white-hot pain was indescribable, like nothing I'd felt before or since, and I'm sure that I blacked out for a second. When I came to, for some reason I was standing and walking toward poor T'Chaka. I could hear Amare screaming for me to get down, but I couldn't stop myself. I had to get to my husband—but before I could take more than a step, I felt him die."

KLAW staggered to his feet, wiping the warm, salty blood out of his eyes so he could find an escape. Behind him, he could hear a fire ax chopping its way through the suite's door. He fumbled through one of his pouches for a grenade and tossed it in the general direction of the doorway. The door gave way with a crack, and three armed accountants rushed in, searching through the smoke for the king. One stumbled forward and saw the grenade rolling slowly at his feet.

"Grena—"

The explosion threw the three of them back out of the room, limbs flying everywhere. Klaw nodded to himself and turned back toward the remaining royals. Ramonda stood blank-faced, staring at him.

NOW, AT this point, my number-one goal should have been to get out alive," Klaw continued. "But I was young, and there was an extra $5 million if I exterminated the entire line, and she was standing right there! One shot, and I've eliminated the mother and daughter. Then I'd tag the kid and his crippled bodyguard, and rappel my way down the wall.

"But you know what they say about best-laid plans…"

KLAW slowly and deliberately lifted his Uzi, and trained the red targeting dot on Ramonda's head. "Night night," he whispered to himself as he began to pull the trigger. But before he could fire, two red-hot pokers jabbed him in his arm, searing him with unyielding heat and unbelievable pain. Klaw dropped down to one knee and screamed, looking around for the source.

THAT damn kid shot me with my own gun," Klaw shook his head. "Can you believe that? Turned out that the last remaining bodyguard had crawled over to where my second Uzi had fallen, threw it to the boy and told him to take his best shot."

Klaw ran his right hand down his left arm, and pulled back the epidermis to show Batroc the metal lying just beneath his skin. "I guess the punk missed my torso and shot me in the arm by accident. But it was enough to convince me that it was time to go. I knew I had to get out of there before I snatched defeat out of the jaws of victory, so to speak. So taking a header out of a seventh-floor window was the better option. I knew I had a team downstairs waiting with an inflatable to cushion my fall, and a helicopter on the backside of the hotel prepped for a quick getaway."

RAMONDA hugged Shuri tight up against her body, tears flowing freely down her face.

"I don't remember much about the aftermath. Most of the official details came from Amare. The backup security team apparently stormed the hotel, but they never could find the man who shot your father. By the time they made it to our suite, I was paralyzed with grief. T'Challa wouldn't let go of that damn gun, and Amare was crawling across the floor trying to get to your father's body.

"T'Challa and I were the only surviving members of the royal family: the orphaned son, the second wife, and her unborn baby. So they hustled us to the airport and rushed us back to Wakanda to safety. The royal doctor checked you and me out, and declared us healthy and untouched by the carnage. They gave me a mild tranquilizer, put *Dora Milaje* at the doors of my suite, and ordered me to sleep.

"T'Challa didn't say a word the whole way, and I'm told he only surrendered the gun at the request of your uncle S'Yan. For months, he didn't speak and barely ate. He eventually got better, but the young joyous boy who wanted to ski with his parents died with his father. He became even more studious and serious, spending all his time improving his body and his intellect, foregoing all of the enjoyments a young prince should indulge in."

Ramonda leaned over and kissed her daughter on the head. "Until you came along. When he was playing with you as a baby one day, I heard him laugh. It was then that I realized that he hadn't laughed since that horrible day. Not once, until you brought it out of him."

Drawing a deep breath, Ramonda continued with her story. "Weeks later, the commission investigating your father's death dragged Amare, still in a hospital bed minus one leg, into an inquisition room and grilled her about the *Dora Milaje*'s failure to protect the king. S'Yan had already informed them of my insistence that we attend the Bilderberg Conference, and several people had heard the *Dora Milaje*'s warnings against it. But under oath, Amare refused to place any blame on me, saying it was the *Dora Milaje*'s responsibility to change the king's mind, and they had failed. The commission came very close to exiling her, but in the end sent her back to her sisters for whatever punishment they deemed necessary.

"As you can see, they made her a general," Ramonda said bitterly. "Our relationship has been… tense ever since. And to this day, no one has been able to tell us who the man was who killed your father. The only name we've been able to find is Klaw."

ALTHOUGH I didn't kill the entire line, my sponsors were grateful enough to hide me from the Wakandans for the next decade or so." Klaw sighed. "After that clawing by the Panther and the gunshots from his son, I was barely clinging to life myself. But the Belgian government took good care of me; they provided me with these enhancements to replace the limb and eye ruined by the Panther."

Klaw gestured at his body. "By the time they were finished, I was what you see today: the world's finest assassin, once again. And now, my sponsors are providing us with the resources I need to take revenge on the Panther—to avenge my family's honor, and the loss of my arm and eye. I will have him, even if we have to work with lazy Nigandans and a group of C-list super villains to get it done."

SHURI hugged her mother tightly again, and let her sob on her shoulder until all of the tears were gone. Then she curled up on her mother's lap, her green eyes looking directly into her mother's gray ones.

"Thank you for telling me all of that, Mom," Shuri said. "I understand how difficult that must have been."

"Thank you, Shuri."

"And Mom? I'll be ready and waiting for the *Dora Milaje* in the gym tonight, don't you worry."

Ramonda stroked her daughter's hair, and smiled. "I never had any doubt, dear."

CHAPTER NINE

ONE ADVANTAGE of being king over crown prince was that T'Challa could now dictate the forms of his own travel, instead of having it forced upon him by his regent uncle. There would be no ten-car escort this morning, no motorcycles with sirens blaring or black SUVs with *Dora Milaje* hanging from the sides carrying automatic weapons. He had instead requested a simple four-door electric sedan from the motor pool. In deference to the *Dora Milaje*—and, honestly, to forestall their inevitable complaints about him being cavalier with his life—he ordered a single black SUV for them and their equipment.

Nakia complained anyway, much to his amusement. The younger of his two most loyal *Dora Milaje* had become much more outspoken and headstrong since their return from the United States, T'Challa thought. Quickly crunching the numbers on her Kimoyo pad, she insisted that the royal sedan, while fuel-efficient and eco-friendly, would not provide sufficient protection for the king in case of attack while outside the palace.

"Do you expect an attack today during my visit to the most secure location in the kingdom?" T'Challa spoke in Hausa, with a twinkle in his eye. Nakia looked down furiously, her dark skin reddening as

she blushed under his stare.

"Our job, Beloved, is to expect the unexpected and be prepared," Nakia stuttered, scuffing her boot on the concrete of the royal motor pool. *"The royal limousine has stronger armor and more communications equipment. We can fit in more options for the royal vestments and weapons in the rear. It makes more sense."*

T'Challa looked over at Okoye, who stood nearby silently, her facial expressions unreadable. Like Nakia, Okoye was wearing her light armor, with several of her favorite weapons strapped on different parts of her body. A short sword hung on her back.

"And you, do you agree with her evaluation of today's security needs?"

"Nakia is right," Okoye said tonelessly, her face blank. *"Unless you give us orders to the contrary, the royal limousine is the correct choice and should be used."*

T'Challa chuckled and walked over to the limousine. *"Who am I to ignore the advice of those who have only my best interests at heart?"* he said, climbing into the back seat. *"Get a driver and let's go. The scientists are expecting us within the hour."*

A few minutes later, T'Challa was savoring the silence as they glided through the city. The sturdy limousine muffled the road noises much better than the sedan would have. T'Challa made a mental note to ask Nakia about the car's soundproofing technology.

As much as he loved his mother and sister, there were times he felt he would go insane if he couldn't get out of the crowded palace, away from the relentless noise made by so many people around the clock. The clack of boots on tile, the whispered conversations, the heavy breathing: It all grated on his hypersensitive ears. And the smells: He'd reluctantly banned the use of cologne and perfume by the palace staff after the cloying scent of Chanel No. 5 worn by one poor attendant got into his room. He couldn't sleep for a week.

Ask Nakia if the soundproofing in the car could be adapted for my sleeping quarters, T'Challa thought to himself as he watched the skyscrapers of the Golden City fade into the distance. The day's trip to the Great Mound was a welcome diversion from matters of state, which had occupied his thoughts for the last few days. He rubbed his temple, feeling a tension headache building up behind his eyes. He could feel the uncertainty of Nakia and Okoye since his pronouncement about the future of the *Dora Milaje.* But he could detect no variation in their usually excellent security work, other than Nakia's willingness to challenge some of his less important decisions.

S'Yan had torn into him later that night for what the former regent called an "unnecessary disruption" of the kingdom's security apparatus. His uncle, raising his voice to him for the first time in years, recited all the times the *Dora Milaje* had saved the throne during Wakandan history.

"Yes, the Panther God has blessed you, T'Challa.

But unless she granted you some previously unknown cloning ability, even you cannot be everywhere at once," S'Yan warned before walking out of T'Challa's office. "Sometimes even a panther needs a pride."

The memory made T'Challa lean back into the soft leather seat and close his eyes. The only sounds he could hear were Okoye sharpening her sword on a well-worn stone and Nakia furiously typing on her virtual keyboard wrist-com. These sounds were soothing to him. Eventually, he drifted off to sleep.

<T'Challa>

He bolted up, heart racing and a taste of bile in the back of his throat. His movement startled the *Dora Milaje*. Okoye immediately pulled a handgun from her thigh holster and began scanning for threats. Nakia leaned over across the seat and placed her hand on T'Challa's leg.

"Beloved?"

T'Challa reached up to his forehead, where sweat had begun to bead. *"Did either of you just call my name?"*

The two *Dora Milaje* exchanged worried glances. Then Okoye resumed watching out the window for potential trouble. *"No, Beloved, no one has said anything for quite a few minutes,"* she said. *"Did you hear something?"*

T'Challa was silent, feeling a familiar twinge at the back of his brain. *"Stand down, ladies,"* he murmured. Sitting back in the seat, T'Challa relaxed his muscles and breathed deeply. Closing his eyes again, he willed himself into a meditative state and waited as the darkness enveloped him.

After what seemed like an eternity, he felt an earthy breeze waft past his nose. He opened his eyes and looked around in wonderment at the lush jungle surrounding him. The limousine was gone, and T'Challa was now in the middle of a clearing. Shaking his head, he heard the chirp of insects and the howls of monkeys and smelled the bitter scent of game. Above, the blue sky was clear and cloudless, with an early-morning sun peeking through the branches. Dry branches crunching under his bare feet, he walked over to an Okoumé tree and poked it with one finger. It was solid.

"Yes, it's real, Beloved," a voice spoke softly from the tree. T'Challa looked up in surprise to see a large panther lounging in the tree's lower branches, grooming herself. At least ten feet from nose to tail, sleek blue-black fur covering powerful sinews, the panther gazed at him with gray eyes for a moment. She then returned to her grooming, her pink tongue scraping across the large claw-tipped pads of her paw.

T'Challa hesitantly bowed before his deity—and realized suddenly that he was naked. "Where are we?"

"Don't you know, T'Challa?" the panther asked.

Without thinking, T'Challa frowned.

"Careful, T'Challa," the panther warned, halting her grooming to stare down at him. "I know you wouldn't have asked if you knew. But I also know you'd figure it out if you stopped being so slack-jawed for a moment."

T'Challa crossed his arms. "I would appreciate it if my mind were my own. This mind-reading can be very annoying."

The panther yawned, displaying her massive fangs and flexing her claws as she stretched. "Asking me to not know what is in my avatar's mind is like asking you not to breathe, my child. It can be done, but not permanently."

T'Challa looked around again, noting the virgin condition of his surroundings. There were no tracks, no excrement, no sign of true life anywhere. "We're in the spirit plane?"

The panther curled up on the branch and locked her eyes on him. "Bravo, T'Challa. I decided this time to give you something you could relate to. I thought that would make our little chat go smoother and forestall some of the questions I knew your inquisitive mind would come up with."

"We've never had these…chats outside of the palace before," T'Challa said. He wandered over to the tree and plucked a leaf, feeling the oily texture as he ground it between his fingers.

The panther laughed and leaped to the ground behind him. "Did you really think I was confined to that structure you call a palace? I'm always watching." She strode up to T'Challa, sniffing at him as he turned and dropped to both knees. Her pink nose twitched, and her tail lashed back and forth when she neared his face, her hot breath blowing on his cheeks.

T'Challa closed his eyes until he felt the panther's rough, wet tongue flick his nose. He opened his eyes. Kneeling before him was one of the most beautiful women he'd ever seen. She was clad only in a simple brown woolen shift that did nothing to hide her supple, curvaceous figure. The woman blinked the panther's gray eyes and smiled, her midnight-black skin contrasting with her wide nose and blush-pink lips. Her curly white hair cascaded down to her shoulders. Her rich, earthy scent wafted by T'Challa's nose, causing him to close his eyes again and draw as much of that enticing aroma into his lungs as possible.

When T'Challa opened his eyes again, the woman was gone and the amused panther was sitting back on her haunches. "You were becoming distracted, my child," the panther chided, laughter clear in her voice. "We have got to get you a queen."

T'Challa snorted and stood up. "The way things are going, that doesn't seem likely. And by the way, I still don't believe any of this is scientifically possible. This is just a self-induced hallucination, with my prefrontal cortex working out some of my most pressing concerns through audio and visual fantasies linked to recent events and worries."

"It's been a long time since any of my Black Panthers have questioned me," the panther purred. "I'd forgotten how...stimulating that can be. This is why

Khonshu prefers to possess the bodies of his avatars. Less explaining necessary, but it can leave a bad taste in your mouth. I've never liked it.

"Anyway...you've grown up, T'Challa, without the benefit of your father's guidance in the more... spiritual portions of our faith. That has led you to a different path. But you are my son, my Black Panther. You will find your destiny—and having an avatar steeped in technology and science instead of faith and mysticism will be truly interesting, if you survive."

The panther walked up to T'Challa and began to wind her way around him, rubbing her silky fur and musky scent against his naked legs.

"I cannot give you a direct warning, T'Challa. But I am allowed to tell you this much: A time of great trial is nearing. That which my people depend on most will be wielded as a weapon by the one-armed man. Stop him and avenge your father, T'Challa."

The panther sat back down and gazed up at him. "You must be strong and diligent, my son, and remember that even you cannot be everywhere at once. You must make a terrible choice, and I would spare you from that if I could. But those you love will stand with you, if you let them."

The jungle grew misty, and T'Challa began to lose sight of the panther even though she was only inches in front of him. "You are my avatar," the panther's voice grew faint, as if she were now a great distance away in an inky blackness. "Even if you don't believe in me, my son, I believe in you."

T'Challa opened his eyes. He was in the limousine, with Nakia and Okoye looking anxiously at him. He rubbed his eyes. *"How long was I out?"*

"You just closed your eyes, Beloved," Nakia said, shooting a worried glance at Okoye.

T'Challa brought his hand to his nose, feeling a slight trace of moisture on the tip. Shaking himself alert, he looked at his watch. No time had passed.

"Okoye, alert the war council that I will be holding an emergency meeting later this evening. Nakia, I want security increased around the Great Mound and the palace immediately. Get some of your sisters to guard my mother and sister and make sure that they're safe."

The two women quickly picked up their communicators and began issuing orders without question. After her second call, Nakia put her hand over her mouthpiece. *"If someone asks why, what do we tell them, Beloved?"*

"Tell them my father's killer is back," T'Challa snarled.

Nakia and Okoye looked at each other, wide-eyed. *"Should we return to the palace?"* Nakia stammered.

T'Challa shook his head and began unknotting his tie. *"No, we don't know whether we're under surveillance. A headlong dash to safety would put us one step behind our opponents again. Let's not tip our hand too soon and cause a public panic. Instead, we will draw them out before we crush them."*

T'Challa pressed a button on his console, and a metal case slid from under his seat. He picked it up and pressed his finger into a thumbprint scanner to open it. Reaching inside, he lifted a leather Panther cowl and held it up for the women to see.

"That doesn't mean we go in unprepared, though," T'Challa said, eyes flashing. *"Only a fool tests the depths of a river with both feet."*

Lesedi M'Boye Fumnaya never planned to be an elementary school teacher.

Lesedi's dream as a little girl was to be an astronaut or a ballerina—or maybe even one of the *Dora Milaje,* a fierce and respected warrior for the kingdom. But her eyesight was not good enough to qualify for the space program, and she grew up tall and bony, all knees and elbows, dashing her dream of dancing for a living. Lesedi M'Boye then threw herself into her studies. A late bloomer, she watched enviously as boys flocked around girls who weren't forced to wear horn-rimmed glasses to see the numbers on their smartphones.

But in college, Lesedi met Peter Fumnaya, a funny, squat garage-band musician. He didn't care that she towered over him, even in flats. She didn't care that he had already started developing a beer belly. They dated for a few years and then married after graduation.

Lesedi's new husband still dreamed of hitting the big time with his guitar, but he made ends meet by teaching music at their village's school. Lesedi joined him at the school a few years later, first as a substitute and then as an elementary teacher, shepherding the youngest children through their alphabets and beginning calculations. She still danced, mostly in the privacy of her own home, and took in students for private lessons every once in a while. She was content with her life, despite its twists and turns.

At least, on most days. But this day, she thought, was not one of them. She shook her head as her charges ran pell-mell around the Great Mound's viewing area, which overlooked the side of the mountain. The children's bright clothes made them seem like butterflies flitting around the massive granite-colored platform jutting out from the side of the mountain.

Usually Lesedi enjoyed the school's field trips to the Bashenga National Park ore-processing plant at the Great Mound, even though she'd seen it hundreds of times herself. The looks of wonderment on the children's faces as they experimented with minute amounts of Vibranium always pleased her. Lesedi liked sparking an interest in science in their still developing minds. But in this year's bunch, there were a couple of rambunctious boys and mean girls who stirred the pot whenever they could. It took everything Lesedi had not to haul off and shake some sense into some of them.

You can handle this, she thought. *Peter promised to make agave margaritas with dinner tonight. You've just got to make it until last bell.*

"Children! Children, please," Lesedi called out in what her husband jokingly referred to her schoolmarm voice.

After pulling one adventurous girl down from a safety railing, Lesedi finally got their attention. For the fifth time that day, she wished some of the parents had come along as chaperones—but she knew many of them had jobs of their own.

"Children, who knows what they mine here at the Great Mound?" she said, tucking a strand of hair back into her tight bun.

Little hands shot up. Lesedi smiled as she pointed to Abdalla, one of her prized students. "Vibranium," he lisped, still trying to get used to the loss of his two front teeth.

"That's correct," she said. "And who can tell me what Vibranium does?"

Hands shot up again, and Lesedi looked around until she caught shy Oluwaseyi's eyes. The girl usually hid behind her long dreadlocks to avoid being called on. Lesedi had made it her goal that year to bring Oluwaseyi out of her shell. She had a fine mind, and there was no advantage in hiding it from the world.

"It absorbs…vibrations?" the girl peeped.

"Very good!" Lesedi said, as Oluwaseyi beamed at her classmates and basked in her teacher's praise. "And why is that useful?"

Hands shot up again, but Lesedi wasn't looking at her students now. Her eyes were on the mountain, where hundreds of birds simultaneously had taken off in panicked flight, squawking and screaming as their wings beat a hasty retreat. "What the..." The children raced over to the railing to point in amazement at the birds as they flew away.

It started as a tiny vibration beneath Lesedi's feet, like the pulsation from a large electric toothbrush. Within seconds, it intensified. The children looked around in fear as the platform began to sway back and forth over the side of the mountain. A hard jolt threw several screaming children to the ground. Lesedi could barely keep her balance, even while holding on to the railing.

The platform creaked and groaned. A long, jagged crack appeared, snaking across the floor. Glass windows shattered somewhere behind them, and Lesedi could hear a cacophony of car alarms shrieking in protest at the disturbance.

Looking up, Lesedi saw broken panes of glass fall from the main building's upper floor, smashing on the platform between her charges and the relative safety of the plant. She looked back at her children and quickly decided that riding it out on the platform was the best plan. As long as the platform didn't collapse and send them hurtling down the mountainside.

"Children, grab the railing and hold on tight!" she screamed, wrapping both arms around a lamppost near the edge and trying to shield several children with her body. Sobbing children, scared out of their wits, grabbed onto the fence wherever they could. The platform shook and crumbled, and glass continued to smash against the stone walkway.

After a few seconds, the shaking stopped and the air grew quiet.

Lesedi uncovered her head and looked around. No one seemed hurt badly, though several children were cowering against their friends. One boy clinging to her leg had a wet crotch. But she soon discovered a more immediate problem. The platform they were standing on had developed several wide cracks halfway between the children and the plant. As she watched, one of the cracks grew even larger, shedding pieces of metal that clattered down the mountainside.

"Children, inside! Now!" she shrieked, pushing them toward the shattered glass doors. Children stumbled and ran toward safety, hopscotching over the cracks growing ever wider on the floor. Lesedi picked up two crying girls and ran as fast as she could, throwing them inside the doors.

Looking back, she saw Abdalla still clinging to the safety railing, frozen in fear. Lesedi started back out, but as soon as she stepped onto the platform, she could hear the groan of the cracking pillars under her feet. She pushed on, but the closer she got to the crying boy, the louder the groans became. She felt a small tremor develop under her feet, which subsided only when she stopped moving.

"Abdalla, honey, you're going to have to walk to me," Lesedi pleaded with the boy. "It's not safe where you are. I need you to stand up and take two steps toward me."

The boy shook his head, tears streaming down his face.

"Baby," Lesedi begged, "I know you're scared. I just need you to be brave for a few seconds. Just take two steps, and we'll figure it out from there."

Abdalla nodded and reluctantly let go of the railing. Lesedi sighed in relief as the boy stepped gingerly toward her outstretched arms, carefully picking his way around what she could now see were open-air holes in the platform.

"Just a few more feet, honey," she said. She lay down flat on the ground and inched as close as she dared to the largest of the jagged cracks. "That's my good, brave boy."

Abdalla looked up at her, a crooked smile on his face.

A second later the outer portion of the platform collapsed underneath him. Arms windmilling in the air, the boy toppled backwards into the chasm, crying as he fell out of sight. Lesedi screamed and started to run toward the edge, ignoring the crumbling platform under her feet.

A black blur suddenly rocketed past her and threw itself off the edge of the platform. A pair of strong arms grabbed Lesedi and dragged her back to safety, ignoring her desperate struggle to get to her charge.

"Do not worry," a raspy voice whispered into her ears.

A teary Lesedi looked back and saw the confidence in the eyes of the muscular woman who had saved her. A metal clank caught their attention as a flat, four-clawed grappling hook sought purchase on the floor in front of them. A smaller woman, dressed in the same uniform, pulled what looked like an enormous staple gun out of her backpack, and began securing the rope to the floor with powerful blasts. Once she was satisfied the rope was stable, the woman inched close to the edge of the fallen platform to peer over the side. She looked back at the woman holding Lesedi's arms and said something in an unfamiliar language.

The woman holding her arms let go and began to grin broadly.

"Your boy is safe," she informed Lesedi, slapping her on the back. The teacher swayed. The woman grabbed her by the arm again and led her over to a wall inside the building, where Lesedi slumped down to the ground between fallen paintings and broken glass. Seconds later, she was mobbed by crying children. She gathered them up in her arms, kissing their heads and hugging as many of them as she could.

The woman stared down at them, a small smile threatening to crest at the edge of her lips. She waited until Lesedi got control of herself and the children before speaking.

"Your bravery in the face of extreme danger is to be commended, ma'am," the woman said. "Please, may I have your name to inscribe in the histories of the *Dora Milaje* as an example of what we should aspire to?"

"Lesedi," she stammered. "Lesedi M'Boye Fumnaya."

WELL, Mrs. Fumnaya," Okoye said, scribbling her name on a small white notepad. "I expect that our king will want to meet with you soon to properly thank you for your courage. And I would like you to dine with the *Dora Milaje*—at your convenience, of course."

"Okoye!" the smaller woman shouted, as she began pulling the rope hand over hand.

"Excuse me, Mrs. Fumnaya, duty calls." The tall woman winked, strode to the precipice, and grabbed the rope. Seconds later, the two women helped the Black Panther claw his way back into the room from over the edge, Abdalla grinned broadly as he clung to the king's back piggyback style.

Okoye pulled the young boy free and watched as he ran over to his teacher, who enveloped him in an enormous bear hug. T'Challa unbuttoned his leather mask from behind and pulled it over his head. The three of them looked on in satisfaction as the teacher and her students were escorted out. The children babbled about having seen the famed Black Panther in action.

"The strength and resilience of the Wakandan people always amazes me, Beloved," Okoye said in a low voice. *"With no special training or abilities, that woman almost threw herself off the side of the building in a futile attempt to save that child."*

"Our people are worth protecting," T'Challa replied calmly. *"All of them, from the youngest to the oldest. And I can't do it alone, Adored Ones. If you two hadn't been here, I would have had to choose between saving the teacher or her student. Luckily, I had backup. Good work, ladies."*

Nakia grinned broadly until Okoye jabbed her with a sharp elbow. *"What now, Beloved?"* she asked as they walked back inside the plant.

"Now," T'Challa said, grinding his teeth, *"we find out what happened."*

KLAW leaned as close to Stancheck's stone window as he dared, with M'Butu and Batroc a few feet behind him. "Report, Igor."

Stancheck's green eyes glowed as he stepped forward out of the darkness, forcing Klaw to back away from the door. "I did as you asked," he said. "I found the atomic wavelength of this piece of metal you gave me, and reached out and discovered a large collection of it nearby. Then I played with it, just a little bit."

Klaw nodded. "Well done."

"What about my toilet, Klaw?" Stancheck

growled. "You promised to get someone in here to fix the damn toilet yesterday. It stinks to high heaven in here!"

"Patience, Igor, patience. I need a few moments with M'Butu here. I'm sure we can get something worked out." Klaw walked back to where M'Butu and Batroc were waiting, a satisfied grin on his face.

"We have our weapon, gentlemen," Klaw said, putting his arms around M'Butu's and Batroc's shoulders. "Now that Stancheck has internalized its signature, he can ignite small portions of the Vibranium, trigger earthquakes, and—if we need— make the whole mountain explode."

M'Butu shrugged off Klaw's arm. "Explode? What type of explosion are we talking about, Klaw?"

Eyes narrowing, Klaw looked over at Batroc. "Nothing extraordinary, M'Butu. Just enough to destroy Wakanda and everything else T'Challa loves."

M'Butu frowned. "Niganda shares a border with Wakanda, as you well know. Will my palace—I mean, my people—be safe from this explosion?"

Klaw looked at Batroc, who was hidden from M'Butu's view. Batroc shrugged. Klaw hesitated, then nodded. "As long as they're not in Wakanda, I think they'll be safe."

M'Butu's mood immediately shifted. "Ha! I do not care if you destroy all of Wakanda. T'Challa deserves every bit of sorrow we can heap upon his head." He shook his hand at Klaw. "But I do not want my people hurt…if we can help it."

Klaw slapped M'Butu on the back. "There will be nothing to worry about, my king. Trust me."

M'Butu blinked and then waddled off, shouting for a girl to bring him grapes. Klaw and Batroc watched him walk out of sight.

"The second we get what we want, get out," Klaw whispered to Batroc, a frown creasing his face. "No matter what happens, I'm bringing the entire country down. I'll know for sure he will be the last Black Panther if I leave his whole country a smoking, radioactive ruin."

"The radius?" Batroc said, doing quick calculations in his head on the fastest form of escape.

"Based on what Igor just did, I'd say anywhere in central Africa would be too close."

Caught up in his vision of revenge, it took a couple of seconds for Klaw to notice the unsettled look on Batroc's face.

"Don't worry, I don't plan for us to be anywhere near Wakanda when we let Igor off his leash. This is a get-in, get-out kind of job, and I plan to live to enjoy spitting on the graves of the Wakandans."

"And I to enjoy my money," Batroc added.

Klaw looked at him silently for a second. "Time to earn it, my friend. Is everything ready?"

Batroc shrugged. "The Nigandans are as ready as they're ever going to be. You've briefed Stancheck, right? And I've given Rhino your marching orders, but I will admit to a teeny bit of concern about him completing his objectives. What's to stop the

Wakandans from just using their air force to bomb him back to Niganda? We'll need some kind of air support, and I don't see where the Nigandans can provide it."

"I wondered if you'd noticed that," Klaw said. "Luckily, I thought of that last night and made a few calls. The solution arrived earlier this morning. Let's go say hello to our air force."

He looked at the Radioactive Man's enclosure as they walked back into the palace. "But first, I've got to find M'Butu and figure out if he's got any expendable plumbers. The last thing you want is a cranky ultimate weapon, you know?"

CHAPTER TEN

T'CHALLA watched impatiently as his scientists fiddled with their seismic equipment and took samples of the soil from the Great Mound.

Still in his Panther habit, he fought against his instinct to take control of the project himself, given that his own scientific training made him one of the world's leading experts on Vibranium.

The earthquake had brought out not only his scientists, but also the war council and his uncle S'Yan, dressed impeccably in a black double-breasted suit and an ivory-colored French-collared shirt. S'Yan was stroking his gray goatee and talking to one of the plant's managers. Once on site, S'Yan asked for T'Challa to step aside and let him gather, collate, and interpret the information, and then present the findings.

T'Challa balked at first, wanting to do the hands-on research himself. But S'Yan plaintively glanced at the *Dora Milaje*. Though standing within earshot, Okoye and Nakia had been trying to allow them privacy. Okoye stepped forward at T'Challa's nod.

"My king," she said in Wakandan for S'Yan's benefit, "now is the time when your people need a king, not a scientist." She exchanged an inscrutable look with S'Yan, then stepped back and resumed her post next to Nakia.

S'Yan almost laughed at the frustrated look on T'Challa's face. "Finally learned how to listen, I see," S'Yan chuckled. "Be patient, my king. I will have something to present shortly." His gold hoop earring shining in the afternoon sun, S'Yan strode off to talk with one of the scientists.

Rarely in his life had T'Challa been forced to wait with no responsibilities, especially while wearing the royal Panther habit, and he didn't like it. His sour mood was deepened by the curious stares of the Vibranium miners, executives, and onlookers who had gathered after being evacuated from the mountain. Nudged forward by Nakia, he'd plastered on a flat smile and neutral voice as he worked the crowd. But he continued to shoot glances back at the huddled scientists, who stood shouting and yelling with S'Yan and now Shuri.

The princess, for some reason, had talked S'Yan into bringing her along to the Great Mound. And from what T'Challa could see, Shuri was holding her own in the conversation, sticking her finger in S'Yan's face once and throwing her arms into the air in disgust at someone else's comment. A feeling of jealousy washed over T'Challa, but he quickly pushed it down as he knelt to speak to a girl in the crowd.

The gap-toothed girl, no more than 10, had shyly asked for a hug. For some reason, T'Challa felt strangely comforted as the elf-like little girl threw her arms around his neck and squeezed with all her might.

"Always watching, Beloved," she whispered in his ear.

Surprised, T'Challa released the girl and looked in her eyes, which flashed gray. The king stepped back, drawing a confused and concerned Okoye near. *"Is everything okay, Beloved?"*

T'Challa looked at her. When he turned back around, the girl was gone.

"Ask him if I can get a hug like that," Nakia giggled to Okoye through her earpiece, getting a death glare from her partner as her reward. Unrepentant, the younger woman stuck her tongue out at her partner, snapping back into protective mode when an amused T'Challa glanced over her way.

T'Challa turned and threw one last wave to the crowd. S'Yan and Shuri had broken away with a small group of scientists and were heading his way. Trailed by Okoye and Nakia, T'Challa led them toward the royal limousine to make sure their conversation would not be overheard. Nakia opened the passenger-side door of the car and toggled a few switches, activating a scrambling field that would keep anyone's smartphone from recording. S'Yan had suggested earlier, and T'Challa agreed, that any of their findings should remain a state secret for now, not to be bandied about in public until they were sure of their conclusions.

Shuri, T'Challa saw, was bursting to speak. But in this forum, she knew the protocol was to allow the one placed in charge—this time S'Yan—to brief the king first. T'Challa thought his little sister could stand to learn a little patience.

"My king," S'Yan began. A raised hand from T'Challa stopped him.

"First, were there any injuries?" T'Challa asked calmly. "Did all of the miners make it out of the mountain?"

S'Yan checked the readout on the tablet in his hands. "The kids got a little banged up, but they're okay. There were no major injuries in the mountain. A miracle, really." He looked at Shuri, shifted his weight, and waited for T'Challa to speak again.

T'Challa looked over at the Great Mound, the source of his country's prosperity. He could hear the returning birds chirp as they searched for their nests among still-upright trees. Down near the mountain's base, several miners stood near a tunnel's mouth gathering equipment that had been tossed aside in their headlong rush for the sun.

"Now, can someone tell me how a mountain made up of vibration-absorbing minerals managed to shake?" T'Challa looked at his scientists, quirking his eyebrows at their silence.

K'Darte Wikdetsari was the first to speak. T'Challa had personally appointed him to the Science Council, despite his youth, because of his quick mind and devotion to pure science over politics. He had met K'Darte years earlier, when the young man was still a promising student, and had taken an interest in furthering his career by sending him as the king's emissary to geological and archeological conferences around the world. Luckily for his young wife, N'Jare, the man spent most of his time in a laboratory or a classroom at the university while complaining about his need to get back out into the field. But his skill was such that more senior scientists said nothing when S'Yan nodded for the young man to begin the briefing.

The husky, chocolate-skinned man cleared his throat. K'Darte wore only an open-necked khaki shirt with a sweaty t-shirt underneath and blue jeans. A smudge of dust on his face, and T'Challa thought he easily could have been mistaken for one of the miners below.

"My king, we've checked for seismological activity that would account for the phenomenon witnessed today," K'Darte said, reviewing figures on his laptop. "As you know, Wakanda does not sit on any fault lines on our tectonic plates. It would take a major geological event somewhere in the world for us to feel tremors of that magnitude, especially considering the dampening effect of the large quantity of Vibranium found in the mountain."

"We've checked," S'Yan spoke up with a grim smile. "California did not fall into the ocean, Mount Vesuvius is still dormant, and Atlantis has not risen from the ocean."

"As if Namor would tell us," T'Challa snorted. He looked over at W'Kabi, who was standing silently on the outskirts of the group. "Underground testing of nuclear weapons?"

"None that we can tell, your majesty. Our sources have reached out tentatively to governments in North Korea, the United States, and Iran, but have been assured by each that no tests were conducted today."

T'Challa took in all of this. "So what this fine collection of minds has discovered after an hour of investigating one of the most shocking events in our country's history…is nothing."

He watched the eyes of most of the group's members drop under his gaze. W'Kabi just looked back at him, arms crossed. T'Challa wasn't sure that K'Darte had even heard him. The scientist was scrolling furiously through his incoming data.

"I have a theory," Shuri said.

She was virtually vibrating with her need to speak. T'Challa looked over at S'Yan, who was frowning and shaking his head at the princess. Shuri refused to meet her uncle's eyes, however. She locked her gaze on T'Challa, imploring him to allow her to continue.

T'Challa sighed, smiling slightly. "Yes, Shuri, you have a theory that your undergraduate study of nuclear physics has allowed you to come up with?"

"You don't need an advanced degree to know that something is wrong with our Vibranium," she said, throwing an irritated look at her brother.

Shuri's words burst the group's silence like a pin into a balloon. The scientists and officers began arguing amongst themselves again. Some shouted that even questioning the viability of the Vibranium was apostasy. Others yelled that testing should commence immediately before something even worse happened. The commotion even made K'Darte stop his typing to glance up at the princess, a look of interest in his eyes.

It was that look that made T'Challa call for silence and urge Shuri on.

"As everyone knows, Vibranium stores the energy expended against it within the bonds between the molecules that make up the substance," Shuri explained, as the group's members nodded. "As a result, kinetic energy is dissipated within the bonds, instead."

Shuri looked down at her boots sheepishly before continuing. "This morning, I might have been experimenting with some of the palace's Vibranium, brother. I added shaved, wafer-thin layers of Vibranium to the interior of my boxing gloves, hoping it would help blunt the impact on my hands the next time I sparred with Zuri.

"So I had a bar of Vibranium in my room this morning, and I was using a laser scalpel to shave off pieces, when all of a sudden I could see the Vibranium move on its own." Shuri looked around at the group. "Now, this is prior to the earthquake. You could see small ripples forming on the bar's surface, as if a wave was crashing through it. I put down my equipment and watched. After a few minutes, it just stopped."

Shuri looked T'Challa in the eye. "And that's when I heard that something had gone wrong at the Great Mound."

T'Challa looked at K'Darte, who seemed intrigued. "I've never heard of Vibranium acting like that, Princess. Are you sure what you saw? Is there video?"

Shuri blushed. "There are no cameras in my bedroom, K'Darte, so no. The only evidence we have to make up our minds is what I have told you."

S'Yan frowned, taking control of the conversation. "Your majesty, I believe the princess, but is this the time for a scientific inquiry into the properties of Vibranium? I think we have more pressing matters at hand."

"More pressing than the makeup of our most precious resource?" Shuri retorted.

"Vibranium isn't our most precious resource, girl." S'Yan was dangerously close to losing his temper. "The Black Panther is. The threat to the king and the kingdom comes first."

"How do you know that what's going on with the Vibranium isn't what's threatening the kingdom, Uncle?" Shuri seethed. "You're not regent anymore, so don't try to push this to the side to make yourself look important. You just want to be somebody again, instead of the other brother."

S'Yan's eyes narrowed at Shuri's words. "I served

Wakanda since long before you and your mother arrived. Don't assign feelings to me, girl."

T'Challa raised his hand, forcing them to be silent. Shuri stepped back to get control of herself. S'Yan stood still and watched the princess pace back and forth, muttering to herself.

After a few minutes, she walked back over and bowed to T'Challa. "Brother, Uncle, please forgive my lack of tact," she said softly. "T'Challa, I would like to lead a team to investigate whether the same phenomenon I witnessed happened with the pure Vibranium ore, and not just with the refined metal. With a small team of experts working with me down the mineshaft—"

"Out of the question!" S'Yan frowned at her before a small growl from Okoye silenced him again.

"This is the king's decision, Uncle" Shuri looked at T'Challa with hope in her eyes. "I would only need—"

T'Challa shook his head. "I'm sorry, Sister. There could be a cave-in. I'm not going to risk sending other miners back into the shaft to save you and your team."

"But T'Challa—" Shuri complained.

"Case closed. Now, S'Yan, take me through the timeline of what happened here. I want to know everything."

T'Challa turned his back on Shuri and headed toward the mine, his entourage following. Okoye gave Shuri a shrug and trailed along behind the king.

"Why won't he listen?" Shuri muttered to herself.

"Because you're his sister," K'Darte replied, folding his laptop and walking up to the princess. The scientist peered down at her over his horn-rimmed glasses. "Keep in mind that to T'Challa, you're probably still that little girl he remembers teasing and playing with from his childhood. He can't help wanting to keep you safe."

"Well, I don't need him to keep me safe. I need him to listen to me."

"Princess, you also have to keep in mind that you're next in line for the throne," K'Darte pointed out. "Risking your life on an…intriguing theory is probably not the best idea to the king right now."

Shuri's eyes widened at K'Darte's words. She grabbed his arm. "You believe me, don't you?"

"I believe something happened to cause a mountain of Vibranium to shake—and outside of a nuclear blast or a meteor strike, I can't think of anything else that would have caused that." K'Darte paused, thinking. "So absent any external influences, the fault has to be in the Vibranium…and a pure sample would be better to work with…"

Seeing the hope rising in Shuri, K'Darte immediately tried to pull back, waving his hands. "I also believe your brother, my king, told you that you couldn't take a team down into the mountain to investigate."

Shuri wasn't to be deterred, however.

"But he didn't tell you, K'Darte, that *you* couldn't

take a team down into the Great Mound." Shuri rubbed her hands gleefully. "We'll keep it small, just you and me, and we'll come back after sunset and work through the night. By the time T'Challa and Uncle know what we've done, we'll have our readings and be on our way—"

"Whoa, whoa, Princess." K'Darte couldn't believe what he'd just talked his way into. He pushed his glasses back up on his nose and tried to figure a graceful way out of this predicament. "I don't know if this is a great idea."

Shuri arched her eyebrow at K'Darte. "You mean, 'I don't know if this is a great idea, *your majesty.*' I can make it a royal order and include not telling anyone else, if that'd make you feel better?"

K'Darte put his head in his hands. "Yes, your majesty," he said glumly, "but I'm going to need you to call my wife and tell her why I'm not at her mother's house for dinner tonight. A call from the princess may make the hell she's going to give me for missing a visit with her mother survivable."

"Deal," Shuri grinned.

THE SETTING sun silhouetted the Black Knight as he knelt for his evening prayers, his Ebony Blade pressed into the black soil tip down. Klaw noted that the man was wearing a full set of scaled armor now, instead of just the cape and helmet. His winged horse, Valinor, was nearby, decked out in a saddle and reins with Christian iconography stamped throughout.

Klaw was loath to interrupt the holy man. But time was now short.

The mercenary team had gathered on a grassy plateau about 50 miles outside of the Wakandan border, at the head of a Nigandan ground division consisting of tanks, armored vehicles, and helicopters. The Nigandans had been instructed to swoop in after the first sortie brought down the Wakandan defenses, and had been given special dispensation by their king to loot and plunder to their hearts' content. After all, it was only Wakandan property that would be destroyed.

The Nigandan soldiers seemed of good cheer, laughing among themselves as they awaited Klaw's order to strike. An hour ago, M'Butu had riled up the men up with a speech about the longtime animosity between Niganda and Wakanda, and a laundry list of what Klaw assumed were made-up atrocities committed by the Black Panther and his kin.

Glory, power, and loot were promised by the king to his soldiers, with special accolades offered to anyone who captured Wakanda's arrogant princess or Queen Mother and brought them back to Niganda— undamaged—to face the king's justice. M'Butu's men had cheered and hooted in response.

Now M'Butu had retreated to his palace to await word of victory. A nervous energy filled the staging area as the men joked about all of the booty—

human and property—they would claim before the next nightfall.

That didn't go over well with Batroc, Klaw noted. Once the king had departed, the mercenary had stalked between the lines, slapping down one soldier after another who claimed to be planning special forms of atrocities against the Wakandans.

Most of the men accepted their chastisement and fell silent. One soldier, his wispy beard betraying him as a surly teenager attempting to impress his friends, spat at the Frenchman's feet. The challenge was clear.

Ten seconds and two swift kicks to the mouth later, Batroc had the boy spitting teeth and blood into the dusty ground. Batroc ordered the boy's friends to haul him to the rear of the formation, where a doctor would be able to reset his jaw. Then Batroc climbed on top of a tank and shouted for attention.

"I am a professional, and while you are under my command, you will act as if you are professional, too—or you will answer to me," Batroc warned. "There will be none of this…unnecessary brutality against noncombatants. If someone attacks you, deadly force is authorized. If you can grab something valuable and take it back home, do so. But if the people you encounter surrender, they will be treated as you would want your family to be treated at the hands of the Wakandans."

Batroc glared at the grumbling men surrounding him. "Break these rules at your peril," he snarled. "Or the Black Panther will be the least of your worries."

He jumped down, seemingly unconcerned about the now-ugly mood of the Nigandan soldiers. Batroc strolled over to where the Rhino waited, testing out the mechanical joints in his armor by stomping on some anthills.

"I never knew you had a bleeding heart, Frenchie," the amused Russian said, shaking a nearby tank with his stomp.

Batroc looked at him haughtily. "This will not be my last contract, Russian. My reputation as a professional toppler of government hinges on what's left behind after a coup. Television images of raped women and beaten children tend to make foreign intervention more, not less likely. It is just bad business."

"Well, comrade, you might want to watch your back," the Rhino snorted. "These boys look like they want to chew you up and spit you out."

"I am not worried," Batroc declared. But he walked to stand alone at the head of the staging ground, a few feet from where the Black Knight was praying.

A few words from a calming voice might reduce the tension, Klaw thought. As he approached the knight, he could hear the man whispering feverishly to himself, speaking some sort of mantra. "And from now unto the hour of our death, in the name of our Lord, amen," he finished.

The Black Knight stood, wiped some spittle

from the edge of his mouth, and waited for Klaw to speak.

"I was hoping we could get you to offer a few words to the troops before we got started," Klaw said, waving back at the camp.

The knight placed his sword in the scabbard at his side. He whistled to Valinor, who neighed and began to trot toward his master. "It's your army, Mr. Klaw," he argued. He gathered his helmet under his arm and reached out to stroke Valinor's nose.

"Yes, but as a man of the cloth, I was hoping you could put it all into context for us," Klaw replied, reaching over to pat the winged horse. "Things are a little tense down there right now, and a bit of inspiration might be good for the men."

"God does move in mysterious ways, his wonders to perform," the knight said, almost to himself.

"Thank you, kind knight." Klaw bowed and walked away.

A few minutes later, Batroc had the Nigandans in formation in front of the Black Knight, who was now completely adorned in his battle armor. Klaw and the Rhino stood off to the side with Batroc. They watched the knight trot his horse back and forth down the Nigandan lines, his helmet under his arm.

"Centuries ago," the knight began in a loud voice, "we brought civilization, commerce, and God to Africa. We dragged this whole continent into the 20th century.

"Now, at the beginning of a new century, Africa

needs our help more than ever. Representatives of four great European nations stand here prepared to do just that: Belgium, France, Russia, and Great Britain. You should give them your thanks." He pointed to Klaw, Batroc, and the Rhino.

"Now, I regret that force is necessary to achieve our goals." The knight leaned forward in his saddle and placed his helmet on his head. "But the people of Africa want the true God in their lives, and with this undefeatable Ebony Blade, we will grant them their wish." He pulled out his sword and held it high in the air. "I'm aware that many of you are fighting for various reasons. Money, glory, power, revenge—or just regular meals. But whatever your reason, know that the hand of God guides us on this holy crusade."

Valinor spread his wings in preparation to leap into flight. Rearing back, the knight began to shout encouragement to the men. "The good book says, 'The Lord will cause your enemies who rise against you to be defeated before you. They shall come out against you one way and flee before you seven ways.'"

Valinor soared into the sky. The Black Knight whirled to look down upon the cheering men. "They will need more than seven roads to escape our justice tonight! Amen?"

"AMEN!" the men shouted back.

"Amen," Klaw whispered. "And so it begins."

CHAPTER ELEVEN

SLIPPING into the Great Mound after hours was so easy, Shuri wondered whether her royal duty required her to leave a note complaining about the lack of security.

Riding with T'Challa in his royal limousine, she'd refused to speak to him the entire way back to the palace. In fact, she pointedly turned her head away from her brother and put wireless earbuds in her ears. She was still annoyed at his refusal to allow her to investigate the flaw in the Vibranium.

Holding up the tablet to block her view of T'Challa, she'd begun looking up classified scientific studies of Vibranium. She wanted to have the most recent information downloaded before they entered the mountain. As deep as she planned to go, she couldn't be sure of wireless reception.

After she had downloaded her second report from the royal library, a message popped up on her tablet.

What are you looking for?

Shuri peered over her tablet at T'Challa. He was meditating, seemingly not bothered in the slightest that she wasn't talking to him. The two *Dora Milaje* sitting with them were occupied with their duties. Okoye, the muscular one, was scanning the environment for danger through the windows, her eyes tracking the passing trees and buildings. Next to T'Challa, Nakia—the tech expert—was typing furiously on her own tablet. She seemed oblivious to the world around them—except for when she would shoot barely disguised loving glances at T'Challa.

Shuri smiled at Nakia, who blushed furiously when she realized the princess was looking at her. Nakia immediately ducked her head and continued typing. As Shuri turned back to her own tablet, a second message popped up.

Yes you, Princess. What are you downloading from the royal library? You know that W'Kabi, as security chief, reviews a log of downloaded information at midnight every night, right?

Confused, Shuri again looked up at Nakia. The young girl wouldn't meet her eyes.

You've got to learn to be a bit more discreet, Princess. I was looking right at you and K'Darte when you came up with your little after-dark expedition, and lip-reading isn't that difficult. It's actually a required portion of *Dora Milaje* training. How do you think we always know what's going on around us?

Shuri shifted in her seat before composing her reply.

Can you help?

The sound of typing across from her slowed down for a moment, and then increased in speed.

I shouldn't. I'd be in HUGE trouble if I got caught, and that's just from Grumpy sitting next to you. But I'm worried that you might be onto something—and the way your brother's acting right now, he's liable to lock you in your quarters if you step the wrong way.

Please, Shuri pleaded silently.

Nakia looked up at Shuri and winked before turning back to her tablet.

If I get thrown in the royal gulag, I expect a pardon, okay? I'll wipe the traces of your "activities" from the library logs. There'll be a car waiting for you outside the west wing of the palace. Keys will be in the glove compartment, and the appropriate equipment in the back.

You'll have to get yourself through Great Mound security, but you're the princess. They'll let you in if you ask, but be sure to tell the guards that it's a QUAGMIRE-level investigation so they'll wait 24 hours before informing the palace. If I were you, I'd be back in my quarters by daybreak, cute scientist or not.

Shuri snorted and immediately tried to hide her smile, causing Okoye to glance over at her. He's married!

Nakia typed back. And you're the Princess. ;)

Nakia was as good as her word.

Once they'd arrived back at the palace, T'Challa announced they'd confiscated the bar of Vibranium in her quarters for further study. Then he stalked off, the two bodyguards on his heels. But Nakia threw her another wink before disappearing around the corner, making Shuri grin at the thought of leading her own personal conspiracy inside the kingdom.

She yawned her way through dinner with

her mother and excused herself early, claiming exhaustion. That should provide an alibi, explaining why no one would see her in the palace that night. And as early as she dared, she dropped down from the balcony of her suite into the royal topiary and headed over the wall.

A black, four-door sedan from the motor pool was exactly where Nakia had said it would be. Shuri expertly drove it a few blocks away from the palace before calling K'Darte on her smartphone to plan the rest of the night.

The hardest part was reassuring the scientist's young wife that nothing untoward was going on between K'Darte and her princess. Shuri, at K'Darte's insistence, came to their condo and shared a cup of tea with N'Jare, who was a bit starstruck by the fact that the Wakandan princess was inside her house. Still in her daywear dress and strappy sandals, Shuri complimented the woman on her lovely home and promised that her husband's presence was absolutely necessary.

K'Darte quickly ushered them out once she completed her tea, receiving a passionate kiss from his wife in the doorway. Shuri could feel the heat rise in her cheeks and looked at the floor until they had released each other. She gave the woman a small wave as she pushed the dazed scientist toward the elevator.

A couple of hours later, she watched K'Darte swear as he adjusted the lens of his molecular microscope over a slide of pure Vibranium ore. The two of them were deep in the mountain, having used a mining cart to haul a portable generator and as much of their scientific equipment as they could down into the narrow, hot shaft.

Lanterns threw uneven yellow light on the walls as Shuri and K'Darte searched for a pure vein of ore, uncontaminated by the refining process. They'd only been working for an hour or so when they discovered their target and assembled their equipment.

K'Darte was pleasantly surprised at how willing and knowledgeable the princess was. He was treating her as a full partner in his work, using her as a sounding board and even incorporating some of her ideas into their investigation.

"You would make a wonderful scientist, Princess, if you ever decide that helping rule a country is too boring."

Shuri smiled, and they kept working.

Finally, they had their result.

"It looks like you were right, Princess." K'Darte pushed his glasses down on his nose as he pulled away from the microscope and wiped sweat away his forehead. "There's some type of subatomic ripple throughout the Vibranium ore. How is that possible?"

"All three samples from different places in the mountain show the same thing?" Shuri asked, frowning.

"They do. And this ripple wasn't there a year ago, per the research you provided. It's a new occurrence." K'Darte scratched his head, embedding dirt into his curly black hair. "This doesn't make sense, even with all we don't know about Vibranium."

"All we don't know?" Shuri was taken aback at the scientist's words. "What do you mean?"

K'Darte smiled at her. "You've done so well tonight, I forgot that you don't study Vibranium for a living. You know it's not a naturally occurring metal, right?"

Shuri leaned back against the mining cart and began ticking facts on her fingers. "I know that the first Black Panther, Bashenga, found the Great Mound and founded our culture around it. I know that the vegetation around the Mound grew in strange and wild ways, leading to the discovery of the heart-shaped herb that gives my brother his powers. I know Vibranium has properties unmatched by any other substance on Earth."

"All true, Princess, but have you never wondered why Wakanda is the only source of Vibranium in the world?" Shuri could see K'Darte slip into professor-mode, and she settled back on the cart to listen. "I'm surprised they haven't gone over this with you yet.

"Vibranium is an alien metal, Princess. As far as we can tell, the Great Mound is really the location of a long-ago meteor strike—the Vibranium is what's left of the meteor. Unlike most meteors, which shatter upon impact and cause massive destruction, the Vibranium core of this meteor absorbed the impact. This is why we don't have the kind of impact crater our friends down in South Africa are studying at the Vredefort Dome. We think our strike was somewhat similar, and the Vredefort crater had an estimated radius of 300 kilometers when it hit the Earth millions of years ago.

"Anyway, I'm getting off-topic," K'Darte continued. "We don't know where Vibranium originated or how to make more. We're still discovering new properties of the metal on a daily basis, so I can't tell you whether this…ripple…is unnatural or not. All I can say is that we've never seen anything like it in our studies so far. T'Challa will be pleased to have this knowledge."

"Yeah, after he reams me out for not following orders," Shuri pouted theatrically.

K'Darte laughed, pulling off his glasses to wipe them on his shirt.

"The king I know will not punish you for bringing him important knowledge, especially knowledge that expands our understanding of the foundation of our country's commerce," he said. "Just remember me when he throws me into prison with my wife's blessing."

For the first time in a long time, Shuri laughed.

T'CHALLA had never been a deep sleeper, even as a child. The slightest thing would rouse him from even a sound slumber.

He was one of the few people who could regularly sense his father's approach, a skill that had prevented T'Chaka from taking unfair advantages in their ongoing tickle wars.

No matter how long he'd been asleep, T'Challa

would awaken at the creak of his door. He would pretend to be asleep, counting the number of soft footfalls between the doorway and his bed. And just before his father would leap onto the bed, T'Challa would curl into a ball and deny his father the tender stomach flesh that he was seeking, forcing T'Chaka to tickle, instead, the soles of his feet or the sensitive spot between his collarbone and his neck.

T'Challa would shriek and thrash anyway, giggling under his father's merciless assault. Growling and snarling, T'Chaka would roll him about the bed, tossing the boy back and forth in an attempt to get to his belly. Eventually, they would make so much noise that Ramonda would appear and begin mock attempts to save the bold prince from the vicious "Panther." More often than not, that led to T'Chaka tickling *her*. Before long, all three of them would be breathless, a fine sheen of sweat clinging to them as they lay together in T'Challa's bed, the rest of the world forgotten in their family's love.

T'Challa thought about those days sometimes while lounging in his imperial bedroom, listening to the quieting sounds of his palace as he attempted to drift off to sleep. Tonight, it likely wouldn't matter how noisy the castle was. He was both emotionally and physically exhausted after the day's activities at the Great Mound.

Shuri had not spoken to him since his refusal to allow her to enter the dangerous mine shafts. She'd vanished by the time he entered the royal dining hall, no doubt sulking somewhere in the palace. He hadn't meant to hurt her feelings, but there were literally hundreds of other qualified people in their country that he could send down into the Great Mound for answers, and none of them were in line for the throne.

But he knew Shuri wouldn't understand that. She'd taken his refusal as a slight to her, her knowledge, and her place in the kingdom. T'Challa, frankly, was grateful to not have to continue their argument. He meditated instead, hoping for another visit from the Panther God. But like any feline, she came when she wanted, not when she was called, and all T'Challa got was a peaceful, quiet ride home.

The rest of the day was taken up with security briefings and Science Council meetings. For some reason, the Nigandan army was on the move, and there were rumblings that major amounts of money were being shuttled to somewhere on the continent. As for the scientists, they had yet to figure out why the Great Mound had shaken. So T'Challa had ordered a halt to Vibranium mining for a week, placing the workers on furlough with full pay until they were sure no one would be hurt underground.

S'Yan warned that any longer of a delay would lead them to miss shipments to S.H.I.E.L.D. and other buyers, but T'Challa felt the slight trouble would be worth it. S.H.I.E.L.D. had another order of Quinjets coming from the Wakanda Design Group and wouldn't squawk too hard—though Maria Hill, their current S.H.I.E.L.D. contact, had a reputation for being a hardass.

So that left T'Challa alone for a pleasant dinner with his mother for once. They had a good conversation about national affairs and palace gossip—for a while. Eventually, Ramonda wanted to hear all about what she called his "misadventure" at the Great Mound, hinting heavily that he should have allowed his bodyguards to jump off the building instead of him.

"When will you learn, T'Challa, that your life is meant for something more?" She looked over at Okoye, who was standing impassive near the dining hall's doorway.

T'Challa stood up and walked around the long table to his mother, and kissed her on the forehead. "All of our lives are meant for something more, Mother." T'Challa hugged her tight, feeling her return his embrace. Then he walked out.

After assuming the throne, T'Challa had moved into his father's suite, which had been used by Wakandan kings for decades. He would have preferred to have stayed in his longtime quarters across the hall from Shuri, but he couldn't think of a logical reason not to take the imperial suite.

Three years into his rule, T'Challa was still not accustomed to the cavernous room. He'd sent as much of his father's furniture down to storage as he dared. Instead of the dark woods and satins preferred by his parents, he'd allowed an up-and-coming designer friend of Shuri's to "modernize" the massive bedroom by ripping out the older material and replacing it with cream-colored marble flooring and columns, with gold-inlaid wall panels in various designs.

The one thing she wasn't allowed to touch was the royal flag of Wakanda, which was mounted in a case that took up the entire wall in front of the bed. The green, red, and black flag with a snarling panther in the center was the last thing T'Challa saw before sleep and the first thing he saw every morning—just like his fathers before him.

After a morning of roughhousing in his parents' bed, a young T'Challa had once asked his father why he kept the flag displayed so prominently in his room.

"To remind me, my son, that the first duty of the king is to his country and his people," T'Chaka told him, ruffling his hair. "Our lives—the life of any king, really—are filled with easy pleasures and noble pursuits, but they all must be weighed against the good of the people. Without their faith in us, we are nothing. We must never forget that, and the flag is a symbol that helps us keep that at the forefront of our minds."

So when T'Challa moved in, the flag was the one thing he told the designer would stay, no matter what. Every night, T'Challa focused on the snarling panther's face until it blurred as he drifted off to sleep.

"Your majesty?"

T'Challa bolted up at the feather-light touch of Nakia's hand on his shoulder. He must have been extremely tired to let the his bodyguard get so close without his awareness.

Absurdly, he pulled the cover up over his naked chest, even though he knew that the *Dora Milaje* had seen him in much less than pajama bottoms. But T'Challa had become more and more aware that the youngest of his main guards was carrying an unrequited crush on her king. It would not be wise to allow her thoughts to go any further than they already had. He watched Nakia's eyes sparkle in the low light of his room.

"Is he awake?" Okoye hissed from somewhere near the doorway.

"I am now, Adored Ones," T'Challa yawned. *"I assume there's a reason you two are inside my bedroom instead of at your posts?"*

The expressions on their faces shocked him awake.

"There is an emergency, Beloved," Nakia whispered as he threw the covers back and swung his legs to the floor. *"You're needed in the command center at once."*

T'Challa strode over to the flag and pressed a button on the bottom of the case. The front panel of the wall slid quietly away, revealing one of the many Black Panther habits T'Challa had stashed about the palace during its modernization. Ignoring Nakia behind him, he stripped off his pajamas and within seconds was encased in his leather-like Vibranium-weave armor. The white eyes of his helmet glowed in the dark as he picked it up from its case.

"Tell them we'll be there in five." The Black Panther pulled on his mask as he strode out of the room.

BY THE time T'Challa made it to the palace's underground security command center, the room was in a state of organized chaos. Men and women rushed from monitoring station to monitoring station, checking and rechecking figures and reports. At the center of it all, on a small platform, stood W'Kabi. He stared grimly at the main monitor screen, showing an infrared map of Wakanda's outer borders.

The massive security chief was in his traditional Wakandan garb. He wore a brown loincloth with a loose blue sash tied around his neck and across his muscular chest. A red headdress held his long black dreadlocks out of his face. W'Kabi would have looked just as comfortable stalking prey on the savannah as he did speaking into his wireless headset and issuing commands to his men and women. Considering most people in the room were dressed in business suits, military uniforms, or casual Wakandan garb, W'Kabi's clothing made it clear why he was there.

Only a man of great confidence would wear a loincloth to a military operation.

T'Challa silently eased into the room behind W'Kabi and waited for a break in the chaos. W'Kabi never turned around, but one of his aides saw T'Challa and announced his presence. T'Challa waved off the genuflection, recognizing the seriousness of the situation.

"Your majesty," W'Kabi gave a small nod in T'Challa's direction, still not taking his eyes off the main screen.

"What's going on?" T'Challa stepped onto the platform next to his security chief. The *Dora Milaje* remained close by, their eyes sweeping the pandemonium.

W'Kabi pointed at a small red blip moving toward Wakanda's border on the main screen. "We've got some kind of bogey headed our way from the Nigandan border, a few miles away from that massing of troops from last night that we briefed you about earlier. We only have a few fuzzy pictures of it from cameras at the far-west edge of the kingdom. I was just about to send up a few drones so we can identify the target."

"Over Nigandan soil?" T'Challa took some fuzzy black-and-white photographs from an aide and looked at W'Kabi, who didn't seem at all concerned about the sovereignty of Niganda's borders.

"They're our newest stealth models, your majesty," he explained. "If the Nigandans have anything that can catch them on radar or shoot them down, they deserve to be able to keep them."

T'Challa squinted at the fuzzy pictures, focusing on the protruding horn at the top of the image. "That looks like a rhino, W'Kabi," he said. "My head of security couldn't deal with a wild animal without waking me in the middle of the night?"

W'Kabi pointed at the rapidly moving red blip. "A rhino that we're tracking at 56 kilometers an hour? I don't think so, your majesty." An aide called out to W'Kabi that they'd be in range soon.

"Put it on the main screen," he ordered.

The infrared map flickered, replaced by a shaky, greenish night-vision view of a grassy plain at the edge of a tree line. T'Challa looked down to one of the monitoring stations, where a young woman was maneuvering a large, two-handed controller. She directed the drone so that its camera caught an optimal view of the oncoming object. Flying her drone about twenty feet off the ground, she pressed a few buttons on one of her control panels, setting it to auto-hover. Satisfied, she began adjusting the drone's camera lens, sharpening the image until T'Challa could make out individual blades of grass blowing in the wind.

"I think that's as good as we're going to get for now, Chief W'Kabi," the drone pilot shouted. "I'm going to toggle on the audio, but there'll be a slight lag to account for the transmission on lower, less detectable bands. I think it's worth it, sir."

"Thank you, Nyah," W'Kabi responded, then leaned over to whisper to T'Challa. "The next-gen drones on order from the Wakanda Design Group not only will have incoming video and audio, but also will be able to auto-project holograms from the command center so we can warn people off. They will be a quantum leap over our current security technology."

W'Kabi shot T'Challa a rare grin. "I am very excited," he whispered to his king. "Do not tell anyone."

T'Challa laughed. "Your secret is safe with me, old friend."

W'Kabi straightened up; in his normal growl, he asked his aide, "How long until we have sight of the target?"

"Any second now, sir. We're getting some audio of what sounds like…footsteps?" Nyah looked over at a neighboring technician, who had thrown on some headphones and started adjusting his feed. "Udo, are you hearing this?"

"I'm picking it up, Nyah—and yeah, confirmed," Udo said. He looked at her and shrugged. "That's exactly what it sounds like."

"You mean hoofbeats," W'Kabi pointed out.

"No, sir," Udo shook his head. "That's a human stride, not a four-legged animal. Whatever's making that noise is running on two legs."

"Target acquired in five, four, three, two, one," Nyah interrupted. She gestured toward the main screen.

They all peered at the screen, which showed nothing that could be making the rhythmic thuds. Then a small greenish cloud of dust floated up in the center of the screen, and the massive armored Rhino appeared, charging hellbent toward the drone.

"Holy crap!" Nyah screamed. She jerked back the controller, hoping to get the drone clear, but it was too late. Without breaking stride, the Rhino leaped into the air. A massive paw clipped the side of the drone, and the onscreen picture flipped over as the machine crashed to earth. The screen flickered, showing an upside-down picture of the departing Rhino and his trailing cloud of dust, before going dead.

The room went silent. After a few seconds, Nyah cleared her throat.

"Bringing drone Beta online and triggering self-destruct circuits on drone Alpha, sir," she said to W'Kabi. "We'll have real-time pictures again in a minute, your majesty."

"Thank you, Nyah," W'Kabi answered. He looked over at T'Challa. "So that's no wild rhino."

"No, it's not," T'Challa said. "The Rhino is normally based in Russia, Europe, and the United States. I know he's a mercenary, but what's he doing in Africa?"

"What's he doing, sir?" W'Kabi snarled as Nyah brought a second video drone online. "He's destroying our outer defenses."

This time, Nyah kept the drone high in the air, giving them a good view of the Rhino charging straight through an electrified metal fence. He knocked down a huge chunk of it without even acknowledging its existence.

"That electrical fence was running enough current to power a small city for a month," W'Kabi whispered, impressed despite himself.

The Rhino slowed briefly to kick off a clinging

piece, hopping in a circle for a moment as he was silhouetted by a shower of electrical sparks. Shaking himself free, the bestial man continued his headlong rampage.

"The minefield will stop him, sir," an aide said. W'Kabi looked at him skeptically.

A few seconds later, Nyah's drone lost sight of the Rhino as he plunged into the half-mile-wide minefield Wakanda had placed along its border with Niganda after that country's last failed invasion attempt. The shockwaves from multiple explosions shook the drone and its video. Clouds of debris and dirt flew into the air, obscuring the view of the ground.

"Yes!" an aide said, pumping her fist in the air. "That settled his hash! All we have to do now is fly a hovercraft in to pick what's left of his carcass out of the dirt."

W'Kabi walked toward the main screen. "If that's so, why do I still hear explosions? Shouldn't they have stopped?"

A strong breeze kicked up on the minefield, blowing the cloud of debris out of sight. The Rhino stood revealed, still slowly stomping his way across the minefield. Explosions detonated under his armored feet, but they only pushed him an inch or so off the ground as he trudged along. The impact of the Rhino's stomps and the detonating mines began setting off still more nearby mines, leaving a massive scorched path behind him.

The Rhino ignored all of this, single-mindedly

marching across the field as fast as he could manage. A few minutes later, he'd reached the far edge. The massive man stopped for a moment to pull out a rag and clean dirt from his visor before breaking into a trot.

Stunned aides watched silently as the rampaging Rhino moved into their land. W'Kabi broke the uncomfortable silence.

"Nothing seems to be stopping him. If he keeps on that trajectory, he'll be in the outer suburbs of the Golden City in…" W'Kabi stopped to consult a map before looking over at T'Challa. "At his current rate, he'll be in populated areas in less than 15 minutes."

T'Challa stepped down from the central platform and walked over to Nyah, who was maneuvering her drone behind the armored super villain. He placed a hand on her shoulder, making sure he didn't break the young woman's concentration. "Clear your drones from the area, Nyah," he said, "and search for any activity behind the Rhino. I don't want you to lose your equipment unnecessarily."

She glanced up at him and nodded, then turned back to her screen. T'Challa looked over to W'Kabi. "If he can't be stopped, we'll have to distract him. Scramble an air attack, and tell the quartermasters to make sure those jets are carrying payload C-15. That'll harry the Rhino enough to give us some time to figure out what his plan is."

W'Kabi snorted as he consulted a report handed to him by an aide. "Plan? From what I see here, the Rhino's muscle for hire, a brute used by others in service of their own plans—not someone you'd expect to come up with something on his own."

T'Challa nodded. "I suspect this is just someone's opening gambit. The real attack will come elsewhere, and we'd better be prepared for it. But until we know more, let's slow down this Rhino."

THE CRAMPED ready room at the air base smelled of sweat and stale coffee. But Captain Sharifa Ashei of the Royal Wakandan Air Force found herself craving that aroma more and more as the days went by. This room was usually used for planning active sorties, so her mind had linked that repulsive scent with action.

She'd been grounded too long if she was longing for the smell of the briefing room, Sharifa knew. Flying was everything to her. It was almost the only thing she had left following her mother's death, the year before.

Sharifa had overcome a lot to earn her pilot's wings, including an abusive father who eventually defected to Niganda to escape justice for the beatings she and her mother had suffered. She'd always suspected that father's abuse was prompted by her light skin, freckled complexion, elfin features, and straight hair, given that the rest of her extended family were all proud owners of mahogany-colored skin. Her mother had always insisted that a recessive gene accounted for her skin color and features, but she was never able to verify that without her father around.

Regardless, her mother was Sharifa's biggest cheerleader through a rough childhood. Other Wakandan children teased her about her sunburnt skin and tangled hair, which her mother could never do anything with because of the unfamiliar textures. Still, Sharifa would hold her head high and ignore her classmates' insults, holding back the tears until she could make it home. Her mother, who worked two jobs to keep them in their ancestral home, would find Sharifa nearly every evening sobbing in her room. Before leaving for her night job, Sharifa's mother would rock her to sleep, singing lullabies and reassuring her daughter that the Panther God loved all her children, no matter what they looked like.

The constant rejection forced Sharifa to become a studious child. Because her classmates never invited her to their homes or their parties, she learned to amuse herself with the library her mother made sure was well stocked. As her body developed, she suddenly got the attention of the boys, though the girls continued to be dismissive of her—only now because their boyfriends would turn and watch Sharifa as she walked by. But she ignored them all. Sharifa preferred the world inside her books—a world of fighter pilots who soared above it all, dispensing justice with machine guns and missiles, untouchable by the evil below. She knew early on that being a fighter pilot was her destiny and worked hard to get the grades that would allow her to enter the Royal Air Force Academy.

Sharifa remembered the wide smile on her mother's face when she posed in her cadet's uniform and again a few years later when she was chosen for the military flyover at King T'Challa's coronation. While the military had little use for war pilots because of the country's isolationist policies, Sharifa continued to train hard to improve her stick and rudder skills, waiting for the day her king would call on her to protect her country in their modified Quinjet X-16s.

So she slept in her flight jumpsuit and hit the floor running when she was called to the ready room. Stepping into the small room, she closed her eyes and inhaled deeply before heading down the stairs. The room was set up like a small movie theater with rows of bucket seats. Sharifa sat down in the front row and looked around at the empty room. Perhaps she was early?

A few seconds later, Captain Joey H'Rham sauntered in and plopped down right next to her. Sharifa liked H'Rham, but he was one of those pilots entirely too confident in his charms. Over the years, he'd made a pass or two at her in the officer's mess, but she'd always shut him down. He just wasn't her type, despite his bronze skin, powerful muscular shoulders, and immaculately shaved bald head. He'd be fun for a weekend, but his type would always come around again and again, grinning with polished white teeth, looking for more. She wasn't ready for that in her life.

Luckily, he'd gotten the message and backed

off. But she could tell he was just biding his time, waiting for the right opportunity.

"You know what's going on here?" He leaned over toward her. He smelled of sweat commingling with hastily sprayed-on cologne.

"Nope," she said, then pretended to gag as she turned her nose away from him. "You take a bath before reporting tonight?"

He shrugged. "Hey, you interrupt a guy's social agenda in the middle of the night, you take what you get." She was ready with a retort when Admiral Wekesa Obasanjo, the nation's most decorated pilot, strode in.

They both snapped to attention, but the gruff Wekesa waved them down. "We've no time to waste, pilots. Gear up and get airborne immediately. We're looking at an imminent attack, and our fellow Wakandans are depending on us to stop it."

"What are we facing, sir?" H'Rham, all humor gone, asked as they gathered their helmets and headed toward the hangar.

"And are we it?" Sharifa added.

"You're the only two on deck who are qualified for urban in-flight warfare," Wekesa said. "I'd go myself, but according to W'Kabi, my time in a cockpit is over now that I've put in for retirement next year. Anyway, I've told him and the king that if you two can't do it, it can't be done.

"And captains?" Wekesa looked serious. "You're facing the Rhino."

The two pilots looked at each other as they walked toward their Quinjets, which were being fueled and armored by technicians. H'Rham looked puzzled. "We're facing a rhino?"

"Not a rhino, *the* Rhino," Wekesa corrected with a small smile. "The Black Panther wants him stopped before he gets too far into civilian areas, so I'd pull out every trick I had if I were you. Good luck, and may the Panther God bless you."

Minutes later, H'Rham and Sharifa rocketed into the air, sensors reaching out and searching for the armored Rhino. The jets made several passes over the city and surrounding countryside before they locked on to their target. He was rampaging through crops and fields outside the suburbs, on a direct line for the city.

Even from high in the air, the Rhino looked massive. He tossed aside farm tractors and dump trucks instead of running around them. He even threw aside an uncooperative bull, leaving the stunned animal on its back.

Sharifa gritted her teeth. Cruelty to animals. Someone dressed as one should know better, she thought.

Sharifa heard H'Rham report to the command center through her helmet-comm. "Target sighted." H'Rham had taken lead on this mission, having received his captaincy a year before Sharifa. "Permission to fire."

The speaker system crackled for a second before

they heard a response. "Pilots, this is King T'Challa. You have permission to engage. Try to limit structural damage as much as you can, and no civilian deaths. But otherwise, do what you must to stop him."

"Yes, your majesty," Sharifa answered as she and H'Rham set their planes to auto-hover. The big propellers embedded in the wings kicked up dirt and leaves in front of the Rhino. The massive man stopped and shielded his eyes from the powerful spotlights the two Quinjets trained on him. The jets' missiles and guns cycled to active and pointed down toward the ground.

"Locked and loaded, Captain," Sharifa announced.

"Gotcha, Captain. Commence with bombardment in three, two…" H'Rham counted down, his Quinjet hovering off her wing. But before they could fire, Sharifa saw H'Rham's plane jerk in midair and begin to pinwheel toward the ground, a line of sparks glittering on its belly as if something had slashed it with a giant claw.

Sharifa immediately disengaged, shooting her plane straight up using her vertical fans as she tried to see what had happened to her wingman. "Command, Captain H'Rham is going down!" she shouted into her microphone.

"Not yet," she heard H'Rham say. He fought to stay aloft, instrumentation sparking in the background. "Captain, what the hell hit me?"

"Searching," Sharifa looked at her scanners,

which were showing empty air in all quadrants. "I'm not picking up any other craft in the vicinity, sir. Switching to infrared."

Using her helmet's infrared scanners, Sharifa tilted her plane and peered over the side of her cockpit. She had to blink and shake her head to make sure what she was seeing was real. She hesitated for a second.

"Uh, Command?" she said. "It seems we have a man on a flying horse attacking us with a sword."

There was silence on their channel for a second. "Captain Ashei, did you say a flying horse?" Wekesa asked.

"Yes, sir." She swung her plane's spotlights over to the rapidly approaching object. "I swear, I'm looking at a man dressed in medieval armor waving a black-bladed sword and riding a horse with freaking wings. Permission to engage?"

T'Challa came on the channel again. "Have you dropped your payload on the Rhino?"

"Not yet, your majesty," she replied. She pushed her plane higher and higher in the air, keeping just out of the reach of the knight's sword.

"The Rhino is your priority, Captain. You've got to take him out quickly before he reaches densely populated areas," T'Challa reminded her. "He'll hit the city before we scramble any other fighters."

"I've almost stabilized my plane, your majesty," she heard H'Rham shout into the channel. She leaned out to see his plane still pinwheeling crazily below her. "If worse comes to worse, I'll drop it on the Rhino's stupid head. See how he likes that."

"Whatever it takes, Captain. Good luck." T'Challa abruptly closed the channel.

Absurdly, Sharifa felt a giggle build up in her throat. "I'm going after a mechanical rhino, you're being assaulted by a King Arthur wannabe," she said to H'Rham. "Not exactly how we expected this to go, is it?"

"Amen to that, sister."

T'CHALLA dropped his microphone and walked over to an unmanned screen. On it, a blip was moving fast toward the city. "W'Kabi, what's that?"

The security chief had pulled several of his aides into a corner. Yelling, he demanded to know how a man on a flying horse made it so far inside their lines without being spotted. His underlings, trying to explain how the knight flew under their radar, were ignoring their stations. Even though the beeping from this panel demanded attention, T'Challa was loath to sit down, knowing it wasn't his place or position.

Noticing her king's consternation, Nakia walked over and looked at the screen. Her skin paled as she slid into the seat and studied the readings.

"Blood of the Panther God!" she turned and screamed at the security chief. "W'Kabi, we've got incoming!"

The security chief ran over to the station, his eyes wide in horror as he started pushing buttons.

"Too late for the missile shield," he muttered to himself, looking at the readouts scrolling across the screen. "I'm showing a large missile, your majesty, Kalu-class, with unknown payload. We're not detecting a nuclear signature, however, thank the Panther God. Possibly a misfire?"

"I'm not taking anything for granted tonight, W'Kabi. Do we have a point of origin?" T'Challa said.

"It's Niganda, sir," Nakia whispered, standing back behind him again, working her tablet. "I'm plotting a trajectory that will take it straight to…" She trailed off as a look of dread swept over her face.

Nakia looked over at Okoye. "Where, Nakia?" Okoye prompted.

"The Great Mound," Nakia whispered.

CHAPTER TWELVE

SHURI was relatively confident she'd gotten away with her audacious research expedition without her brother's knowledge. Now, if she could only get K'Darte to stop talking, they could get out of the Great Mound.

After working for hours, she and her co-conspirator were packing away their equipment. Their testing had identified some type of subatomic wobble in the samples of pure Vibranium taken from the mountain. They had been arguing for the last hour about the possible causes of it. The young scientist wasn't really as interested in speculation as she. He preferred to haul their samples back to his laboratory to recheck their work and get second opinions from his colleagues.

Shuri didn't want to wait. She knew that T'Challa would make her account for her actions. Giving him as much information as possible might mollify her brother and make him less disappointed in her for finding a way around his royal decree.

But their actions had ignited a small ember of adventure in K'Darte's heart that he was loath to let die. He'd already started planning their next excursion even before completing the first.

Shuri shook her head as she listened to him

babble while she packed the computer equipment lent to her by Nakia. K'Darte was going on about how their night sneaking around the Great Mound had reawakened in him the need for fieldwork and how he now realized how much he had come to dislike being stuck in a laboratory or a classroom.

If he had anything to say about it, K'Darte insisted, he would be trading in his lab coat for hiking boots and mosquito repellent at the earliest opportunity. After getting permission from his wife, of course.

"Not that you need a job, but I found that you make quite an enjoyable associate in this endeavor, Princess," K'Darte said offhandedly. He carried an armload of tools back to the motorized rail buggy that would drive them out of the tunnels. "Perhaps, with the proper persuasion, your brother might be convinced to assign you as permanent lead on a geological project such as this."

Shuri shook her head in frustration. Even her unindicted co-conspirator was now planning her life for her—although it *did* sound tempting.

"Somehow, I don't see T'Challa and my mother agreeing to me living a life scrabbling around in the dirt," she sighed as she helped him roll up their various maps.

"What about what *you* want, Shuri?" The scientist placed his hand on her shoulder and looked her directly in the eyes. "I don't mean to cause offense, but just this little time with you tonight has shown me that there is much more to you than you like to reveal."

K'Darte was silent for a moment. The only sound in the dark tunnel was the crinkling of their maps as they rolled and stored them in the cart.

"A mind caged is a horrible thing, Princess," K'Darte continued as he piled their equipment in the bed of the buggy. "At some point, they're going to have to realize you are a young woman with a fine mind and a thirst for knowledge. Why hide that? And even if you don't want to do fieldwork, there is so much you could do to promote the sciences or math for Wakandan girls. Even in our progressive society, girls sometimes need special encouragement to engage in the hard sciences. You could be a role model, regardless of whether you ever become queen."

Shuri silently continued to gather their things. She considered what he'd said. Being a Black Panther might not be her destiny, as she had once thought.

But there was more than one way she could serve, wasn't there? Perhaps that's what T'Challa had been trying to tell her that morning in the gymnasium. But why didn't she hear it then? Maybe, just maybe, the time hadn't been right.

But now she heard it loud and clear. Shuri smiled.

"If I go back into the field with you, we're going to have to drag your wife along," she snickered. "I don't think she truly trusts me alone at night with you."

"Forgive her, your majesty. It's the hormones."

K'Darte's eyes shone with pride as he laughed. "We've been keeping it quiet for a while…but she's pregnant."

Shuri jumped up and down clapping and gave the embarrassed man a quick hug. "Congratulations!"

K'Darte grinned and turned back to their work. "You'll probably have an easier time convincing King T'Challa to let you back into the field than I will convincing my wife, Princess," the man admitted. Now imitating his wife's high, squeaky voice, he said, "'You're going where? And for how long? And with HER?'" K'Darte put his hands on his hips and glared at Shuri. "'And your plan is to leave me behind, looking like a calabash gourd, to sit around and wait for you to come back?'"

Shuri broke down into giggles at K'Darte's silliness, feeling a great weight lifted from her shoulders. "I'll run interference with your wife for you, if you do the same for me with my brother," she said.

K'Darte smiled. "I don't think that's quite the same thing, Princess," he said. "Your family, your problems. But if the king asks my opinion, you'll get a glowing recommendation."

K'Darte bent over, gathering some of their equipment to throw into the cart. "Anyway, that's the last of it. Let's get topside. I'm sure my wife is beside herself with worry by now. And consider staying for breakfast this morning, Princess. For a scientist, my wife makes a mean eggs Benedict."

Shuri chuckled, and headed around a corner to

retrieve a forgotten pickax—when an alarm started shrieking, and flashing sirens threw an eerie reddish glare over the tunnel. She clapped her hands over her sensitive ears and ran back to the mining cart. K'Darte was hyperventilating, now that the reality of being caught in the forbidden underground tunnels had become real.

She ran up to the scientist and shook him slightly, just to calm him down. His eyes were still slightly wild. "Looks like our unauthorized excursion has been discovered," he moaned. "How will I explain being thrown in prison to my wife?"

"Don't worry—I'll tell my brother it was all my fault." Shuri shouted to make herself heard over the blaring sirens. "He'll forgive you if you tell him I blackmailed you into doing it."

"But what about my wife? We lied to her as well."

"I can't help you there, partner." Shuri grinned. "Your family, your problem."

"Funny," the man replied, calming down at last. "I'll just have to throw myself on the mercy of the court. Let's get out of here."

Climbing into the rail buggy, Shuri aimed the cart up toward the tunnel's exit. They were trucking along at a brisk pace when a massive explosion erupted above them. A dull roar reverberated through the rock; they could hear the tunnels above collapsing and compacting in on themselves like falling dominos.

The rail buggy began to tremble and shake as the ground shifted beneath them. Chunks of the ceiling fell, forcing Shuri to shield her eyes as falling rocks threw up dirt and debris in their wake. Miraculously, their way was unimpeded at first by the collapsing tunnel, though a dropping rock glanced off K'Darte's head, leaving a wound that gushed blood into his eyes. Shuri fumbled for the cart's first aid kit and handed the man a pressure bandage as she continued to urge the cart forward, one-handed.

Finally they could drive no more. A jagged boulder sat in the middle of the tunnel in front of them with only enough room around it for a person. The rumbling had stopped, leaving a dusty haze in the tunnels that made it hard to breathe. Shuri pulled out another clean bandage and wrapped it around her mouth to keep the rock particulates out of her lungs, then jumped out of the cart. K'Darte was still a bit dazed from his injuries; he moaned quietly, rocking himself back and forth in his seat. Shuri walked around to his side of the cart and checked his injury. It seemed to be clotting nicely, despite his moans of pain.

"I'm going to check to see if we can get around this rock," Shuri's voice was muffled by the bandage, but she felt confident that K'Darte could make out what she said. He nodded as she tied a bandanna around his mouth to help keep out the dirt.

Shuri walked up to the rock pile and tested it, pushing slightly on its side. A few pebbles dropped from the ceiling, but she had no discernible effect on the rock. Carefully scrambling up the pile, she peered over the top and was relieved to see a relatively clear tunnel ahead, leading into one of the main underground caverns—although a strange light was flickering against the walls.

"Can you see anything?"

Shuri looked down to see K'Darte standing at the base of the pile, looking up hopefully.

"Yeah, clear tunnel. Come on up, it looks like we're going to have to hoof it from here."

Shuri reached down to give the man a boost; they carefully picked their way over the rocks, mindful of the pile's loose and shifting nature. Shuri realized she had been holding her breath when her feet touched the ground on the other side. One wrong shift could have brought more rocks down on them, trapping them underground until Nakia confessed to helping her and sent a search party.

K'Darte looked sadly back at the cave-in, undoubtedly wishing he could save their research, which they had left in the cart. But now was not the time for regrets. She pushed the scientist toward the main cavern, and they began to walk.

A few minutes later, as they stepped out into the tunnel into the cavern, they could see the extent of the destruction they had only heard from below ground. Shuri whistled as she stumbled over smoking rocks and the remains of jagged timbers that once had braced the walls. Even though the massive cavern they were standing in was two to three stories underground, she could now see open sky. A hole had been punched through to the floor where they stood, revealing the honeycombed levels of the mine above them, making it impossible for them to walk out. Above, the early morning sun tried to burn through some of the previous night's mist.

Shuri thought she might be able to scale the open face of one of the sides of the pit and make it out the top. But when she glanced over at K'Darte, she realized the scientist would never make it out that way—and his pride would make him try. They would have to wait for rescue.

"Look!" K'Darte pointed at something through the smoke. "A ship!"

Shuri squinted in the direction K'Darte was pointing. Sure enough, there was a large metallic object in the center of the cavern. "What is that?" she asked, inching closer. K'Darte followed, right on her heels.

"It must be some kind of manned ship," K'Darte coughed into his bandanna as they crept closer. "Likely that's what hit the mountain and caused the cave-in. But I thought the airspace was restricted around the Great Mound."

Shuri halted a few feet away. "It looks more like a missile to me."

The scientist moved past her and began pressing on the sides of the metallic craft, looking for an opening.

"K'Darte, be careful," Shuri warned.

"It's still warm," he pondered. "It's been a while—it should have started to cool down by now."

K'Darte walked around the craft, running his hands along the hull. "Perhaps it has a radio that we can use to call for help," he called around to Shuri, who was now out of sight behind the ship. As K'Darte stepped closer, he noticed a circular seam moving counterclockwise, as if someone was unscrewing a cap from the inside. He leaned forward, placed both hands on the ship, and pushed. A hatch popped inward.

"I found the door," he called out, using his hand as a fan to clear away the smoke. He poked his head inside the craft.

"Hello?!" he shouted into the craft. He crawled halfway inside the circular, missile-like tub, blinking as his eyes adjusted to the greenish interior glare. "Is anyone hurt?"

A few steps ahead, a man lying down inside the missile reached out for K'Darte's hand. "You there, sir, are you all right?" the scientist said, stretching out for the man. Suddenly a death grip clamped down on K'Darte's arm, and a sick burning feeling enveloped him as if he were standing too close to a furnace.

"I am just fine, Comrade," the man said in a thick Russian accent.

"What the…" K'Darte looked down at his arm. The skin where the man held him began to blacken and peel, and the smell of burning flesh and hair assaulted his nose. He looked up in horror. The man's glowing eyes narrowed and pulsed as he drew the scientist close.

"You're…you're green!" he stammered. The man lifted his other hand and brought it close to K'Darte's face, the heat from his fingers scorching K'Darte's eyebrows and superheating the sweat running down his brow.

"And you're dead," the Radioactive Man sneered, before pressing his hand into the scientist's face.

K'Darte's face sizzled and popped, the man's death-screams muffled by Igor Stancheck's unrelenting grip on his jaw. When the man was finally still, Stancheck grabbed him by his neck and threw him back out the hatch. The dead body flopped unceremoniously on the ground, smoke rising from the ruined black-and-red mess lolling at the top of his shoulders.

Shuri clamped a hand over her mouth, muting her own scream as she looked at her smoldering friend, the stench of his roasted flesh wafting in the air. A glowing green leg appeared in the hatch, followed by the rest of the immense, jumpsuited man. He stretched and looked around through the smoke and haze. His green, hawkish eyes caught sight of Shuri.

"My first kill of the day." Stancheck smiled grimly at her, freezing Shuri in her tracks like a frightened deer. "But he won't be the last, my dear."

W'KABI sighed in relief as he looked over his monitors. "We're picking up no sign of an explosion at the Great Mound, your majesty. It looks as if the missile just rammed into the ground, causing a collapse at the leeward side of the mine. There should be no casualties, given the mine's closure yesterday." He looked back at T'Challa, hope in his eyes. "Maybe it was a dud?"

"Maybe it's not a bomb." T'Challa concentrated on the screen showing the now-ruined side of the mountain, tapping his hand on his jaw. "Evacuate the guards from the site; have fire and EMS crews at the ready," he called out.

He looked back curiously at Nakia and Okoye, who were in a corner having an intense argument. The furious Okoye seemed to be tearing into the younger woman, who looked as if she were about to cry.

T'Challa took a step toward them to ask what was going on—but Nyah, the drone operator, called for him. "Your majesty? We have visual from the border. Something you should see."

W'Kabi moved over to her screen. "Blood of the Panther God," he muttered. "On screen, Nyah."

The room's main screen filled with the sight of tanks and troops. The Nigandans were picking their way through the remains of the electric fence the Rhino had destroyed earlier that night, heading down the blackened path through the middle of the minefield.

"We have visual of several battalions of Nigandan

troops pouring over the border," the security chief called out. "Tanks, armored ATVs, Jeeps, and foot soldiers—all headed here."

"And the Rhino? Where is he?" T'Challa questioned.

"I'm still on him, your majesty," Captain H'Rham's voice crackled over the intercom. "We're now about three klicks out of the outer suburbs. He's plowing straight through a heavily populated area, civilians and military. I've put a couple of rounds into him, but he's shrugging them off like they were flies. Don't want to bring out the heavy stuff yet. Too crowded down there."

"I'm on your six, Captain," Sharifa called out. "Be careful—I'm seeing major smoke still pouring out of your number-two engine. And I'm still playing hide-and-seek with this flying-horse guy. He's making a real nuisance of himself every time I try to line up a shot."

"Just keep him off me, Sharifa. I've got something for the Rhino, if we can get a clear field of engagement."

"Keep on him," W'Kabi ordered. "We'll clear the surrounding area."

He turned to one of the aides standing behind him. "Pull everyone not needed for evacuation away from the Rhino and send them to plug those holes at the border. I want those Nigandans stopped before they hit the suburban areas. Leave the Rhino to air support."

He turned to T'Challa. "At least now we know one of the players."

T'Challa nodded. "M'Butu. How many planes do we have in the air now?"

W'Kabi looked down at a readout. "A dozen, your majesty, with more on the way."

T'Challa stared at W'Kabi and spoke with a quiet voice distorted slightly by his Panther mask. "I know what I must do, W'Kabi, and you know what you must do." The *Dora Milaje* fell in behind him.

"Keep the two currently engaged on the Rhino and send the rest to take out that column from Niganda," T'Challa ordered. "As soon as it's clear, tell H'Rham and Sharifa to drop their bombs on the Rhino, then return to base for resupply and reengagement.

"And get M'Butu on the phone," he snarled.

M'BUTU popped a grape into his mouth and chewed leisurely as he inspected the sumptuous breakfast spread his chef had prepared for him. Roast pig and pheasant on one end of the table; more traditional flapjacks, assorted fruits, and wine at the other end. And grapes, his favorite, throughout.

He must really remember to thank the chef for her work in her time of need, M'Butu thought. The woman's son had lasted a whole hour after fixing Stancheck's toilet, breathing his last out in the courtyard as the radiation poisoning cascaded through his body. M'Butu had ordered the body disposed of before his chef found out about it: There was no need to lose someone of her talents over simple grief. And he knew he'd need a good breakfast this morning, on this of all days.

The operation was going quite well, as far as he could tell. The Rhino was tearing a path of destruction through the Wakandan border defenses, leaving a clear opening for the brave Nigandan troops to reclaim the riches so unfairly stolen from their ancestors. And now that the Rhino had made it to populated sectors, he could continue to wreak havoc, knowing T'Challa would never use his heavy weapons, and the Black Knight would keep conventional airborne assaults at bay.

The modified missile transport had struck true, delivering the Radioactive Man right to the heart of the Vibranium mound—in optimal position to destroy all of Wakanda, if the others failed. And then there was Klaw, he thought, popping another grape in his mouth.

The Wakandans had yet to reckon with Klaw.

"Your worship!" A young girl ran into his dining hall, breathless. He'd whipped this one last month for not moving fast enough. Good that she'd learned her lesson. "Your worship, there is an urgent call from Wakanda. The Black Panther would like to speak to you."

"He would?" M'Butu smirked. "Then by all means, let us see what the cat king has to say. Have them set up the link in here. I will not allow my breakfast to go cold."

M'Butu chewed leisurely on a pheasant leg, one leg thrown up over the side of his dining-room throne, as he watched his technicians scramble to set up a video link around his table. He flicked bits of meat off his suit as one of his public-relations ladies puffed foundation makeup on his face. He'd purged several of them a few years back when he watched his first international interview on *60 Minutes* and noticed the sickening wet pallor and shininess of his skin.

The ones who were left knew better by now.

A young boy wheeled in a large-screen television with a video camera on top and fiddled with something behind it, then activated the power. The screen flickered and focused in on a dark room. T'Challa stood—in full costume, no less—with his sycophants scurrying around behind him.

M'Butu laughed as the boy pointed at him to indicate the line was open. "T'Challa," he called out. "How are you this glorious morning?"

T'Challa just stared into the screen, the white eyes of his Panther mask boring into M'Butu. Without a word, he pressed a button on the side of the mask, and the face shield slid open. Now M'Butu could see the undisguised fury in the young man's eyes.

"I just wanted to thank you, M'Butu," T'Challa ground out.

"Why?" M'Butu hooted. "Was the crown weighing

too heavily on your swollen head already, young king?"

T'Challa continued as if M'Butu had not spoken. "As you knew and were likely depending upon, Wakanda does not interfere in the affairs of other governments, no matter how foul they are. So we have endured the stench of your regime next to ours for far too long. We'd hoped that your people, who have suffered under your reign of terror, would have risen up and beheaded you on their own. But now you've given us an excuse to do it."

M'Butu leaned forward into the camera before spitting out a grape seed. "You're not half the man your father was, T'Challa, and Klaw killed him. Now he's coming for you, and I'll be spitting into the grave of your precious kingdom soon enough!"

M'Butu slashed his hand across his throat, and the picture went dark. He reached down to the table, picked another grape off the bunch and tossed it into his mouth. "That went well," he said to himself, smiling.

No one in the room had the courage to tell him otherwise.

KLAW!" W'Kabi said thoughtfully. "So now we know who the real enemy is."

T'Challa reengaged his face shield, again closing himself off from the world. "Prepare my skybike. I would have words with M'Butu."

W'Kabi looked at him in confusion. "Your

majesty? You're leaving Wakanda…now?" The security chief appeared distraught. "But we need you here."

T'Challa stared at W'Kabi.

"Your majesty, don't allow your emotions to dictate your actions." W'Kabi stepped forward to block the king's path out of the command center. "That's what they want."

Okoye pushed W'Kabi back with a snarl, as Nakia raised her machete from its scabbard to W'Kabi's neck. The room went silent, until W'Kabi slowly backed out of T'Challa's way. T'Challa waved down the *Dora Milaje*, and started up the staircase.

"Emotional?" He stopped and looked back from the doorway. "I'm happy. I finally know where all of my enemies are."

Then T'Challa disappeared into the light.

T'CHALLA ran his hand over his custom-built black skybike and readied it for takeoff for Niganda.

As T'Challa prepared, Okoye and Nakia stood at the side of the hangar, watching him silently. Nakia's eyes were red-rimmed as if she had been crying, and Okoye's stony demeanor was even more rigid than usual, if possible. Neither woman said a thing to him as they watched him prepare to jet off to Niganda. T'Challa hoped they understood that there wasn't space for them on his skybike, and there was no time to prep any of the other vehicles his engineers had been working on.

Despite what he'd told W'Kabi, this was personal. By the end of the day, he hoped that two major pieces of unfinished business would be taken care of permanently. He had full confidence in Wakanda's ability to repel the Nigandan troops and invading super villains, so he wasn't worried about his people. But it was time for M'Butu's reign to come to an end. How could Wakanda justify improving the lives of people across vast oceans when their brothers and sisters a few miles away were living in squalor?

No, it was time for M'Butu to step down—willingly or not. In fact, T'Challa hoped that M'Butu struggled and gave him an excuse to eliminate him. In the best of all possible worlds, M'Butu would have planned for Klaw to be his last line of defense in Niganda, and T'Challa would be able to kill two birds with one stone.

He coiled one of his electro-whips and placed it in the last remaining space, then closed up the compartment. He threw his leg over the saddle, grasped the handles, and activated the ion drive. The engine, most appropriately, purred.

"Adored Ones," the Black Panther began, as he dismounted and walked over to Nakia and Okoye.

But Okoye shocked him by raising her hand to silence him. As she stepped forward, T'Challa saw a fierce light in her eyes and determination on her face. Her hands were clenched into fists, and she was almost trembling with anger.

"Do not tell us that we must remain behind as

you go fight for our kingdom, Beloved. DO NOT," she hissed venomously. *"If you would go end your life, do not leave us with the dishonor of not having been at your side when you left to meet the Panther God. I will not live as Amare does, with the shame of having outlived her Beloved."*

T'Challa shook his head. *"I cannot bring you, Okoye. I ride swiftly this dawn, and cannot afford even the slightest delay. I leave you with my most precious possessions: the protection of the Queen Mother and the crown princess. Guard the palace and await my return, Adored Ones. That is my charge unto you.*

"We cannot, Beloved. Shuri is not at the palace." Nakia trembled and looked at the hangar's concrete floor, her confession seemingly coming at great cost to her. *"The princess is in the Great Mound."*

T'Challa stalked over to Nakia and pulled her chin up to look in her eyes. *"The princess is where, Nakia?"*

Nakia forced herself to look directly into the Panther mask's white irises. *"The Great Mound, Beloved. She left last night and has yet to return to the palace."*

"And you know this how, Nakia?" T'Challa opened his face mask and looked down at the young woman, the betrayal clear on his face.

"She asked me for my discretion and help to investigate the flaw in the Vibranium." Nakia looked unrepentant. *"I gave it. The Dora Milaje is always faithful to the desires of the king and his family, even*

when the king is not faithful to us and our duties."

"I see," T'Challa growled in Wakandan. "This we will discuss later."

T'Challa pulled open his communicator, hooked the headphone over his ear, and pressed several buttons on a handset before getting a connection. "Shuri? Shuri?" he called into the microphone. Static crackled on the line. T'Challa could hear soft footfalls and the rustling of cloth. Then desperate breathing, as if someone were holding their hands over their mouth, trying to quiet any sound.

"T'Challa? Shhhh," Shuri finally whispered back, static crackling in the background.

"Shuri, are you all right?" T'Challa said in a low voice. "Were you trapped in the cave-in?"

"T'Challa," Shuri whispered desperately, her voice echoing slightly. "I'm sorry for disobeying, brother. Don't blame Nakia—I made her help me."

T'Challa glared over at Nakia, who was still standing at attention. "I will deal with all of that later. What's wrong? Can you get yourself out?"

"The missile destroyed the elevator and the stairwell, and collapsed several of the tunnels," she whispered again. "I don't know what's left."

"Why are you whispering? Can you speak up?"

"No! Lower your voice," she quietly. "I'm hiding from some Russian guy with green skin. He's walking around talking to himself about what he's going to do when he catches me."

"Green guy?" Nakia asked.

T'Challa waved her closer. "Green Russian man in the Great Mound," he whispered to her as she fired up her tablet. "Look it up." She began typing furiously.

"He calls himself the Radioactive Man," Shuri said, a small sob escaping her. "Brother...I saw him melt K'Darte's face off."

"You took him down there with you?" T'Challa said heavily. "Oh, Shuri..."

Nakia tapped T'Challa on the shoulder and maneuvered her tablet so he could read her report. "Igor Stancheck, the Radioactive Man," he read to Shuri. "Exposed to radiation, glowing green skin, power to manipulate radiation across the spectrum. Can emit it as heat, hard radiation, and hypnotic light."

"Yes, yes," Shuri said urgently. "Can you come get me, T'Challa? I need help."

T'Challa sighed heavily and muted the channel. He closed his eyes for a second and began to pace. There was no good decision. If he didn't go to Niganda, M'Butu's troops and super-powered mercenaries would fight to the last man, killing untold numbers of his people. But if he left Shuri, and something happened to her, he would never forgive himself. Either way, someone would be at risk.

He opened the channel again. "Shuri, the kingdom is under attack, but I assure you help is on the way. Keep as far away from Stancheck as possible. Quiet as night, swift as an antelope. Remember?"

"Hurry, T'Challa," Shuri whispered one last time before dropping communication.

T'Challa looked down at the floor, despair in his eyes. When he looked up again, Nakia and Okoye both involuntarily took a step back. The determination in his eyes made them glow, and an animalistic vibe seemed to radiate from his body.

"You want orders, Adored Ones? Here are your orders," T'Challa said quietly, voice dripping with power. *"There are only three people Klaw has ever failed to kill: my sister, my mother, and myself. He's going to be targeting the palace eventually, and I will not leave my mother defenseless. Okoye, you must defend the Queen Mother. Pull in my uncle and the rest of your sisters if you must. But I charge you, one of the greatest warriors of my kingdom, with her protection.*

"Okoye," T'Challa warned, a small growl building in the back of his throat. *"If my mother dies and you survive, you will answer directly to me. And I will not be as kind as they were to your general."*

Okoye nodded, and T'Challa turned to her partner. *"Nakia, you will go to the Great Mound. The defense of the princess is your goal. Keep her alive and safe by any means necessary. You got her down there, you get her out."*

T'Challa looked at the two women. *"This night, you will be the Panther's fist—the tip of the sacred spear. I was told by the Panther God I must trust those I love to do what needed to be done. I will not forsake my mission, Adored Ones. Do not forsake yours."*

"*T'Challa,*" Nakia whispered reverently, dropping to one knee. "*I will not fail you, Beloved.*"

Okoye fell to her knees as well. "*T'Challa,*" she repeated. "*I will not fail you, Beloved.*"

The Black Panther nodded, climbed aboard the skybike, and ignited the engine. Dropping his faceplate back into position, he gave the two women one last glance before rocketing off into the morning sun.

CHAPTER THIRTEEN

THE WIND whistled around the Black Panther's armor as he pushed his skybike faster and faster toward Niganda and M'Butu's palace. The day promised to be hot and bright, with few clouds in the sky. The houses and fields of Wakanda rushed by below him as his bike shrieked through the sky. Although he continued to monitor the different battles taking place in the kingdom through his helmet-comms, T'Challa felt grateful for a few moments of solitude to ponder the previous night's happenings.

The king could see oily black smoke rising in front of him, where Wakandan ground and air forces had engaged not only the regular invading Nigandan armed forces, but also the pair of super-powered mercenaries hired by M'Butu to escort his troops into Wakanda.

The armored Rhino and the zealot Black Knight, flying astride a winged horse, were the vanguard of Niganda's invasion, sent to disrupt Wakanda's defenses and distract from the second strike: the missile that had delivered the deadly Radioactive Man to the Great Mound, the country's sole source of Vibranium.

T'Challa had yet to figure out why M'Butu and Klaw—the hidden hand behind the day's activities—wanted the Radioactive Man inside the Great Mound. Perhaps he planned to irradiate the mountain, making it harder to mine and throwing Wakanda's economy into turmoil?

It wasn't a strike against the royal family, which T'Challa expected was Klaw's main goal. The fact that Princess Shuri had spent the night in the Vibranium mines and was now trapped in there with the Russian was an awful coincidence, not a well-thought-out plan. No one, not even T'Challa, could have predicted that his little sister would disobey his direct commands and enter the mines on a scientific inquiry—assisted by his own *Dora Milaje*, at that!

No, T'Challa thought as he redlined his skybike's engine, there had to be more to this attack than was immediately apparent.

They had yet to see Klaw himself. M'Butu was a brute and an opportunist, but he was no strategic mastermind. The true opponent had yet to rear his head, and so the Black Panther must force his hand, T'Challa thought grimly.

So deep was T'Challa's concentration, he almost missed the alarm beeps from his proximity scanners, warning him to change trajectories. He leaned over the side of his craft to see what could possibly be approaching him from that angle. Then he saw it.

"Blood of the Panther God!" T'Challa swore, immediately putting his bike into a power dive.

A refrigerator hurtled over his head, followed quickly by the matching freezer.

The Rhino must be close by, T'Challa thought—and frustrated that the Quinjets sent to slow him down were staying out of his reach. T'Challa banked his skybike toward the ground. Time to end the man's rampage.

A few seconds later, T'Challa was skimming the treetops, trying to get an idea of the tableau beneath him. He adjusted his helmet-comm to the pilots' frequency. They cursed as they bobbed and weaved their jets, trying every trick they could to push back the Rhino and dodge the Black Knight's attacks.

The two Quinjets assigned to stop the Rhino had the super villain pinned down in a suburban cul-de-sac. The tasteful, middle-class homes had been evacuated, and the jets had opened up their guns in an attempt to keep the Rhino from advancing farther. The asphalt road leading into the circular street was now pockmarked with holes.

The pilots—Sharifa and H'Rham—had achieved minor success, but the Rhino had taken shelter from their bullets inside a three-car garage. Frustrated with the pilots, the Rhino had started bombarding them with anything he could get his hands on. That explained the flying refrigerator and freezer.

"Whoops, here comes the kitchen sink!" H'Rham joked, pushing his smoking plane higher into the air to dodge another missile from the Rhino. The villain roared up at the planes, then retreated again to the ruins of the house.

"Pay attention, idiot!" Sharifa, the other pilot,

chastised him. "Flying horse at your six!"

Her Quinjet banked hard, targeting the flying animal and its rider with a barrage of bullets. The horse gracefully dodged and weaved, but the maneuver forced the Black Knight far enough out of range that he could not strike at either jet.

The air was clear for the moment. The pilots put their Quinjets in hover-mode and circled the cul-de-sac. They opened fire on the Rhino's hiding spot, shredding the walls around him in an attempt to draw him out.

T'Challa, however, had a better plan. "Pilots, this is the Black Panther," he radioed. "Use your missiles to deny him his hiding spot. I'll take it from there."

"Yes, sir," Sharifa called back, pulling her jet back up in the air to line up a shot. "Missile locked and away!"

The explosion collapsed the roof of the Rhino's house, forcing him to stumble out into the driveway to avoid the falling debris. As soon as he saw the armored man, T'Challa began his bombing run, toggling a special missile to readiness as he dived out of the air.

The Rhino just laughed as T'Challa's skybike swooped toward him between the two Quinjets.

"You got something for me, kitty-cat?" The man pounded his chest. "Bullets can't hurt me; missiles only slow me down. As the kids say: What you got, comrade?"

T'Challa smiled under his mask. "Sleeping gas."

A specially tipped missile streaked out from under his skybike and exploded on the ground in front of the Rhino. T'Challa aimed his skybike back up into the air as a green-tinted cloud billowed out and enveloped the man. The two Quinjets maneuvered around the Rhino, using their horizontal flight stabilizers to keep the gas cloud swirling around the staggering villain.

T'Challa banked and looked back down to see the Rhino with his hands around his throat, slowing falling to one knee. "Unfair," the man choked as he tried to stand and stagger his way out of the gas cloud. "That's—that's…cheating."

"As the kids say: Tough," T'Challa said quietly. He watched the man faceplant on the ground.

He maneuvered his skybike to hover above the defeated Rhino. "W'Kabi," he radioed back to the command center. "One down. Get a Vibranium null cage for this one, and quickly. I don't know how long the gas will keep him out.

"Captain H'Rham? Disperse this gas for me, please. We don't want any of our soldiers falling asleep on the job, do we?"

As T'Challa pulled his skybike back around, he could hear the grin in the pilot's voice. "No sir, we surely don't. Vectoring down." T'Challa could see the jet maneuvering its way back toward the Rhino, its nose tilting slightly in the air. The Quinjet's hovering fans began pushing the cloud away. "We should have blue skies again in five, your majesty."

"H'Rham! Look out!" Sharifa called out—too late. The Black Knight, the sun at his back, swooped down on the hovering Quinjet and sliced his Ebony Blade across the wing, causing a massive explosion.

"I can't believe this," H'Rham shouted, struggling to keep his plane aloft. "He's got me. I'm going down!"

The Black Panther could only watch in horror as H'Rham tried to maintain control of his spinning Quinjet. It weaved in the air like a dying bird. A few seconds later, the Quinjet nosedived into the roof of a nearby house, throwing smoke, flames, and debris into the air. T'Challa felt the shockwave as the house ignited in a massive blast, leaving no hope for the doomed pilot.

H'RHAM! *No!*" Sharifa shouted, aiming her plane toward the burning house.

"Captain Sharifa, stop. He's gone," T'Challa said sadly. "There's nothing we can do for him."

Sharifa watched the twisted metal of the Quinjet collapse among the ruin of the house. She sniffed in her helmet and angrily batted away tears. H'Rham was a jerk, but no pilot deserved to die like that.

"Nothing, your majesty, except avenge him," she snarled, looking around for the now-vanished Black Knight.

"Captain, I have a different mission for you," T'Challa said urgently, moving his skybike to hover off her port wing, scanning the skies to make sure the horse was not within sight. "Leave the flying swordsman to me, and I promise you your wingman will be avenged. But for now, your kingdom needs your services."

Sharifa looked at the Black Panther through blurry eyes, smoke from H'Rham's funeral pyre billowing up behind him. *Damn it all,* she thought.

"Promise me he'll pay," she whispered.

"I promise," T'Challa replied. "But this is what I need you to do…"

VALINOR'S wings beat confidently against the air as he and the Black Knight soared away from the battle, staying just above the suburban houses, parks, and fields to keep under the Wakandans' radar. The evacuation of the Wakandan people had served the attacking force well, because it delayed eyewitness reports of their progress into the heathens' hands. This gave the night a better chance to reach his goal before any appreciable defense could be mounted against him.

Valinor, whose nose emitted warm steam in the cool morning air, was able to move at a much faster clip now that they didn't have the Rhino to protect any longer. The knight was still amazed by the armored man's defeat at the pagans' hands.

He was surprised that he felt sadness at the pilot's unintended and unnecessary death. The heathen had had no chance to confess his sins and receive forgiveness for his pagan worship. But the knight's grief was tempered by the knowledge that the man was a soldier and had died following orders. He knew the comfort that gave a person, being a professional soldier himself.

But he was a man of the cloth as well, and it was incumbent upon him to bring the light of the Lord to these people through any means necessary. The violence and death was regrettable, but the Wakandans had been led astray by their animal-worshiping leaders for far too long. Klaw had promised him a chance to convert as many of them as he could, and the knight had several ideas about how to subvert their traditions and celebrations. He smiled to himself. Perhaps they would name this day a holiday of religious freedom.

But first he needed to complete his current mission. Now that the Rhino had fallen, he had to make it to the Vibranium mountain post-haste.

Just ahead of him, he could see the Great Mound. A tug on the reins, and Valinor circled down and around through the low-hanging clouds. The jungle terrain around the mountain made it difficult for the knight to see. He peered through the morning mist, trying to spot the Radioactive Man's missile transport.

M'Butu and Klaw needed to be sure that Stancheck had made it inside the mountain. But radio communication was spotty because of the man's internal radiation and the depth of the mines. The

Black Knight could see a smoking hole in the side of the mountain where he assumed the missile had struck and bored into the ground, but no life was immediately apparent.

Having been warned about the reach of the man's radioactive touch, the knight was loathe to bring his horse much closer to the impact crater. But he knew he would have no choice if he was to fulfill his mission. He patted his horse on the neck, and Valinor began slowly drifting toward the ground.

"Surrender!" a voice called out.

The Black Panther was dropping from the sky behind him on the back of a flying mechanical contraption. The night shook his head. In the confusion of his attack on the jets, he had not paid attention to the Panther's vehicle. Just like a heathen to use a manmade creation instead of one of God's wonders, like Valinor.

"Bring your worst, varlet!" The knight unsheathed his Ebony Blade threateningly, aiming it at the approaching man. Valinor screamed as they swung around, pushing the knight higher in the air toward his enemy.

The Panther pulled out of his dive. He sounded amused as he toggled a switch on his handlebars. "Did you just call me a varlet?" he goaded as he fired a missile at Valinor.

The Black Knight ignored the taunt and leaned forward, pushing Valinor down under the missile. At the last second, he reached up and sliced it in two with the Ebony Blade as it soared over his head. The pieces tumbled out of the sky and into the jungle below, landing seconds later with a muffled explosion.

The Black Knight looked up at T'Challa in triumph, brandishing his sword. "See the speed and power my God provides me?" he sneered. Valinor reared up in the air, whinnying a challenge at T'Challa.

The Black Panther hovered in place for a moment, seemingly contemplating the knight's words. "I see metal armor, a genetically modified horse, and an enchanted sword—none of which seem particularly holy to me." The Panther pressed another button on his control panel.

The skybike lurched down as if the power had been cut. Then the Panther swept back up in an arc behind the Black Knight, quicker than the man or the flying horse could react. A grappling hook shot out from the belly of the inverted skybike, snaking across the sky toward the night. Before he could get his sword around, a magnetic clamp at the end of the grappling hook had latched on to his armor.

The Panther revved his engine and took off in a climb, unceremoniously jerking the Black Knight out of his saddle and leaving a confused Valinor flapping aimlessly behind him. The knight, buffeted by the wind, tried to swing around and use his sword to cut the cable. But T'Challa kept weaving his skybike to keep him off-balance.

"I wouldn't do that if I were you," T'Challa

called down, shooting higher and higher in the air. "Unless you're willing to bet that your armor will help you survive a headlong crash into the ground from a couple hundred meters in the air."

T'Challa drove faster and faster, circling around, whipping the Black Knight back and forth at the end of the cable. "A few minutes ago, you said God was on your side," the Black Panther called back in a conversational tone. "Now that you're losing, has God abandoned you?"

"Blasphemer!" the knight cried back.

"It was just a philosophical question," T'Challa responded, speeding up again and diving toward the Great Mound. "And something else that's been bothering me: You Christians like saying that no weapon formed against you shall prosper. Seems like my weapons are doing pretty well, wouldn't you say?"

"That's—that's not what that means," the knight sputtered.

T'Challa shrugged. "Just wondering."

JUST ahead, the Black Panther could make out the knight's flying horse, still circling where they had left him, awaiting his master's command. T'Challa aimed his bike toward the horse, flipping the knight around so he could briefly see his faithful steed.

Immediately, the Panther swung the knight around again and put his bike in a power dive toward the winged horse.

"Well, this conversation has been interesting, but I have other things I must do before nightfall," he shouted back to the trailing knight. "Now, drop your sword or I'll blow your horse out of the sky."

The Black Knight froze his cape flapping around him. "You…you wouldn't," he called.

The Black Panther's voice dripped with menace as he targeted the horse. "I wouldn't? You and your friends have cost me at least one life this day, a pilot of some great promise. That's not counting the men and women out in the field defending Wakanda from your friend M'Butu, and the dead inside the Great Mound. All of that blood is on your hands. Balanced against that, the life of one freakish horse means nothing to me.

"Bike, autonomous mode," T'Challa called out as they drew near Valinor.

"Confirmed, your majesty," the onboard computer replied. "Kimoyo controls activated."

"Target organic anomaly 20 meters ahead; prepare a missile spread, heat-seekers and sunburst. Confirm when set."

"Targeting organic anomaly, countdown to positive target lock in 20, 19, 18…," the Kimoyo computer counted down.

The Black Knight's struggles intensified wildly. "You savage!" he screamed. "You'd kill an innocent animal!"

"Typical European, more concerned about an animal than your fellow man, whom you were about to gleefully plunge into a war that could have cost thousands of lives." T'Challa's voice was cold. "Well, you brought your horse onto the field of war, and you can save him, if you really care for that animal. For myself, I hold all life sacred, not just that of my pets. So if you really care—"

"Stop, stop!" the Black Knight shrieked. "I surrender! Don't shoot!"

"Drop your sword," called T'Challa. He'd flipped the skybike around, flying backwards to keep an eye on his unwilling passenger. "And hurry."

The Black Knight's head dropped in defeat. With a flick of his wrist, he sent the Ebony Blade whistling down toward the impact crater. He and T'Challa watched silently as it disappeared into the ground.

"Kimoyo, cancel firing sequence. Confirm," the Black Panther said.

T'Challa looked down at the Black Knight, sulking at the end of the cable, then turned back around and grasped his handlebars.

For a second, he stared down at the Great Mound, his desire to find his sister overwhelming. But no, his people's safety and welfare must come first, T'Challa thought sadly. *May the Panther God protect you, little sister.*

"Now, Sir Knight, we're going for a little ride," the Black Panther aimed his skybike toward Niganda. "I need to speak with your boss."

ROSS burst into the crowded Pentagon conference room, pushing through a crowd of suits and aides, straightening his tie. He shot Reece a look, and got a clear "It's his show now" vibe back from her. Matigan tapped a coffee mug on a table to call the room to order, then handed the mug to his attaché— Lieutenant Wilson—and waved at her for a refill.

"What's going on?" Ross asked as he slid into a chair next to Reece.

She tapped a perfectly manicured nail on the table, the unpleasant look on her face never changing. As she leaned over toward him, the strong smell of lilacs in her hair surprised him. They'd never actually been this close to each other before, Ross realized. She'd always been at the head of the table, and he'd been at the end with the other analysts.

There was a new pecking order, apparently, and she'd lost out to Matigan. Washington was like that, Ross knew. Ups and downs came fast and furious in the political world.

Reece had been good to him, and she still made a good ally. Ross didn't have enough of those to turn any away. He reached for a pitcher of water and poured two cups.

"There's been an attack on Wakanda," Reece said. She never took her eyes off of Matigan. "Be ready.

Ross looked back at her in confusion, swinging around in his chair. "Be ready for what?"

"Ladies and gentlemen, may I have your

attention please?" Matigan cleared his throat as the room settled down. Ross looked around at the faces; besides Matigan, Reece, and Wilson, he didn't know any of these people. He had no idea how they'd even gotten into the Pentagon after hours.

"We have actionable intelligence that there is an ongoing conflict, possibly a state of war, between Wakanda and Niganda as we speak," Matigan continued. "Our intelligence shows that a small force has moved in from Niganda, using that country as a launching pad for an invasion of Wakanda."

The general turned around and nodded at a projection of M'Butu on the screen behind him. "M'Butu's an idiot who can barely feed his own people without foreign aid, so we're pretty certain that the Nigandans don't have the stones to pull this off on their own."

Reece leaned forward. "Then who is behind it, William?"

Matigan looked at a man sitting directly to his left, chewing on a toothpick and grinning like a cat that just ate a canary. "Our…sources indicate that the men are being led by professional mercenaries employed by one Ulysses Klaw, a notorious Belgian mercenary," the man said.

Matigan slapped both hands down on the table, and looked directly down at Ross, who was sipping on his water.

"There's no way we're going to let a bunch of waffle-makers play us out of position in Wakanda, people," Matigan insisted. "We need to send in support troops to aid our Wakandan allies right away. Ross, I want you on the next plane out."

Ross spit out the water he'd just sipped as Reece frowned. "Out?" he exclaimed. "Out to where?"

"To our carrier group off the coast of Africa, son. Put-up-or-shut-up time." Matigan smiled. "Dr. Reece says you're the expert. Get into some fatigues and get out there and put that knowledge to good use for once. I want our troops to know where they're going and what they're doing when we assist our brave Wakandan allies.

"Dismissed." He looked around the table. "Ross, don't miss your flight."

The room emptied, leaving Reece and Ross alone at the table.

"Dr. Reece," he stammered, "I am sooo not an in-the-field type of guy. What's Matigan thinking here?"

Reece looked at him grimly before answering. "I believe he's thinking he's outmaneuvered me, and now he's outmaneuvering you by stashing you somewhere he—or anyone else in the administration or the media—can't hear your advice anymore. Can't run complaining to the White House or CNN from the middle of an ocean, can you?

"And the sad thing about it is that he's right for all the wrong reasons. Our boys will need your expertise if they set one foot into Wakanda uninvited." She sighed. "The best we can do now, and this goes for you especially, is try to keep this situation from blowing up in our faces."

Ross looked down at his hand and fought back the urge to start biting his nails—a habit he thought he'd outgrown years ago. "I'll try," he promised.

M'BUTU had been trying to get a call through to his benefactors since his last chat with T'Challa. But somehow the Wakandans were jamming his telephone lines, his satellite receivers, the internet, and his palace's cable television. So other than word of mouth from a few disreputable runners, he had no idea how his assault on the neighboring kingdom was going.

Frustrated, he retreated upstairs to his office, carrying more of his grapes, and slammed and bolted the door. Through an intercom, he demanded to be left alone by his staff until they had real news of his victory—which he expected them to deliver soon.

It would be a good day, he insisted to himself as he paced back and forth. He loved his office. His soundproof, wall-length plate-glass windows kept the world at bay yet allowed him to keep an eye on the people down below who existed to do his will. Some of his best work was done in here, from the questioning of rebels to the training of household staff to the editing of incorrectly written copy by local newspapermen. He looked at his correcting rod on the wall, and sighed. Good times.

M'Butu thought good news had to be coming soon. The plan was genius. Rhino and the churchman would do the heavy lifting, carving a path through the Wakandan defenses for his troops, while Batroc and Klaw eliminated the royal family. The Radioactive Man would hold the rest of the world at bay by threatening to destroy the Vibranium mound, until M'Butu had his puppet government in place and was ready to open the doors of commerce and religion.

Everyone would win, he thought as he pulled a snifter of brandy and a glass from his desk and reclined in his chair. And best of all, the world would be less one pretentious, overbearing, righteous cat king.

M'Butu was no fool. Nigandans had tried invading Wakanda before with no success, so there was the possibility his mercenaries would fail. If so, M'Butu had set himself up nicely to rebound in the eyes of the international community. His troops would be a sad loss, but his people were already drafting the speech he would give at the United Nations calling them a rogue unit under the influence of European mercenaries. Any that survived, he'd purge himself to make sure there was no one left to present an alternative story to his.

What, they would ask, about the super-powered mercenaries on his lands? And he would reply: How was he to know what happened in every corner of his kingdom? Did the United States control every mutant, Inhuman, and powered individual within its borders? How did the world expect a lowly African president to do so, if the world's most powerful nation could not?

The missile launch? A sad mistake…no, a grievous error committed by his young troops. They'd been trying to retake a missile compound near the palace from mercenaries, but regrettably were too late to stop the mercenaries—no, terrorists!—from launching against his honored neighbors. He hoped there'd been no loss of life in Wakanda, offered them his most sincere apologies, and promised to use every resource available in the war against terrorism.

M'Butu stuffed another bunch of grapes in his mouth. He was familiar with the necessary routine—and quite frankly, he thought, he danced quite well. But there would be no need for such apologies this time around, because the plan was going to work. By nightfall, he'd be inside Wakanda sitting on that pretender's throne.

Life was good, M'Butu thought as he walked over to his windows and watched his people scuttle down below. Several men in the courtyard were scrambling back, pointing at him in the window. He couldn't hear what they were saying, but the looks on their faces told him everything. They saw him and were afraid.

Fear and respect were good, he thought, and he deserved it all. Yes, this was going to be a good day. He popped one more grape into his mouth before the windows shattered.

Shards of glass pelted M'Butu in his face, seconds before a black-caped body knocked him over his desk and sent him sprawling on the floor. He tried to push the heavy armor off him, but the body inside seemed limp, unmoving. Pieces of glass cut into M'Butu's hands every time he tried to brace himself.

Almost unknowingly, M'Butu took a second to untangle the cape from around the figure's body. The Black Knight's unseeing eyes looked back at him through the medieval helmet. The man's head lolled to the side, and drool ran down his unshaved chin.

The graphic display of the knight's failure infuriated and reinvigorated M'Butu. He managed to roll the knight off of his body and stand up. Was there nothing upon which he could depend? The windows, he thought indignantly, were supposed to be bulletproof. Surely that meant body-proof as well, didn't it?

A small part of M'Butu laughed at himself. *The things that go through one's mind when facing death!* And death was what he saw in the Black Panther's white-eyed mask as the Wakandan gracefully climbed down a cable into the Nigandan king's office.

M'Butu had never actually seen T'Challa in the Panther habit. He had to admire the grace with which the Black Panther was able to walk through the crushed glass and around his desk to face him.

T'Challa clenched his fists, and silver claws slowly extended from his fingers. M'Butu's mind snapped back to business. The damnable Panther never spoke, just crept closer and closer to M'Butu—who, despite himself, could feel his gut start to tremble and quake, the grapes roiling in his stomach.

T'Challa extended his hand to M'Butu's desk and dragged it along the surface, leaving four deep gouges in its wake. M'Butu imagined that T'Challa was licking his sharp canines under his mask, anticipating sinking his teeth into M'Butu's ample neck as a panther would a gazelle. He could feel the hairs sticking up on his back and knew running would be futile.

Staring death in the eyes, M'Butu decided he would show T'Challa what real courage was all about. "These are not office hours, T'Challa," he managed to sputter—bravely, he thought.

T'Challa's arm moved faster than M'Butu could see, leaving throbbing heat blossoming on his cheek. M'Butu's hand flew to his jaw, feeling his blood coat his fingers and drip down on his ermine carpet. Another flash of T'Challa's claws, and four matching scars were gushing scarlet blood on the other side of his face.

"I will not tell you anything, boy," M'Butu gasped through the wetness and pain. "Someone will come for me."

The Black Panther looked at his hand. His silver claws were now painted red with M'Butu's blood. The white slits of the mask turned back toward M'Butu, and he could imagine the satisfied smile on T'Challa's face. Without warning, the Panther lunged at him and dragged all eight claws from

M'Butu's forehead to his chin, making him scream pitifully.

"What will they find when they arrive?" T'Challa asked calmly in his metallic voice. He knocked M'Butu to the ground and pounced on top of him, slashing the Nigandan king across his chest, stomach, and arms. The fat man flailed about pitifully.

After a few seconds, T'Challa dragged M'Butu to his feet and lifted him up into the air, claws pressed into the man's neck. M'Butu kicked his feet feebly. Blood gushed from his face, running down his chest, arms, and legs. He almost lost consciousness from the pain.

M'Butu looked out through bloody eyes. He could see the horrified look on his own face in one of his wall-length mirrors that had escaped destruction. The sight of himself in tears and pain, a look he'd etched into the faces of many of his own people in this very office, broke his will as much as the pain that the Panther was causing.

"In the few seconds you have left, you must make a decision," the Black Panther cocked his head as he squeezed M'Butu's neck tighter and tighter. "You can keep your silence and die. Or…"

He dropped M'Butu, who fell to the floor on his hands and knees. He looked up at T'Challa, trying desperately to find the escape hatch. People begged when facing destruction, M'Butu knew, and sometimes it helped. But before he could make his throat work, he remembered what he'd done the last time someone begged him for mercy: a quick bullet in the back of the head.

He spat blood out on the floor instead, and watched it pool under him. He'd never thought he would be down on his knees in his own office, desperately trying to find a way to survive his own machinations.

T'Challa crouched down, sank his claws under M'Butu's chin, and forced his gaze up. "Or you can tell me where Klaw is, and I will leave you what's left of your wicked life…for now."

The white eyes of the Black Panther's mask filled M'Butu's world as he held in an agonizing scream. "Choose," T'Challa snarled.

M'Butu talked.

CHAPTER FOURTEEN

SHURI'S hands scrambled for purchase as she pulled herself over a pile of rubble left behind in the tunnel, her breath coming in jagged gasps and her eyes watering.

Maybe if she made it over the top, she thought, she could escape her pursuer, whose mocking laugh she could still hear echoing in the dark behind her. When she crested the top of the rubble, she glanced back over her shoulder, hoping to see nothing but darkness. The pile shifted under her weight, sending rocks tumbling around her feet. Shuri pressed up against the pile and peered back over the top, wiping sweat and dirt from her eyes.

Please, please, please, let me have lost him.

But there it was: Radioactive Man's sickly green glow, pulsing and throbbing through the dust cloud, overpowering the tunnel's emergency lighting. She could hear his heavy tread, the cracking of his aura, and worst of all, his mocking laugh as he walked unerringly toward her hiding place.

"Little girl, where are you?" Igor Stancheck mocked, running his hand along the tunnel walls. "Are you not tired yet?"

Truth was, yes, Shuri was getting tired.

She'd been on the run since speaking to

T'Challa, with the Radioactive Man dogging her steps. Somehow he always found her, despite her attempts to mask her voice, her scent, and her breath behind rocks and walls, and inside crevasses. The mine's collapse had turned the underground complex into an unfamiliar maze for Shuri. Now she had to contend with caved-in passages, unexpected drop-offs, and broken ladders that led to nowhere.

Her brother had told her to stay alive, and Shuri was trying her best. She was smaller, faster, and lighter, and she could cover more ground than Stancheck could. Without his radioactive abilities, Shuri would have been willing to pit her martial skills against the heavyset Russian, fairly certain she would win such a contest.

But playing cat-and-mouse inside a now-unfamiliar mountain against a glowing green Russian with a death touch and an apparently psychic ability to pinpoint her location? That made things more difficult, Shuri thought. She ducked behind the rock pile and slid down to the ground, the rocks gouging new wounds on her legs.

T'Challa, where are you?

As she hit the floor, the underground breeze carried the stench of burning rock through the gaps in the pile. Like she'd seen before, the Radioactive Man was using his deadly touch to superheat the molecules in the rock, literally melting his way through the mound to get at her. In a minute or so, the thick-accented Russian would be on the other side, having not exerted a single bit of physical energy climbing over the pile as she had.

So Shuri headed deeper and deeper into the mountain, hoping the darkness would hide her—or at least give her an advantage against the Radioactive Man and his deadly blasts. She'd purposefully moved away from the impact crater where the Radioactive Man had smashed into the Great Mound in his specially built rocket. With her training, she could easily scale the crater to the wide gap and freedom—but she knew the Radioactive Man would microwave her halfway up and send her smoking, barbecued corpse plunging back to the ground.

So Shuri ran.

"You will die slowly, Princess," Stancheck called through the molten slag, which threw bright red-and-yellow lights on the tunnel walls behind her. "Not quick like your friend, but slowly and painfully, as is deserved by the bourgeois reality-TV swine that you are."

The Radioactive Man waded through the melted rock, impervious to the heat. He called down the tunnel into the darkness where Shuri disappeared, seemingly unconcerned about her hurried flight into the bowels of the mine.

"You will die alone in a hospital—teeth rotting, skin peeling, hair falling out—as your body eats itself from the inside," he promised. "The pain will grow greater and greater until you beg someone to end your life. You can't outrun my radiation forever, little girl. Be nice to me, and I may end your life quickly instead of handing you over to M'Butu. But if you make me run…"

Shuri ran faster, her headlong dash taking her around bends and through caverns she'd never seen before. The tunnels sloped down, then back up, and then down again, leaving her lost and disoriented. But with every turn she made, every time she backtracked, every fork she took, the Radioactive Man followed in her footsteps with little problem.

"Are you wondering how I am finding you so easily, Princess?" he called. "Did you know that the human body absorbs and emits radiation in small quantities? I can see this radiation. It stands out like a beacon in this dark, dank mine. You cannot escape, girl."

Shuri turned a corner and scrambled up a ladder in an elevator shaft overlooking the tunnel she'd just fled. A couple of floors up, she found another cave-in—but this time the rocks were scattered horizontally across the floor, with several medium-sized ones near the shaft.

"Time to stop running," Shuri muttered to herself. She knelt down to pick up the heaviest boulder she could move. Straining under the weight, she duck-walked the massive rock to the top of the shaft's ladder, mentally thanking Zuri for the thousands of reps he had forced her through. Looking down, she could see the Radioactive Man's telltale glow coming down the hallway.

"Little girl, I will kill you fast if you are nice," the Radioactive Man teased. He peered up the shaft and grabbed the ladder. "They showed me your last appearance on TMZ. That backless dress with the feathers was horrendous. You should thank me for ending your public pain."

Shuri smirked as she stared down into the darkness at the glowing man, who had scaled halfway up to her location. "I'll give my designers your critique," she called as she shoved the rock over the edge.

The boulder careened down toward the Radioactive Man, who realized the danger a second too late. By the time he raised a hand to blast the rock, it had smashed him directly in the nose with an awful crunch and an explosion of green blood. Shuri watched with a smirk as he toppled backwards toward the bottom of the shaft, arms flailing as he fell.

The base of the shaft was only a few floors below. She peered down to see what she hoped would be a broken villain at the bottom. While it was hard to see through the cloud of dust kicked up by the Radioactive Man's impact, the drop should have been long enough to incapacitate him. Cocking her ear toward the bottom, she heard nothing except the clattering of rocks. Hope rising, she wiped the sweat from her brow and sighed—then heard, faintly, the Radioactive Man cursing in pain in the shaft's rubble.

"Damn," she muttered. "Still alive down there, huh?"

She looked down at Stancheck, who was testing to see whether everything still worked. Shuri ducked her head back as he spit blood from his mouth and nose. He pressed down on his chest and groaned, as if a couple of his ribs were cracked or broken.

"*Kakogo chyorta*," he groaned as he staggered to his feet and looked hatefully up the shaft at Shuri, who dodged backwards as he sent a sizzling blast up at her.

"That's it," he promised her. "You will not see the sun again, Princess. You try to kill me, I kill you."

"Only if you can catch me, Igor," Shuri yelled back down the shaft. Then she broke into a run. In front of her, a red "Exit" sign flickered and sparked on the wall. She darted down that hallway, hoping it would lead back into the main cavern with the rocket. With the Radioactive Man now several floors behind her, she should be able to make good progress out of the mine before he caught up to her again.

If nothing else goes wrong. T'Challa, you better be saving the world, since you're not here saving me!

WHAT do you mean you haven't rescued my daughter?" Ramonda seethed as she swung her legs out of her bed, into slippers, and yanked a nearby robe around her nightgown.

"Never fear, Ramonda, there is an operation underway to recover the princess." S'Yan stared at her impassively from across her bedchambers. "The king radioed me personally and told me to keep my eyes on you until the *Dora Milaje* are mobilized for your protection. You may not know what occurred during your sleep last night, Ramonda, but the kingdom is under attack. Men and women are dying out there to keep our borders inviolate. And instead of being out there fighting with the troops I've commanded for the last decade as regent, I'm here babysitting you.

"I don't want to be here any more than you want me here, Ramonda. But my king, your son, ordered me to ensure your safety by keeping my eyes on you. And I don't plan to be derelict in my duties to my liege this time, no matter what you say." There was fury in S'Yan's eyes. "I owe the memory of my dead brother that much."

Ramonda stared at S'Yan for a minute. Then her expression softened. "Forgive the emotions of a mother worried about her children, S'Yan," she said quietly. "What is being done to keep my son safe?"

"The job of the king of Wakanda is not to be safe, Ramonda, but to be smart," S'Yan said calmly. "T'Challa said he had a plan that would keep as many of his people alive as possible, as long as we trusted him and followed it. And that's what we're doing."

"And what part of his plan involved saving his sister?" Ramonda asked. "I've lost one member of my family. I don't plan on losing anyone else."

S'Yan walked over to the doors and picked up a spear leaning against the wall where he'd left it.

He twirled it expertly, thrusting and jabbing it at imaginary opponents.

"Neither does the king. He delegated the rescue of his sister to his most trusted *Dora Milaje*, just as he assigned them to you," he said. "There are a couple of them outside your suite right now, standing guard, while Amare and Okoye prepare an overall defense plan for the compound. Funny how all of our plans revolved around the king being inside the palace, not out stalking the person causing our troubles."

She stomped over to her door, only to find it stubbornly refused to open. She pulled harder, but to no avail. Ramonda turned back to S'Yan, put her hands on her hips, and glared at him.

"Let me out of here, S'Yan," she hissed. "Our people—and my children—are in trouble, and you expect me to sit in my bedroom and wait to hear what is going on? I can fight as well as the next person."

"No, your majesty," he replied calmly. "T'Challa suggested you might try something like this and ordered a lockdown on your quarters. No one in or out."

Ramonda straightened her back and walked over to stare up into S'Yan's eyes. "I am still the mother of the king, S'Yan," she said coldly. "You don't outrank me anymore, and I'm giving you a direct order. I WANT OUT."

A small smile crept over S'Yan's face as he stared her down. "You know, I've been waiting years for this moment," he said. "You've always resented the fact the country turned to me as regent instead of letting you rule as queen, as you thought was your right.

"But you don't know what I gave up to take control of the country, the lonely nights when I had to leave my dying wife to make sure national business got done—while you sat in your suite grieving. My nonexistent relationship with my son, who fled all the way to New York City and the Wakandan ambassadorship to the United Nations to get away from me, because I wouldn't push him publicly as the next ruler of Wakanda instead of T'Challa or Shuri."

S'Yan pointed his finger in Ramonda's face. "And all the while knowing that the Panther God had not chosen me to be anything beyond a caretaker. You don't know how it feels to be ignored by your god, Ramonda. No matter how hard you work to prove yourself worthy…"

S'Yan caught his breath and stepped back from Ramonda. "Your king, OUR king—the anointed of the Panther God—has ordered that you stay in your quarters, Ramonda," he said quietly. "Like it or not, here you stay."

S'Yan smiled, showing all his teeth and clutching his spear. "Unless you think you can make me move."

Ramonda stared at him for a second, her face impassive but anger showing in her eyes. "Your sacrifice," she ground out, "was appreciated, S'Yan. I understand how hard it must have been controlling one of the greatest civilizations on this planet while I mourned my husband's cruel death.

"And I can't speak for the Panther God, but I think you would have made a fine king. However, that was not your fate. It fell to my son, who is out there right now fighting for his people, while your son is safe in New York City. We are survivors, S'Yan, you and I—we go on despite never hearing from our god. But that doesn't make our efforts meaningless. We can fight for what we believe in just as well as anyone else, but we can't do it from in here. I'm going to protect my son, my daughter, and our people, and you'll have to knock me out to stop me."

Ramonda stalked over to a monitor screen on the wall. She pushed a button, and the face of a Wakandan communications officer appeared. He paled when he saw Ramonda's face, then quickly covered his expression with a blank look.

"Your majesty," he saluted.

"Let me out of here, officer," said Ramonda, glaring over at S'Yan.

"Ummm," the officer said, looking profoundly uncomfortable under Ramonda's steel gaze. "Sorry, your highness, keeping you secure in a crisis situation is rule number one. You cannot leave the safe room without express orders from…"

"The Black Panther," Ramonda sighed. "Well, get him on the phone, then. I want out of here."

"Yes, ma'am." The guard turned to pick up a phone, but before Ramonda's shocked eyes, a thin, shiny rope dropped over his head and pulled backwards. The man's hands flew to his neck; he croaked and struggled, flailing about in his chair and gagging. After a few seconds, his eyes rolled up, and his head dropped to the side.

Ramonda watched in horror as the officer was unceremoniously shoved out of his seat and out of the picture. A Frenchman with a pencil-thin mustache and sunglasses plopped down in the chair and grinned through the screen at her.

"Don't worry, madame, we will open the door for you in the time-honored way," Batroc laughed. He tossed a grenade up and down in one hand.

"S'Yan!" Ramonda screamed, almost falling as she backed away from the screen. S'Yan rushed over, caught Ramonda as she tumbled backwards, and threw her away from the monitor toward her bed. He leaped on top of her, covering her body with his own.

The explosion tore through the doorway, overpowering the death cries of the bodyguards outside. Smoke and blood poured into the Ramonda's suite, and bits of wood and concrete covered the floor and the bed. Ramonda looked down to see a dazed S'Yan trying to collect his wits on the floor.

He grabbed onto her arm to hold her out of sight. But Ramonda had to know, so she peeked over the mattress with dread creeping in her heart.

Through the haze, stepping carefully through the debris, was a face Ramonda had not seen in decades—though it had haunted her dreams and froze her heart.

Klaw surveyed the landscape majestically as he strolled into Ramonda's room. Spotting the queen behind the bed, he lifted his right arm and flexed his fingers, electricity arcing menacingly between the bionic digits. Batroc ran in behind him, a smirk plastered on his face.

"Your highness," Klaw bowed mockingly in Ramonda's direction. "Long time, no see. We have unfinished business, you and me."

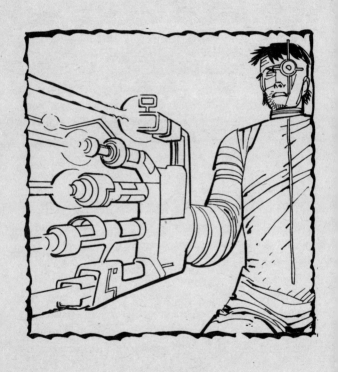

CHAPTER FIFTEEN

THE BLACK PANTHER dragged M'Butu to the middle of his office floor, rolled him over on his back, and turned his head to the side so the blood wouldn't pool in his mouth and accidentally cause him to drown. M'Butu had spilled every secret he could think of when his mortality was on the line, so T'Challa had no real reason to kill him other than personal pleasure.

He had actually been looking forward to that, T'Challa realized.

There was no time for personal concerns, however. He activated his communicator for an urgent message back to his commanders.

"W'Kabi, we have invaders in the palace," T'Challa warned as his war chief's face appeared on his screen.

"In the palace? Impossible!" W'Kabi insisted. He was still in the command center, directing the Wakandan troops in their clash with the invading Nigandans.

"It is true." T'Challa slid open his helmet so W'Kabi could see the seriousness in his eyes. He nodded toward the sobbing, bleeding mass on the carpet. "M'Butu told me everything, from the invasion to the Rhino to the location of Klaw. Get everyone you can to the queen's bedroom. That's where they're going to strike next."

T'Challa heard W'Kabi shout orders around the control room, and the mad scramble to follow them. "Nyah, hand control over to your replacement and get all available troops to the royal wing of the palace." The old man's voice was much softer and more secretive as he turned back to T'Challa. "How did they get into the palace?"

"Our worry now is not how they got in, but what their plan is now they're inside," T'Challa said. "And unfortunately, even with all of that, we have larger problems to deal with at the moment. W'Kabi…"

"Yes, my king?"

"Prepare one of our pinpoint thermonuclear missiles. One of the lowest-yield ones will do. Target…" T'Challa said sadly, "…the Great Mound."

W'Kabi almost dropped his communicator at T'Challa's words. "Sire, inside Wakanda?"

T'Challa nodded. "Yes, inside the Great Mound itself. They have figured out a way to use radiation to trigger earthquakes in the Vibranium deposit; explosions, if they use a high enough dose. That's why M'Butu and Klaw sent the Radioactive Man into the Great Mound, to hold it hostage or to destroy the country. We can't let that happen, W'Kabi."

The older man just shook his head and walked into a corner where no one could hear his whispered pleas. "Your majesty, there must be another way. Your sister—"

"Is still in the Great Mound, I know," T'Challa finished for him. "But Shuri would be the first one to tell you, if a choice came down to her death or the rest of the country, it should be her.

"Old friend, can I trust you to do this?" T'Challa asked grimly. "The king has launch authority, but I need one countersign. And I tell you, this may be the only way to save our country now, and in the future. Will you trust me?"

W'Kabi turned and leaned his head against the wall, so his staff would not see the tears welling up in his eyes. "Yes, your majesty," he whispered. "Now and forever. Give the order and I shall obey."

"Good," T'Challa said, walking back toward the broken window and the cable that led up to his hovering skybike. "We will discuss the particulars when I arrive back at the palace, and—" He stopped as a cold voice interrupted his train of thought.

"Leaving so soon, T'Challa?" Klaw teased from a computer screen on M'Butu's desk, having hacked through the Wakandans' security blockade. "Why, it looks like we must have passed each other on the way. There you are in Niganda's presidential palace, and here I am in your mother's bathroom. Imagine that?"

"Klaw." T'Challa snapped down his faceplate as he looked into the monitor. Klaw had his mother by the throat with one hand and was threatening her with the other, which hissed and vibrated only inches from Ramonda's jawline. His mother was trying to look strong in the face of her attackers, but T'Challa could see the fear in her eyes.

"W'Kabi," he whispered, "Are you aware of the security breach in my mother's chambers? Where are S'Yan and the *Dora Milaje*?"

Klaw pulled Ramonda closer to the screen and laughed. "I can hear you, you know. And if you're worried about that old man that was in here before us, well…"

Klaw panned the camera around the room to show Batroc holding a severed leg, the top sliced through smoothly and still smoking from a laser-hot cutting tool. Klaw wiggled his pinky finger, which was still cooling down and emitting small wisps of smoke.

"I'm afraid he doesn't have a leg to stand on anymore." Klaw smirked at T'Challa. Batroc chuckled as he dropped the limb next to a broken spear. S'Yan moaned and writhed on the floor, clutching his bloody stump.

"Now," Klaw ordered smugly, "Let me speak to M'Butu."

The Panther swung the camera around and pointed toward the floor, focusing in on the sobbing, bleeding black man cowering there. T'Challa stalked over and dragged the man to his feet, displaying his ruined face and chest dripping with his life's blood.

Klaw whistled. "Is that M'Butu? I can hardly recognize him."

The Black Panther dropped the Nigandan king

back down on the floor with a thud. M'Butu let out a strained moan of pain. "He is still very much alive, which is better than the fate in store for you, assassin.

Klaw shook Ramonda, causing her to whimper in pain. "You have no leverage here, T'Challa. I have your mother, and I have your kingdom. No more tough talk, or you'll lose another parent."

Despite her pain, Ramonda gathered up her courage and stared grimly into the screen. "I've lived plenty, son," she called out through gritted teeth. "I'll die fighting. Just do what you need to do to save Wakanda."

Klaw *tsked,* pulling her face close to his. "Such a brave woman. That's what I remember about you from Bilderberg, your majesty. Your courage in the line of fire. I've always been impressed." Klaw placed a small kiss on Ramonda's head before she could jerk away.

"But for you, O king of Wakanda, it's not that simple. I've got more than your mother hostage." With an evil smile, he put on a headset and pressed a button. "Let me show you."

IGOR STANCHECK had crawled several floors up the elevator shaft, grumbling to himself, when his communicator buzzed. Wiping green blood from his hands, he scrambled up a couple more rungs to an empty floor and flopped down before pushing the answer button on his earpiece.

"Igor, this is Klaw." The headset crackled and spit, but the Radioactive Man ignored the interruptions. With his powers, he was lucky to get coverage at all. Stancheck spit a huge glob of blood to the side before he spoke, and tested his sore ribs, bending over as a sharp pain shot through his midsection.

"Of course this is you," he answered crankily through the throbbing. "Who else would be calling?"

Klaw hesitated, hearing the pain in Stancheck's voice. "Is everything okay down there? Still on schedule?"

"*Da, da,*" Stancheck muttered. He stretched his back, unable to muffle a little groan of pain. "The princess here in the mountain, Klaw. She dropped a rock on my head, unt I plan to kill her for it. Any problems with that?"

"Did you hear that, T'Challa?" Klaw said, more quietly now. "I have your mother, my associate has your sister, and now you have this to deal with." Then, louder: "Shake things up a bit, Igor. Just a bit…to send a message."

"*Da, da,* just a moment." Stancheck stood, moaning a little bit as his body protested.

The Radioactive Man closed his eyes and stretched out his hands, concentrating on the particular switch in the back of his mind that felt like Vibranium. His eyes rolled back in his head, and he ground his teeth as he found the frequency. Taking a deep breath, he pulled back mentally with a sharp jerk.

As he opened his eyes, he could feel the vibrations

begin beneath his feet. The mountain started to sway and rumble. Hopefully, Stancheck thought, the mine would drop a rock on that damnable Shuri's head before she made it too far.

SHURI ran as fast as she could through the tunnels, trying to take advantage of her hard-won head start. The terrain was beginning to look familiar to her, and she could feel fresh air cascading down into the tunnels.

So close. So close.

Shuri turned a corner and saw daylight. She put on an extra burst of speed. Rocks clattered under her feet as she slid into the main chamber, greeted by the morning sun peeking through the massive hole in the Great Mound. Everything was exactly as she'd left it when she began her long dash away from the Radioactive Man.

Shuri dropped down to her knees in exhaustion, trying to control her breathing. Sweat poured from her head. Huffing, she looked around the massive chamber to the point where the Radioactive Man had first appeared near the missile. Sadly she ran her eyes over K'Darte's dead body.

Rage began to build as her exhaustion faded. He deserved better, Shuri thought. He, his wife, and baby child, whom he now would never see, deserved to be avenged. And the Radioactive Man deserved to die.

But, her rational mind warned—speaking in T'Challa's voice, as always—first she had to get out of here and find a weapon that would kill Igor Stancheck. *So why are you still standing here?*

Shuri had taken a couple of steps toward the ragged cavern wall when a jet-powered roar echoed from above, and a jagged wind pushed dust and debris down on her head. Covering her eyes, Shuri looked up. For the first time since the quakes began, smiled.

Dropping down through the ragged crater at the top of the Great Mound was a Quinjet, expertly piloted by an intense-looking woman. She weaved the jet back and forth, barely clearing the rocky sides. The jet's wing-mounted, horizontal fans slowed down and sped up as she tilted the plane's nose at the appropriate moments to maneuver down the huge shaft.

As the Quinjet dropped, its massive floodlights illuminated the cavern, searching for signs of life. Shuri began jumping up and down. She ran out over fallen rocks to the middle of the cavern floor, cheering and waving.

The Quinjet's loudspeaker clicked on. Shuri looked up in amazement at the voice that came out.

"*Princess Shuri?* Oh, thank the Panther God you're alive," the excited voice said. "It's me, Nakia! Belove…the king sent me and Captain Sharifa to get you out of here posthaste."

Shuri peered up through the lights. She could

see Nakia sitting behind the pilot, grinning broadly down at her.

"Give us a minute or two to get the jet down. Sharifa says it's going to be a tight fit, but we'll be able to make it. Back away from the landing grid—we don't want to come down on top of your head." Nakia laughed. "Oh, and don't let me forget: T'Challa sent me to pick up something for you to use if we need it. We'll chat about it in the plane."

Shuri took a couple of steps back and sagged down to her knees as she watched the plane descend slowly. It was almost over, she thought, closing her eyes. Once they were out of the Great Mound, T'Challa would send in a squad of shielded soldiers—or maybe some of those new automated Panther robots the Science Council had been talking about—to flush out the Radioactive Man and make him pay for what he'd done.

Shuri felt it first, a small tremor vibrating through her hands and legs.

She opened her eyes and saw small pebbles and rocks begin to clatter on their own, moving faster and faster as the ground began to sway and rock. Subsonic waves shook her bones as she scrambled to her feet, watching in horror as boulders began to detach from the cavern roof and cascade down around the descending Quinjet.

"Nooo!" Shuri shrieked. She ran toward the Quinjet, gesturing frantically at Sharifa, trying to wave her off before the falling rocks trapped the three of them in the mines together with an angry Radioactive Man.

"Oh my god—Sharifa, look out!" Nakia screamed through the loudspeaker. The pilot jerked back the throttle, swerving the jet just enough to avoid a bus-sized boulder dropping from the roof. Other rocks ricocheted off the hull, clanging and grinding as they tumbled off the sides.

SHARIFA winced as a rock fell into the starboard stabilizer fan and shot out at enormous speed, smashing itself to bits against the cavern wall in a cloud of debris. The pilot looked back at Nakia and shook her head. The plane's engines revved and pushed down a cloud of dust and fuel-tainted smoke.

"Hold on down there, Princess," Nakia said as the jet began to climb back up toward the cavern opening. "Sharifa says we can't land during an earthquake, so we're going to pull out and hover until the tremors subside. We'll be right outside, and we'll come back to get you as soon as things are quiet again. I promise."

Shuri huddled on the floor, trying to protect her head from the falling rocks. The ground rocked back and forth, sending debris and small boulders cascading down around her. She peered up, catching sight of the Quinjet just as it pulled out into a beam of sunlight.

Nakia's voice echoed down into the cavern. "We won't leave you, Princess. Oh, and speaking of forgetting—Sharifa, pop the hatch once we're clear."

Shuri looked up questioningly. The *Dora Milaje* wasn't about to try to parachute down, was she? She'd break both her legs if she did. Shuri stood up to yell and try to stop her.

Instead of a woman, a shiny black object plunged through the air and embedded itself into the rock with a thunk. Shuri walked over and looked at the object. It vibrated along with the cavern, having easily cleaved the rock and sunk halfway into the ground. All she could see of it was a bright-yellow hilt and grip.

Shuri reached down, and easily pulled the Ebony Blade free. She held it in the air.

"T'Challa said you might find that useful." Nakia's voice was fainter now.

Shuri swung the Ebony Blade back and forth as the earthquake subsided. Looking behind her, she could see the telltale green glow pulsating from one of the tunnels.

The Radioactive Man had found her again. But this time, she had a weapon of her own.

YOUR majesty, we're detecting a major earthquake in the capital," W'Kabi shouted into the communicator, his voice shaking with the underground command chamber. "A 5-pointer so far, but it's still building. The epicenter… This can't be right! The Great Mound?"

LOOK!" Sharifa nodded forward as the Quinjet hovered above the Great Mound, swirling through circular dust clouds. Nakia ran up to the cockpit and peered out.

The two women watched, openmouthed, as the ground heaved up and away from the Great Mound like ripples in a pond, knocking down trees and opening up rifts. As they stared, a monitor in the Quinjet showed the ripples hitting the capital's towers and spires, making the entire city sway.

"By the Panther God," Sharifa swore. "If it looks like that from up *here*, what does it feel like on the ground?"

KLAW stared directly into the camera at T'Challa as the palace rocked, his hand still clamped on Ramonda's neck. Paintings fell from the walls of Ramonda's room; glass shattered, and vases broke.

Throughout the chaos, Klaw never moved, staring right at the screen. Batroc, however, looked nervously at the cracks in the ceiling, then braced himself against the wall until the tremors subsided.

"See, T'Challa?" Klaw said once the room stopped moving. "I am the new ruler of Wakanda. If you don't agree, I'll collapse the entire country into a big pothole. Makes no difference to me.

"You have no moves left, my young king." Klaw shook Ramonda, making her teeth rattle. "I have your mother. Igor has your sister. Your regent is bleeding out on the floor. Your country won't survive another second without my permission. But they'll all survive if you do one thing for me, T'Challa.

"Go find a knife. I know M'Butu has several in his office. Find a nice sharp one—or a dull one if you want, I don't care—and kill yourself." Klaw smiled, hatred glowing in his eyes. "Now."

CHAPTER SIXTEEN

KLAW stared at the Black Panther through the monitor, his mechanical hand crackling next to Ramonda's head. A smell of ionized energy and sweat blended with the sweet scent of the roses tossed from broken vases on the floor.

Behind Klaw, Batroc noticed a white rose lying in the debris. He picked it up and sniffed it; with a quick movement, he snapped the stem and jauntily tucked the flower into his khaki shirt. He stroked his mustache and preened as he watched Klaw deliver his ultimatum to the Black Panther, who was stuck in Niganda while his enemies had overtaken his home.

"What are you waiting for, T'Challa?" Klaw demanded, shaking Ramonda. She sagged, offering no resistance to the assassin.

"I told you to find a knife and kill yourself. If you don't, I'll kill everyone you care about, starting with mommy dearest here. Then I'll kill your uncle and order the Radioactive Man to torture your sister in the most painful way he can think of before he triggers an earthquake that will trap her underground and destroy your anthill of a country. If you do what I say, you'll at least die with the hope that I'll spare some of your family and the people of Wakanda.

"Resist, and you'll watch your mother die

right now. And before you return, I'll have the microwaved corpse of your sister hanging from the front of the Vibranium mines. Then you'll watch as all of Wakanda collapses into the ground, its people screaming and cursing the name of their selfish king, who put his life ahead of theirs.

"So what are you waiting for, T'Challa?" Klaw sneered. "Do it!"

The Black Panther looked at his mother's stoic face, bravely trying to hold the fear inside as she dangled from Klaw's hand. He stared into the maniacal eyes of Klaw, whose craggy and scarred face had been etched into his dreams ever since the Belgian assassin had killed his father so many years ago.

He and his mother had lost so much at this man's hands. The child T'Challa was, the man he would have been. Klaw had taken it all away when the bullets tore through his father's midsection and took his life.

T'Challa could see it so clearly: the Wakandan throne room where he stood proudly at T'Chaka's right hand, back straight as his father ruled the kingdom wisely and justly. Ramonda and Shuri smiled from their thrones and offered sage comments that endeared them to Wakanda. Behind T'Chaka, Amare—whole and gorgeous—stalked back and forth, warily looking out for any danger, her trainees Okoye and Nakia watching her every move.

Above them all, a huge gray-eyed panther

lounged in one of the windows, its tail swinging back and forth. The large cat seemed to smile down at them as she faded into the night.

T'Challa shook his head, pushing away the vision and returning to the present. Klaw was threatening what family T'Challa had left, but he put his hate aside as he looked into his mother's eyes. He knew what he had to say.

"Or what?" the Black Panther said.

Klaw cocked his head and looked into the camera with a puzzled expression. A slow smile crept over Ramonda's face. T'Challa could see her pride shining through the screen.

"What do you mean, 'Or what?'" Klaw demanded. "I told you—"

The Black Panther laughed, the cold sound echoing through the speakers. "That you would kill my mother? You will do that anyway. That you will destroy my kingdom? You will do that as well."

T'Challa brought his mask close to the camera, his white eyes almost filling the screen. "It really doesn't matter what you do, Klaw," the Black Panther said softly. "I'm still going to kill you. So what's your leverage?"

Klaw's mouth dropped open as he stared into the screen. Batroc shifted uncomfortably in the background, looking down at S'Yan on the floor. The older man was still in pain from his severed leg, but a smirk was developing on his face as he listened to the exchange.

Ramonda snorted. "That's my boy!"

Klaw's confusion quickly turned to anger. He shook Ramonda again, pressing his cybernetic hand against her forehead. She yelped as he sent a small surge through her head.

But Ramonda no longer cowered from him. She laughed at him again as her son stared at them through the satellite feed.

"I don't see why you're so happy," Klaw growled. "Your son just sentenced you to death."

"No," Ramonda retorted, "My son just sentenced you to death, Klaw. And no matter whether I live to see it, I'll die knowing that the Black Panther— T'Challa, son of T'Chaka—killed you slowly and painfully."

T'Challa backed away from the camera and crossed his arms, claws flashing in the light. "By the way, Klaw, a common criminal like you has no right to use my proper name. You can refer to me by my title: the Black Panther."

T'Challa's wrist communicator beeped, and he looked down at it for a second before turning back to the camera. "And your presence is not welcome in my lands, Klaw," the Black Panther said. "But if you and your compatriot surrender now, I may show you the same mercy that M'Butu received."

At the sound of his name, the Niganda king gurgled on the floor.

"If you do not surrender, I will not be responsible for your fate," T'Challa continued. "Throw yourself on my mercy, assassin. And do it quickly. Time is running out."

Klaw sent another surge through Ramonda's head, making her quiver and tremble. A small cry of pain escaped her mouth.

"Klaw," Batroc warned.

Klaw stared into the screen. "I have all the cards, T'Challa," he sneered. "What do you have?"

T'Challa's mask shined in the light of the screen. "Someone who has been waiting years to see you again, Klaw."

AS T'CHALLA spoke, a compact cylinder soared into the room and clattered across the floor, rolling in a small circle. "Grenade!" Batroc shouted, diving behind the bed.

The grenade exploded with a deafening bang, sending clouds of noxious gas billowing into the room. Klaw stumbled back, using Ramonda as a shield. He pushed her to the ground and looked around, seeing no new damage. Batroc kept his head low, just in case.

"It's just a smoke grenade, Batroc," Klaw coughed, shielding his mouth with his free hand. "Get back over here before someone takes advant—"

There was a wild scream as Amare flew out of the smoke. The *Dora Milaje* general, who had been waiting for her chance in the hallway, threw herself at the Belgian assassin, slamming him and Ramonda to the ground. Closing in behind her was Okoye, wielding her short sword and a heavy gun strapped to her back. She stepped over the bodies of her fallen sisters, sparing them only the slightest mournful glance, then looked around to assess the situation.

Ramonda, gathering her wits, rolled out of the way as Amare kneed Klaw in the groin. Amare scrambled to pin his arm to the ground, preventing Klaw from pointing his deadly hand in her or Ramonda's direction. A feral snarl rumbled in Amare's throat as she pounded Klaw's head on the ground again and again, taking out years of frustration on the man.

"Handle the fool with the mustache," Amare shouted, a wild gleam shining in her eyes as she punched the dazed Klaw repeatedly in the face. *"I'll take Klaw."*

"Agreed," snarled Okoye. She stalked across the room toward Batroc, who scrambled to his feet.

"Klaw? Now the ladies are beating you up?" Batroc mocked. He looked the young woman up and down as they started circling each other. He danced back and forth, clearly hoping to throw her off-balance—but Okoye just stared and waited for him to commit himself.

"I don't see you doing so well," Klaw shot back. He blocked Amare's throat punch and dazed her with a left-handed backhand.

"But this one is young and ripe, unlike yours," Batroc laughed. He snapped a quick kick at Okoye, striking her hand and sending her sword clattering across the room. "This one, she is made for loving, not fighting."

Peering over his sunglasses, Batroc licked his lips, looking appreciatively at Okoye's battle armor. "Beautiful women should be kissed, not kicked." He blew a mocking kiss at Okoye. "I do appreciate your... form, young lady. However, in thees circumstance, I think we have to make an exception, right?"

Batroc snapped a second kick at Okoye. But this time, the *Dora Milaje* blocked with her arm and drove her foot into the side of his knee with a snap kick. The Frenchman screamed in pain and stumbled back.

"You talk too much," Okoye growled. She leaped at Batroc.

Klaw pushed Amare off his body and scrambled to his feet, trying to reset his jaw from her pounding. Noticing Ramonda creeping away, Klaw lunged over and grabbed her by her hair, pushing her between himself and Amare—who was trying to get a good shot at Klaw with her gun.

Klaw spit out a glob of blood and pulled at Ramonda's hair. She cried out in pain, caught between him and the *Dora Milaje*. Almost as an afterthought, he sent a searing blast across the room. Okoye rolled to one side, avoiding the laser, and continued to grapple with Batroc.

"Do I know you?" Klaw stared at Amare, trying to place her face. "Why do I get the feeling that... Oh, I remember you now. And I can see you've had some improvements done as well. Nice leg, lady. If you make it out of here, you can advise the regent there on the latest models."

Klaw shot a laser blast in Amare's direction. She dodged, using the smoke as cover. "What a reunion we're having here tonight, Ramonda! Almost everyone who witnessed your husband's death is in your room. One has to appreciate the symmetry of that, my queen."

"The only symmetry I'm concerned with is a life for a life," Amare snarled. "Your life for all the friends you've cost me, assassin."

"If you think you can claim my life, make your move, woman," Klaw smiled, pressing his metal fingers into Ramonda's head so hard she had to muffle a cry of pain. "Of course, you'll cause the death of your queen. So if I were you, I'd back off."

"Never." Amare pulled out a Vibranium knife and wove it between her hands expertly. "There's blood between us, assassin. If I have anything to say about it, you won't live to see the sun set.

"Look out the window," Amare continued, breathing hard but calmly. "Even if you make it out of this room, there is a legion of *Dora Milaje* stationed around the palace. You shamed us by allowing me to live while you killed King T'Chaka. That won't happen this time. We all swore a blood oath that you would die if we ever encountered you again, and not a single one of us will stop until we separate your head from your body and watch your blood soak into the soil of our homeland."

Klaw concentrated. Energy built up in his right hand, charring Ramonda's skin as he dragged her between himself and the furious Amare, wrapping his left hand around Ramonda's neck.

"Your life isn't worth a damn to anyone in this palace, old woman," Klaw said wildly, pressing his hand to Ramonda's temple. "Let's see how they feel when I blow your head—"

Amare grinned as Ramonda dropped her feigned helplessness, slammed her fist into Klaw's crotch, and squeezed. Klaw screamed. His face turned red, illuminating the white claw marks on his cheek as he doubled over. Ramonda punched him in the groin a second time, sending Klaw to the ground in a ball rocking back and forth, moaning to himself.

"Come on!" Amare screamed. She grabbed Ramonda by the hand and bolted for the door.

Seeing their flight, Okoye tried to disengage from Batroc, swinging wildly at his head. Batroc dodged, and booted Okoye in the stomach, doubling her over. "Bad training," he huffed, closing in to finish her off. "Rule No. 1: Always keep your eyes on the opponent."

Okoye waited for Batroc to get in range, and then used the last of her strength to strike him with a powerful uppercut that rattled the Frenchman's teeth and sent him toppling into the bed. Okoye stood slowly, her hand cradling her stomach. She slapped plastic cuffs on Batroc to immobilize him.

"Rule No. 2: Keep your mouth shut," she muttered. She walked over to the prone S'Yan, who was still lying on the suite floor, his severed leg next to him.

"S'Yan, you must stand." Okoye reached down to rouse the wounded man and drape him across her shoulder. She jerked a sheet out from under Batroc and covered the man's severed leg, then tucked it under her arm. "We have to get you and the Queen Mother to safety."

Okoye and S'Yan stumbled for the door, carefully stepping around the moaning Klaw, still rocking back and forth on the floor.

"Shoot him in the head," S'Yan muttered as they passed the assassin. "Shoot him in the head now for what he did to my brother."

Okoye frowned as they passed through the doorway and over the dead bodies of her warrior sisters. "That would be too kind," she said, casting one last look at the assassin as they picked up speed down the hallway. "The king has plans for that one, and a quick death isn't one of them."

SHURI slowly climbed up the wall of the destroyed cavern, her newly acquired Ebony Blade strapped to her back.

When she'd seen the Radioactive Man's green glow heading toward the main cavern, her first instinct had been to test the sword her brother had sent her.

She'd pictured herself crouching above the mouth of the tunnel and slicing down through Stancheck's head as he stepped into the cavern, green blood and brains spilling out across the floor. She would send him screaming to meet his ancestors for the death he'd caused in the Great Mound.

But then her rational mind had taken over—once again speaking in T'Challa's voice, to her annoyance—and told her to put as much space between her and the Radioactive Man as possible while she waited for Nakia and Sharifa to return to her rescue. So that's what she did. She began climbing up the honeycombed walls as high as she could, as fast as she could.

The Radioactive Man stomped toward the cavern wall, intending to crawl up behind Shuri. He was confident that he would get close enough to kill her before she got away. But as he closed in on the wall, his communicator buzzed. He sighed and placed the earbud in his ear.

"Igor!" Klaw wheezed, as if he was speaking through pain himself. "Igor, can you hear me? Bring the whole thing down! Do it now, before they can escape. Bring it down!"

"Escape? She is escaping right now, Klaw." Stancheck stared venomously at Shuri, who was still free climbing the rock face. "I will kill her and then her country. You just be ready to dig me out of this dung heap once I bring it down on her charred corpse."

"Igor?! Igor? Stop and focus on the job at hand! You can kill her along with everyone else—"

"Leave me alone until I'm done." Stancheck pulled his earbud out and fried it with his radiation. He walked across the cavern floor, kicking boulders out of the way, until he could look directly up at Shuri. She was several hundred feet above him.

"You climb fast, little girl, like a monkey!" His voice echoed around the chamber.

"Like a panther, actually," Shuri called back down, pressing herself against a ledge to provide less of a target for his deadly blasts. "And you—Igor, is it?—I heard you say that you're going to kill my country? Tell me, nightlight, how are you going to do that when you can't even kill little old me?"

"Do not make fun of me, little girl," Stancheck warned, sending a sizzling blast past her ledge. "You are just making your inevitable death that much more painful."

Shuri dodged, then stuck her tongue out at the super villain. The picture of nonchalance, she leaned back against the ledge and began to examine her nails.

T'Challa always said she had a special skill at getting on people's last nerve. Finally it was coming in handy. An angry opponent is a sloppy opponent, Zuri had often said. In that lay her advantage.

"It seems to me we have a standoff." Shuri looked down contemptuously at the angry Stancheck. "All I have to do is wait—someone will be coming for me. You? They're just going to kill you."

"I can bring thees whole cavern down on your head," the Radioactive Man snarled.

"And the second you try, I'll drop one of these boulders on your head...again," Shuri retorted, with a grin and a small shake of her rear end.

With a roar, he sent another blast at her. It sailed harmlessly into the ceiling. "I will kill you!" he shouted again as he reached for handholds in the wall to make his way up.

"Come and get me, big boy." Shuri blew a kiss at him and backed up against the far wall. Now that she had him mad, all she needed was a little help from her rescuers. Shuri was confident in her skills, but a monster like the Radioactive Man was out of her league in a fight, even with a magic sword on her side. She could hear him cursing to himself as he scrabbled for handholds on the rock face. She took a chance and peered over the side. His green, glowing form was slowly making its way up toward her, grumbling and muttering the whole time.

Don't let me down, girls, Shuri thought. She backed away from the ledge and looked hopefully toward the sky. With the Quinjet as a distraction, she would be able to take him out, but her chances alone were much more limited. Either way, she wasn't going to just surrender. She unstrapped the Ebony Blade from her back and tested its heft in her hands.

I could get used to this weapon, she thought—and then the scratching of fingers on rock interrupted her. The Radioactive Man had arrived.

His hands searched for purchase on her ledge. Shuri thought for a second about rushing him with the sword, possibly chopping off those hands and watching him fall. But before she could take more than a step, Stancheck's hands flared with energy. Getting close to them would be deadly for Shuri. He pulled himself up to the ledge and stood before her.

"No, Princess, there won't be any more sneak attacks." His face turned up in a malevolent smile. "I will look into your eyes as you die cursing your parents for bringing you into this world, and your brother for not being able to save you."

The mention of her parents infuriated Shuri. She pointed the tip of the Ebony Blade at Stancheck's neck. "Bring it," she spat at him.

The Radioactive Man shot a blast of energy at her with one hand, but Shuri dodged to one side and swung her sword to keep him back. He pointed again, and a second blast sailed past her on her opposite side. It dawned on her what was happening.

"You're toying with me, aren't you?"

"Maybe," he shrugged. "There nothing you can do about it, is there? That toy sword you're holding can't hurt me—and you can't escape, can you?"

He shot a couple smaller blasts at her, seemingly as an afterthought. She dodged easily, but his radiation was beginning to make her sweat.

"Turn your back and climb, and I'll fry you. Run, and I'll fry you. Fight me with that sword, and the same thing will happen. You're alone down here, Princess." The Radioactive Man cracked his knuckles and prepared to send a massive two-handed blast at

Shuri, one that would probably end her life. "The last thing you'll see is my hands around your neck; the last thing you'll smell is your own roasting flesh as you sing with the righteous pain I'll be causing you. That's what you have to look forward to, Princess. No one is coming to save you."

Shuri closed her eyes briefly. She raised the Ebony Blade, sending up a quick prayer to the Panther God that the sword's strange properties would defend her against the coming blast. As she opened her eyes and looked up, she heard a familiar roar. Hope flared in her eyes.

"I'm not as alone as you might think!" she shouted. She pointed at the top of the cavern, where a Quinjet was weaving down toward them. In a few seconds, the plane was hovering within firing range. The Quinjet's cannons rotated down as Captain Sharifa took careful aim at the Radioactive Man. Rocks bounced up around Stancheck's feet as she peppered him with shells to get his attention.

"Surrender, foreigner," Nakia's voice boomed out of the Quinjet's public address system, "and you may survive this day."

"Never!" the Radioactive Man screamed. He whirled around and sent a massive blast at the Quinjet. It tried to maneuver out of the way, but the blast clipped its wing, sending smoke pouring out of its engine. "I will kill all of you damnable women one at a time!"

The second Igor Stancheck turned his back,

Shuri lunged with her sword. The man's aura crackled with energy as he prepared to strike out once again at her protectors. Grimly, Shuri thought: *They wouldn't be down there if not for me.*

"For K'Darte!" she screamed as she struck out, barely able to hear herself over the Quinjet's engines. She stabbed up and into the Radioactive Man's back, amazed at how easily the blade slipped into and through the man's hide and bones.

A SMALL gasp slipped from Stancheck's mouth as he looked down at the black blade protruding from his stomach, coated with his steaming green blood. Shuri pushed again, and the sword slid into his body up to the hilt. Blood began to gush from both sides of his body. She stepped back, panting hard, a little bit queasy.

Stancheck slowly turned around. His hands closed on the point of the Ebony Blade, trying to push it back out. But he only managed to gash his hands, drawing more blood. He staggered backward, his eyes filled with disbelief and sadness at the fact that this little slip of a girl had bested him and ended his life. He tried to call up a surge of radioactive energy to take Shuri with him—but when he raised his hand, nothing came forth but blood, flowing out of his hand onto the floor.

Cursing himself, Stancheck searched his mind for the Vibranium frequency. Maybe he could trigger an explosion that would destroy the mound and his tormentors, or at least cause enough destruction to force this country to remember his name and the wound he inflicted upon their land. But as he closed his eyes, he began to cough and spit up blood, heaving and vomiting as his muscles began to tremble and quake. He tried to straighten up, but found he couldn't stand to look at the blade in his midsection. He raised his head and saw Shuri standing a few feet away from him, a look of cold anger in her eyes.

"You've killed me, little girl," he rasped.

SHURI'S eyes flashed, and a low growl erupted from her throat. She yanked the Ebony Blade free of his body, then kicked the Radioactive Man directly in the teeth, sending him plummeting silently over the edge and down to the cavern floor. His body lay splayed out grotesquely.

Shuri looked down at the dead body. "Welcome to Wakanda, bitch," she whispered.

The Quinjet's engines whined, breaking Shuri's reverie. The plane reversed, and a ramp in the back slowly dropped open as it lowered itself close to the ledge. Shuri spared a second to send a sad glance toward the caverns, where K'Darte's body still lay. Then she took a couple of steps backwards and took off in a running leap to land gracefully on the Quinjet's ramp, where Nakia stood waiting on her.

"Excellent form, your majesty," Nakia yelled

over the Quinjet's roar. She took Shuri's hand and escorted her into the plane's cabin.

"Thank you, Nakia," Shuri acknowledged. The ramp whined shut. "We need to land and recover a body from the Great Mound, and then we can get out of here."

Nakia frowned and shook her head, bracing herself as Sharifa maneuvered the plane out of the mines. "No time, your majesty. We have to get you back to the palace. The country's at war, and my orders are to get you to safety immediately."

"T'Challa?" Shuri worried. "My mother?"

"The king is on his way, Princess. There's been some type of attack on the palace, and we're to rendezvous with him there to take on the architect behind all of this evil."

Shuri looked down at the green body lying on the cavern floor, getting smaller and smaller as they rose. "Idiot. If T'Challa doesn't kill him for this, I will," she swore, placing the Ebony Blade at her feet.

THE BLACK PANTHER strode into the command center, the chaos of the room quieting at his presence. He'd pushed his skybike to its limit to get back to his palace to discover the fate of his mother, but specks of blood still dripped from his wind-swept claws.

Okoye strode over to meet him, silent and wary. T'Challa removed his faceplate, searching the stoic face of his bodyguard anxiously for any hint of his family's fate. Okoye met him at the base of the staircase, W'Kabi at her heels. Without saying a word, she dropped to her knees in front of T'Challa. His heart sank, and he reached out an unsteady hand to Okoye as he looked at W'Kabi for strength.

"T'Challa," a voice called weakly from a dark corner of the room.

T'Challa looked around, and quickly zeroed in on the source: Ramonda, seated on the floor, looking utterly exhausted. Surrounding her, protecting her, were several *Dora Milaje*. Amare stood beside her, eyes shining brightly at T'Challa as she rubbed a bruised lump on her face.

The king ran across the room and swept up his mother in his arms. The *Dora Milaje* whispered "Beloved" reverently around him. Ramonda, safe in her son's arms, began to cry as T'Challa rocked her back and forth.

"It was him, T'Challa," she whispered over and over, as if in a trance. "It was him."

"I know," he said, eyes grim. "He will not live beyond today."

"He certainly won't, even if I have to kill him myself," a loud voice announced.

T'Challa looked up to see Shuri bounding down the stairs, followed by a grinning Nakia and a clearly uncomfortable Sharifa.

Smiling broadly, T'Challa pulled Shuri into a smothering bear hug with their mother, holding on to his family as tightly as he could. Ramonda teared up again. Shuri worked hard to keep her composure as she buried her head in the comforting olive-oil smell of her mother's hair.

"Are you okay?" she whispered anxiously to her mother. "Nakia and Okoye told me what happened."

Ramonda sniffed and looked up at T'Challa, a small smile on her face. "I am—thanks to General Amare, Okoye, and the sacrifices of the *Dora Milaje*."

She straightened up and looked over at Amare. She stood silently a few feet away, watching them stoically.

Ramonda cleared her voice and spoke in her royal cadence. "This family might not have lived past today if not for the *Dora Milaje*, son. They are one of the greatest assets of the crown, and should be treated as such."

T'Challa looked into his mother's eyes, a smile crinkling at the edge of his mouth. Then he looked down at Shuri. She shrugged and punched him in the arm.

"Hey, one of your *Dora Milaje* brought me a magical sword that allowed me to avenge my friend by killing one of the greatest threats our country's ever seen," Shuri pointed out. "If that doesn't show you what's what, then you're a bigger idiot than I thought you were."

Shuri smirked up at T'Challa. Okoye growled softly at the girl's impudence. Nakia only grinned again, bouncing up and down on the balls of her feet.

T'Challa chuckled as he stepped back from his mother. He stood up straight, lifting his chin to project his voice across the command center.

"W'Kabi," T'Challa called out, "I'm giving battlefield commendations to Captain Sharifa and the late Captain H'Rham for their fine piloting. And to General Amare, Okoye, and Nakia for keeping the royal family safe. I'm also awarding Jade Claws to them, and our soldiers and pilots, for their fine work today."

W'Kabi nodded, making notations on a pad. "Yes, my king."

T'Challa looked over at Okoye and Nakia, one stoic and the other bright-eyed, both awaiting their next orders. "I will have a further announcement once my palace has been cleared of its current infestation. W'Kabi, where is Klaw?"

W'Kabi pointed to the monitor. It showed a 3-D representation of the palace with several different-colored dots bunched around the royal family's wing.

"The *Dora Milaje* and the palace guard still have him and the Frenchman pinned down in the royal family's suite. No casualties yet, but it's only a matter of time before Klaw gets desperate and does something foolish." W'Kabi licked his lips in anticipation, and pulled out a short sword from a scabbard strapped to his waist. "Permission to kill intruders, your majesty?"

T'Challa shook his head grimly, looking over at his mother. "No, my loyal W'Kabi," he said, looking down at his fists and extending silver claws from his black-gloved hands. "There is a blood debt between Klaw and myself that must be repaid."

T'Challa raised a hand to forestall the arguments poised on Shuri's tongue and in his mother's tearful eyes.

"T'Challa, I can't lose someone else to that man," Ramonda began.

"I have just as much right to vengeance—" Shuri objected.

T'Challa shook his head. "I will brook no argument in this," he said firmly.

He looked over at Shuri. Surprising her, T'Challa hugged her again tightly, pulling her body close enough to whisper into her ear.

"If I fall, protect my people, my sister," he said softly. "The Panther God will show you the way. I have always believed in you, Shuri, as I did today. Continue to make me proud."

Shuri released him and took a step back, looking into his eyes. Silently, she nodded and stepped aside.

T'Challa turned around and kissed his mother's head softly, reaching up to wipe away some of her tears. "I will return in triumph, with my father's soul at rest. And then we will talk," he said confidently.

"To my side, Adored Ones," T'Challa called in Hausa. Amare, Okoye, Nakia, and the other *Dora Milaje* in the command center gathered around their king, faces sharp in anticipation of their his orders. *"Amare, I thank you and Okoye and your sisters for my family's lives. Know that you more than proved your*

worth as the Panther's fist this day, and your efforts have been acknowledged by no less than the Panther God herself. General, I charge you again with the protection of my mother and the crown princess. I am sure no harm will come to them while in your capable hands."

Amare's single eye shone with pride. *"It will be as if you were here yourself, Beloved."*

"Okoye, Nakia." T'Challa turned to his most loyal *Dora Milaje.* *"I want you with me. The* Dora Milaje *deserve a chance at redemption as well."*

The two women looked at each other, and then back at T'Challa. They nodded at him as their sisters began to pass them reloaded weapons.

T'Challa snapped shut his faceplate, the Black Panther's white eyes glowing in anticipation of the upcoming kill. "Let's end this," he said.

CHAPTER SEVENTEEN

THE BLACK PANTHER crept through the palace, his footfalls muffled by the Vibranium soles of his boots. His eyes narrowed as he witnessed for the first time the damage the *Dora Milaje*'s battle with Klaw had done to his childhood home. Walls were scorched by fire and pockmarked with bullet holes, paintings destroyed in the Hall of Kings. Broken tile and marble lay everywhere, scattered about by weapons fire that still rang out occasionally from the palace guard as they attempted to keep Klaw corralled in the royal suite. A painting of T'Chaka, wearing his crown and formal business suit, was on the floor, slashed down through the figure's chest—a bad omen, T'Challa thought as he neared the conflict zone.

Behind T'Challa strode Okoye and Nakia, weapons snapped up and at the ready. Their eyes surveyed every corner, monitored every bit of movement as the three of them maneuvered past the Wakandan Royal Guard and the other *Dora Milaje*. The bodyguards snapped smart salutes as they neared Ramonda's suite, where Klaw was still holed up.

Just down the hallway, Ramonda's oaken double doors lay fallen from the earlier grenade attack. Bodies of the *Dora Milaje* killed in that attack were still in the rubble, limbs sprawled, eyes glassy and unmoving within burned skin.

"Report," T'Challa hissed. A palace guard, a young stringy youth with a wisp of a beard, looked over at a *Dora Milaje* warrior, who looked back at him and nodded.

"Your majesty, we've been trying to get close to the royal suite to rescue your *Dora Milaje* hurt in the blast." The guard's voice cracked with tension. "We don't know if anyone is alive outside the inner rooms. Every time we get close, the hostile fires some type of energy out of the room—and sir, he has wicked aim. We've lost a couple of people just trying to rescue and assess the wounded.

T'Challa looked at the middle-aged *Dora Milaje*, who nodded her sandy-brown eyebrows along with the report. *"Beloved, he has a strong defensible position at this moment. We have him pinned down inside, but that's all. As much as I would love to recover the bodies of my sisters, it would only cause more deaths if we tried to take the room from this position."*

"No, no more deaths," T'Challa said grimly. *"I will go in alone and eliminate the threat. My father's honor demands it."*

T'Challa turned to the sweaty palace guard. "Hold your men back. Make sure the perimeter is secure, and there is no opportunity for the hostile to be reinforced by anyone, from any angle. I'm pretty sure we've defeated all his plans, but I don't want to leave anything to chance. The *Dora Milaje* will hold the front line until we've recovered their sisters, but your job is to make sure the hostile doesn't leave these lands. Understand?"

The guard snapped a salute and moved back down the hallway to carry out his orders. T'Challa felt a soft hand on his shoulder and looked back to see a worried Okoye staring directly into his eyes. Next to her, Nakia looked anxious.

T'Challa knew what was coming and shook his head to forestall their arguments. He opened his faceplate and reached out for their hands.

"You know honor demands I face my father's killer man-to-man," he said softly, feeling their heartbeats pound through their skin. *"With you at my side, there is nothing that can defeat us, nothing in this entire world. I would take on whole countries with just you two and your sisters at my side. But this is something I must do alone. I will not insult your oaths by ordering you to stay behind, but I humbly request that you allow me to face this danger on my own.*

"You have proven your worth this day, my Adored Ones. I must now prove mine." He released their hands.

Okoye swiped angrily at a tear, while Nakia dropped her head and looked at the floor. Pulling themselves together, the two women looked at each other, communicating silently. Finally, Okoye nodded, and Nakia stepped forward to pull T'Challa into a fierce hug. Okoye was next, squeezing him as hard as she could and then patting him on the cheek.

Nakia gave him an intense look. *"You have two minutes, Beloved, before we come in after you,"* she growled, in a good replica of Okoye's voice.

T'Challa looked at her askance, and quirked an eyebrow. *"I could order you to—"*

"But what good would giving that order do?" Nakia interrupted. *"Your honor demands you go in alone. Our honor demands we keep you safe. Do you think for one second we need permission—even yours— to do our jobs?"*

T'Challa fought back the urge to grin, and decided to surrender gracefully. *"I might need a little more time than that,"* he allowed, looking at Okoye for help.

Okoye put her hand on Nakia's shoulder and smiled. *"We can stretch it to five. But if we hear something we don't like, we're coming in guns blazing— no matter what you say, Beloved."*

"Agreed," T'Challa said, snapping shut his faceplate.

"Good luck, Beloved," Nakia murmured as the Black Panther crept down the hallway toward his mother's suite, his silver claws flashing in the light.

KLAW raged back and forth through the rubble of Ramonda's suite, listening to the barrage meant to keep him immobilized. He wondered how it all had gone so wrong, so quickly. His options for success, escape, and even survival were dwindling fast.

His best man, Batroc, lay unconscious and handcuffed on the bed. No one else was answering his calls—not M'Butu, the Black Knight, or the Radioactive Man.

Wakanda wasn't a smoking pit of destruction, which meant that Igor was dead or neutralized. No one had heard from the Black Knight, which eliminated one avenue of escape. Klaw assumed he'd lost all his hostages, since no one had attempted to contact him to negotiate the release of the princess. And, of course, Ramonda and the former regent had been rescued by those damnable female bodyguards.

He'd stuck his head out of the door a couple of times, and almost lost it to crossbow arrows and bullets. Those bodyguards seemed to have him surrounded. Klaw had wounded a few *Dora Milaje* who'd gotten too close, but he was well and truly trapped—with no mission, no way to escape, and no team to bail him out.

All that was left was a Belgian cybernetic assassin, stuck in a woman's bedroom with an unconscious Frenchman, hemmed in by the African Estrogen Guard, under fire and waiting for a man in a cat suit to come kill him. If it hadn't been so dire, it would be absurd.

And T'Challa was coming, Klaw knew. It was just a matter of time before the king of Wakanda would arrive to exact his revenge on the architect of this misery and destruction. Klaw could beg, he could offer up the people who financed his operation, he could offer penance for the young king's pain. But he knew it would be for naught.

The Black Panther was coming, and his only option—just as it had been for his illustrious namesake who first laid eyes on this forsaken land—was to fight. Klaw looked down at his hand and cycled some energy through the servers. His reserves weren't inexhaustible, but he had enough left to make a good showing of himself. And perhaps, just perhaps, if he could wake Batroc and get the upper hand on T'Challa, he'd be able to bargain their way to freedom with the Wakandan king's body.

Those were his only choices. Fight and win.

Or die.

THE BLACK PANTHER raised his hand, and the barrage aimed at his mother's suite halted for a moment.

He crept toward the doorway, casting sad glances down at his fallen *Dora Milaje*. They had died trying to keep his mother safe. He said a quick prayer to the Panther God for their souls as he sniffed the wind, hoping that his olfactory skills would give him some idea of what was waiting for him inside. But all he could smell was ionized air, gunpowder, and the coppery tang of blood.

"So I don't hear any more bullets," a voice called out from Ramonda's room. "I'm assuming that means that you're out there, T'Challa, and you're coming this way. Don't bother sneaking up, pal. My enhancements allow me to track you, so you can forget the silent act.

"But before we get started, I want to remind you of something. Remember back when I killed your father? You remember that day, T'Challa? I do."

T'Challa gritted his teeth. He crept closer and closer to the taunting voice, activating his smoke grenades.

KLAW backed away from the door, preparing for T'Challa's inevitable attack.

"You were such a little punk that day, T'Challa," Klaw sneered. "Snot running out your nose, bawling like a baby. I bet your father was *so* disappointed in his little boy—horrified, even. Imagine: The last thing he hears is his only son crying like a baby, instead of running to help his mother and father.

"And your beloved father, T'Chaka? The man you've spent your whole life revering? I want you to know he died like a coward. When I shot him in the gut, tears spilled from his eyes like blood, and the most pitiful moan—like a kicked puppy—came from his mouth.

"And do you know who your father looked at with his last breath? It wasn't you. It wasn't your mother. It was that one-legged female bodyguard I saw earlier, who attacked me with such passion. She took T'Chaka's death really hard, didn't she? What do you think happened there, T'Challa? The king and the bodyguard, sneaking around behind the foreign queen when she was fat and pregnant? A little bit of court intrigue, boy? Maybe your sainted father had feet of clay?

"Do you really want to waste your life avenging a man you didn't know, T'Challa?" Klaw's voice echoed. "We can both walk away today, Panther, and never see each other again. We don't have to do this. Let me back into Niganda and I'll disappear, never to be found again. You know I can do it, T'Challa. All you have to do is say the word, and my people will make it happen.

"But if you walk through that doorway, T'Challa, I'll kill you the same way I killed your father. And you know that your sister will want to avenge you, and I'll kill her, too. Think about it, T'Challa, because you're dooming both yourself and your baby sister if you walk through that door."

Klaw took careful aim through the gathering smoke and haze surrounding the doorway.

"What is going on?"

Klaw looked over to see a revived Batroc sitting up on the bed, tugging at his plastic cuffs. "Klaw, what is happening?" he asked. "And why does my mouth hurt?"

Klaw put his finger to his lips, hushing the confused mercenary. Black smoke billowed in the doorway, with wisps floating into the room. Klaw wiped his eyes, backing away as he tried to target through the smoke.

"We can work this out," he called, trying to

catch a glimpse of his prey. "C'mon, T'Challa, what do you say?"

A black blur hurled itself through the smoke. A clawed fist connected with Klaw's jaw, faster than he could follow or block. The dazed Klaw found himself flung head over heels across the room into the wall; the energy he'd been building up in his cybernetic hand discharged harmlessly into the wall. A clawed glove clamped around his throat, cutting off his breath, and slowly pulled him up off the floor. A pair of white eyes bored into his soul, and a metallic voice whispered through the mask.

"I say you die," the Black Panther hissed before doubling Klaw over with a punch in the stomach.

Klaw choked, trying to get his breath. He brought down his cybernetic hand, crackling with bluish energy. The Panther blocked it, pushing it to the side as he threw Klaw down to the floor and pounced on top of him. T'Challa raked his claws across Klaw's face, drawing blood from the assassin's forehead. Klaw fired wildly again and again, missing the dodging Panther each time.

One blast sizzled past Batroc, who was still struggling to work his way free from his cuffs. "Watch where you're pointing!" Batroc screamed as a second surge sailed past his head.

The Panther pinned down Klaw's cybernetic hand, forcing Klaw to halt the blasts. "Fast," Klaw croaked, concentrating on his weapons systems. "But speed isn't everything."

A jolt of energy ran through his arm and into the Black Panther. The king cried out in pain and released Klaw's hand. The Panther's armor crackled as the energy surged through his body, making him quiver and lose his grip on his enemy.

Klaw followed up with a punch to the Panther's head, the blow landing on T'Challa's helmet with a metallic clang. The king staggered.

The Panther quickly recovered and tackled Klaw again, moving too quickly for the assassin to keep him in his range of fire. Snatching one of the draperies off the wall, the Panther bound it around Klaw's head, blinding him and cutting off his breath.

"Time to wrap this up, evil one," the Panther growled. He pulled a Vibranium knife from a pouch and plunged it through Klaw's metal hand. "The Panther God will devour your soul before this day is done."

Klaw struggled under the heavy cloth, flailing with his free hand and trying to pull in a breath. All of a sudden, his body went still. A red glow began to flare from under the drape.

The Panther sensed the heat—just barely moved his head out of the way before a laser blast burned its way through the drape. Klaw blinked and focused his cybernetic eye, and a second blast tore through the drapery, scorching a smoking line across the ceiling.

Bracing himself, Klaw pulled the Vibranium knife free of his metal hand and clamped his fingers around the Panther's neck. T'Challa fought, unable to break the mechanical grip.

"I'm going to give you a choice, T'Challa," Klaw snarled, looking at the Panther through the hole in the cloth. "I can either squeeze until my fingers meet in your throat, or I can use my eye to burn a hole in your head. Both are painful ways to die, but at least it'll be quick. What's your pleasure?"

Using all of his strength, the Panther began to pry the cold metal fingers from his throat. "So death by laser," Klaw muttered. "Fine by me."

The Black Panther struggled with Klaw's iron grip, moving the assassin's hand back and forth in an attempt to dislodge it from his body. At the last second, just as Klaw fired his eye laser, T'Challa pulled free and pushed the assassin's hand into the beam, severing it from his body.

Klaw screamed. He pulled the drapery from around his head and looked down angrily at his hand hanging from a mass of sparking wires at his side.

T'Challa used the distraction to retrieve S'Yan's spear, which was still laying on the floor where the former regent had dropped it earlier in the day. T'Challa hefted it into the air and spun it in a circle, then turned back to Klaw.

The assassin was still raging at the loss of his hand when the Black Panther approached with his spear. Klaw sneered when he saw the Panther's weapon—but T'Challa ignored him, weaving the spear back and forth as he approached his enemy.

"You couldn't help going back to your jungle roots, could you, T'Challa?" T'Challa pushed the sound of Klaw's voice to the back of his mind as they circled each other. The prattling from his enemy continued, but the Panther paid as little attention to it as he could.

"A country full of technology, and you pick up a simple stick in hopes of defeating me? That's just like your father, boy," Klaw kept talking, obviously hoping to rattle him, a small voice in T'Challa's head said. *Ignore him and wait for the right moment,* he thought.

"Stuck in an antiquated past of honor, and sacrifice, and courage, when the rest of the world's passed you and your obsolete religion by," Klaw continued. "It was a good thing your people stayed hidden from the world—it would have crushed Wakanda long ago. The only thing your father did right, T'Challa, was to die and force Wakanda back into its shell for a few more years. What will *your* death do for your country, hmmm?"

A red glow appeared in Klaw's eye; he leaned forward to send out a blistering bolt that would end the Black Panther's life. But at the last second, the Panther ducked down below the beam and sprang forward with the spear, shoving it straight into Klaw's belly.

Klaw cried out and looked down at his midsection, mouth open. His hands grasped the hilt of the spear. Blood bubbled from his lips, and he fell to his knees, blood pouring from his wound.

The Black Panther sidled up close to Klaw, and bent over to whisper in his ear. "We'll never know, will we?" T'Challa activated his helmet release and stared Klaw in the eye.

Klaw slumped over, the pain visible in his face. He tugged at the spear unsuccessfully. With his last breath, he spit a huge glob of blood on the floor. "I hate this land," he muttered, and went limp.

T'Challa dropped his helmet to the floor and sagged against the wall, his limbs suddenly heavy with exhaustion. "That was for my father, villain."

He kicked Klaw's body over, wrenched the spear free, and used it to brace himself as he hobbled toward the doorway.

He stopped for a second, sniffing the air, then turned around and closed his eyes. When he opened them again, a huge blue-black panther was curled up in the window, looking particularly well-fed. She burped, and a muffled scream escaped from her throat before she could close her mouth again. T'Challa could have sworn she smiled.

Then she faded away in the daylight.

A noise brought him out of his reverie. Batroc was sitting up in his mother's bed, unabashedly staring at T'Challa while wincing from the beating he had received.

"I do not mean to intrude on what must be a powerful moment," Batroc began, "killing the man who killed your father and all. But we both need medical attention, *oui*?"

T'Challa just shook his head. Okoye and Nakia rushed the room, weapons drawn. He waved them down and sagged into their arms. The palace guard dragged Batroc away roughly, and pulled one of Ramonda's sheets over Klaw's body, which lay in a pool of blood in the middle of the room.

But T'Challa only had eyes for his family as they helped him walk out of the room.

"Thank you, my Adored Ones," T'Challa said. *"Did I beat the deadline?"*

"By 20 seconds, Beloved," Nakia teased. *"Okoye was very concerned, and was about to charge in.*

"Me?" Okoye laughed. *"You were on pins and needles the whole time, girl. Beloved, I don't think Nakia listens very well. We might want to figure out some extra concentration training for her. She obviously has a problem not only listening but following orders."*

T'Challa chuckled, doubling over in pain from the movement. *"Don't make me laugh, Adored Ones."*

"Well, don't die yet, Beloved," Nakia turned serious all of a sudden, cupping her hand over the earphone dangling in her ear. *"Listening to W'Kabi in the command center, there seems to have developed one more task for you to perform."*

"For the life of me, I can't figure out what that could be," T'Challa admitted.

Nakia looked at Okoye, then back at T'Challa. *"The Americans are here."*

ROSS stared off into the ocean one last time before tipping his baseball cap at the aircraft carrier's flight crew. Then he headed up to the bridge, spitting salt water out of his mouth the whole way. He'd been airlifted to the *U.S.S. Langley* just a few hours earlier, and they'd been twiddling their thumbs off the coast for the last few hours, watching Sky News and trying to piece together what'd been happening onshore.

The ship's captain, a gruff fellow named Dearborne, had given Ross free run of the ship and its equipment, within reason. But the ship had gone to battle stations when the first missile flew from Niganda. At that point, the captain had politely but firmly suggested that his guest find somewhere else to stand besides the bridge.

So Ross had decided to head out on deck and stare at the African coastline for a while, knowing that this might be as close as he'd ever get to the focus of his years of study, Wakanda. But now he'd been summoned back to the bridge—because something big had happened, he assumed.

Ross walked onto into the middle of a video conversation between Dearborne and General Matigan, the man who had banished Ross to the Indian Ocean in the first place. Matigan and Dearborne were arguing, and Ross had to step nearer to make out their frenzied voices.

"Send the boats *now*, Captain," Matigan ordered. Dearborne shook his head.

"I don't think sending American troops into

a hostile zone without permission or adequate information is the best idea, General," Dearborne replied. "And since they're *my* boats, they're not moving until I'm comfortable that their mission has been authorized and signed off on by the commander-in-chief."

"I speak with the president's voice on these matters, Captain," Matigan ground out, "and I say we'll never have a better chance than now."

"If I could interject here, as the expert on the region?" Ross stepped up into the conversation, surprising both men. "The absolute worst thing we could do here is to show up uninvited on Wakandan lands. We know from past experience they take that very poorly. Don't we, General?"

Onscreen, Matigan just ground his teeth and sulked.

"The *best* thing we can do, Captain, is put a call in to Wakanda and ask them if they need assistance," Ross continued. "If they don't answer, we've done our due diligence beforehand. If they answer, we can work from there instead of getting into an unnecessary shooting war that could cost American lives."

Dearborne nodded his head in agreement. "That's exactly what I'm talking about, General," he said. "No unnecessary risks with my men and women."

Matigan harrumphed. "Let me know when it's done," he said before abruptly cutting the connection.

Ross shook his head. "That guy's a jerk," he said,

drawing a few chuckles from the carrier's command crew.

"That he is, that he is," Dearborne laughed. "Now let's get someone in Wakanda's government on the line."

It took a few minutes before they reached a man named W'Kabi—*Is that a loincloth?* Ross wondered—who agreed to put them through to his superior. A few seconds later, the Black Panther appeared on their video screen, a reserved and somewhat exhausted expression on his unmasked face.

"I am King T'Challa, and I bring you greetings from Wakanda," the king said softly. "What can we do for you, American vessel?"

Dearborne stepped forward, nodding his head slightly toward the camera in a show of respect. "King T'Challa, I am Captain Dearborne of the *U.S.S. Langley*. We've noticed a…disturbance on your shores, and we wanted to offer our assistance to one of our most important allies. We're going to send a squadron or so of men to help you secure your borders and assist in disaster relief. They can be there within the hour."

"I think we have it under control, Captain," the king replied, cocking his head to one side. "Thank you for your kind offer, however."

"It's no problem at all, your majesty," Dearborne retorted. "In fact, we insist."

For the first time, an emotion—anger— flickered across T'Challa face. Wearing his entire

Panther habit except for the helmet, T'Challa made a striking figure in his throne, leaning forward with his claws extended on the armrests.

"Captain, pass this message along to your handlers in the government and in business. Wakanda appreciates the offer. However, your help is *not needed*. If a single American crosses the Wakandan border today, he will be considered the vanguard of an invasion force and will be treated accordingly. Do you understand?"

Dearborne froze, mouth open. Ross shrugged and waved for the captain to answer.

"Ummm, message received, Wakandan control," Dearborne stuttered. "We'll be heading back out to sea. You have a nice day now, you hear?"

"And you as well, Captain," T'Challa glanced around and locked eyes with Ross briefly, then cut the connection.

"Well now, friend Ross, it doesn't seem like they want our help," Dearborne chuckled, running his hand through his hair.

Ross turned around and headed back out, shaking his head. "No, they don't," he said with a wry grin. "It sounds to me like they have everything under control."

A question from Dearborne stopped him in his tracks. "Ross? There are very few people who get away with turning us down like that, especially with the size of the egos back in Washington. What are you going to say in your report?"

Ross smirked at the captain. "I'm going to say that the king of Wakanda has repelled his enemies from his shores—and that we don't want to ever be included in that group."

CHAPTER EIGHTEEN

T'CHALLA stood looking out over the cheering throngs outside his palace. A smile came over his face as he walked forward, waving to the excited crowds. In the distance, he could see the construction cranes and scaffolding covering half the capital city as Wakanda worked feverishly to rebuild its infrastructure.

The work was going well, T'Challa thought as he adjusted his white flowing robes. With the proper persuasion, perhaps the people would come to accept the idea of a tourist hotel and a foreign embassy complex among the reconstructed facilities.

Wakanda had held itself separate long enough, T'Challa thought, leaving too many brothers and sisters vulnerable to the wickedness of the world. His father and mother had had the right idea, just at the wrong time.

Okoye had argued strenuously against the idea, supported by Zuri and W'Kabi. But T'Challa's proposal had the backing of his mother, the crown princess, and the former regent, with the quiet support of Nakia and Amare. And so it had passed the ruling council by a comfortable margin.

T'Challa looked over at Nakia. She was using her custom-made sunglasses to scan the crowd.

Okoye stood in the shadows of the balcony, also watching for danger. Now that the *Dora Milaje* question had been settled, T'Challa found that his two main guards were quite knowledgeable about affairs of state, and gave excellent advice—even though they rarely agreed with each other. That was another thing S'Yan had been correct about during his recovery—the first being, of course, the use of minute amounts of Vibranium in his prosthetic leg to eliminate almost any jarring from the metal when they sparred in the gym.

Where they *all* agreed was that there were people using their power to make the world a better place—people like Dr. Richards and his family, and these new Avengers he was hearing so much about. If a group of individuals could work that way for the benefit of mankind, think how much a properly motivated king with the resources of a country could do. T'Challa made a note to himself to look further into the Avengers, then put it out of his mind and smiled as he glanced back and saw Shuri and Ramonda striding out to join him.

It was time.

T'Challa raised his hand for silence. Within a few seconds, the raucous crowd had calmed down enough for him to hear Shuri's anxious shuffling behind him. He gave her a reassuring smile, and turned to speak into the microphone.

"People of Wakanda, we are here today to celebrate our victory over our enemies." T'Challa looked out over the silent crowd. "Through careful negotiation with the new Nigandan government, a cease-fire has been established. Once again, we will have peace!"

The crowd roared, a wave of pure adulation that rattled the palace and set T'Challa's sensitive ears to ringing. Looking over at Shuri, he saw she had stuck her fingers in her ears but was grinning broadly at him. Ramonda frowned at her daughter, and Shuri's face fell. Then Ramonda winked and laughed broadly herself.

A large weight had fallen from Ramonda in the days since Klaw's death. Yesterday T'Challa had seen her carefully restoring a repaired painting of T'Chaka to the Hall of Kings, with Amare standing protectively nearby. The two seemed to have resolved their differences, and now were as inseparable as two such radically different women could be. Even now, the *Dora Milaje* general stood just inside the palace, watching the festivities and the work of her prize pupils quietly, her metal prosthetic leg gleaming in the dark.

T'Challa turned back to the crowd. "It took all of us, my brave Wakandans, to survive this cowardly attack not only on our country, but also on the royal palace and the symbol of our strength, the Great Mound. We would not be here today if not for your bravery and courage, but I want to single out some people for their extraordinary work over the last few days."

T'Challa nodded to Shuri. She walked over to a table on the side of the balcony and returned with a case filled with medals. She pulled out two medals and held them out to T'Challa, sadness in her eyes. He took them, and held them up for the crowd to see.

"I am awarding our country's highest military honor and our highest civilian honor posthumously to two brave sons of Wakanda, Captain H'Rham of the Royal Wakandan Air Force and Chief Science Officer K'Darte, who both gave their lives selflessly to protect our country in this most recent attack. Without their sacrifice, we would not be here today. We will always remember them."

A roar of applause rolled through the crowd as giant viewing screens stationed throughout the plaza showed pictures of the deceased men. Shuri looked down into the reserved section and saw N'Jare wiping her eyes with a cloth, a small bulge visible on her stomach. Shuri made a mental note to invite the grieving woman to tea at the palace, to tell her how brave and kind her husband had been.

"I would also like to recognize the brave men and women of the Wakandan armed forces—especially Captain Sharifa of the Air Force and Security Minister W'Kabi—for their tireless efforts to keep this country safe from harm. We owe them an unpayable debt of gratitude, and today we honor them!"

The crowd cheered again as T'Challa handed the medals back to Shuri. He nodded at Nakia, who stepped behind a curtain, pulled out a second case, and handed it to Ramonda, who stepped forward to speak. Shuri looked questioningly at T'Challa, who smiled at her.

Ramonda spoke in a soft voice. "People of Wakanda, this cowardly attack on our great country was conceived and led by the man who killed your beloved king and my husband, T'Chaka." Gasps of surprise rose from the crowd.

"Ulysses Klaue, an assassin for hire, targeted and killed King T'Chaka years ago, and returned to finish the job here inside our own palace. But he not only wanted to eliminate the royal lineage of Wakanda, he sought to scar our country in a way that would never be forgotten: by destroying one of our greatest resources, the Vibranium found inside the Great Mound. He sent a man to explode inside the Great Mound, a man who caused much of the damage you see from the recent seismic activity. The two of them thought they would destroy Wakanda, and there was nothing anyone could do to stop them. But they did not realize that Wakanda has not just one hero, but two!"

Ramonda turned around and beckoned a stunned Shuri forward. She stumbled slightly, and her brother gave her a small shove forward. Nakia, her trademark grin on her face, walked up behind Shuri and placed a jade panther necklace around her neck. T'Challa pulled out the Ebony Blade and bowed to Shuri, holding the handle outstretched to her.

"With this sword, my daughter slew one of the greatest threats in our country's history," Ramonda announced. "In saving our country from destruction, the crown princess performed above and beyond the call of duty. I am proud to present her with our country's highest award and name her a Hero of Wakanda."

Ramonda took Shuri's hand and kissed it, tears welling in her eyes. "And I want her to know I am so, so proud of her, and am looking forward to seeing what majestic feats she achieves in the future."

Shuri, tears flowing down her face, pulled her mother into a powerful hug. They rocked back and forth as the crowd exploded with delight. Ramonda kissed her daughter on the forehead, then released her and stepped back from the microphone. Shuri tackled T'Challa with a bear hug, and kissed him on the cheek. Then she stepped back with a smile, patting the Ebony Blade's scabbard as she strapped it around her waist.

T'Challa walked back to the microphone and raised his hands for silence again.

"There is one more matter of official business before we conclude," T'Challa announced, looking back at his bodyguards. "Okoye, Nakia, Amare: Step forward, please."

T'Challa took great pleasure in seeing the shock on the three women's faces as they moved slowly toward the front of the balcony, into view of the expectant crowd. Their backups, two young women named Ayo and Aneka, silently slipped into protective position behind them and began scanning the crowd for trouble.

T'Challa looked at his most trusted *Dora Milaje*:

the proud Amare, standing tall despite her many injuries; Okoye, her stoic features cracking with fear from this unknown situation; and the young, nervous Nakia, shifting her weight back and forth in an attempt to calm herself. He didn't know where he'd be without them, and as he cleared his throat, he knew that the world deserved to know that.

"Since time immemorial, the *Dora Milaje* have served Wakanda. They were the glue that held our many tribes together through their service to the king." T'Challa looked out over the crowd, their faces questioning as they listened. "Their order has evolved into a protective force for the crown, becoming the most loyal subjects of the king, putting their lives and their sacred honor on the line time and time again without asking for recognition, recompense or even a simple 'Thank you.'

"But that time has passed," T'Challa announced. "It is time to recognize the *Dora Milaje* for what they are: my strong right arm, my closest advisors, my eyes and ears in the world—and most important, my proxies in time of need. Ladies and gentlemen of Wakanda, I declare the *Dora Milaje* as the Fist of the Black Panther."

T'Challa turned and bowed to the three women. *"Adored Ones, the Panther God smiles upon your order,"* he said quietly. *"Ask it, and if it's within my power, it is yours."*

The three *Dora Milaje* looked at each other, keenly aware of their younger sisters behind them listening to every word. Amare gazed at T'Challa, then back at her pupils, and they nodded as she stepped forward.

"Our only desire, Beloved, is to continue to serve the crown as its protectors," Amare said.

"So be it, Adored Ones," T'Challa said with a smile, standing up. *"So be it."*

The king walked back to the microphone, and looked out over his people. Every one of them gazed up at their protector.

"People of Wakanda, we have been tried and we have been tested," T'Challa said. "And we've come out the other side a stronger people—and a stronger nation. The man who took our former king from us is now dead, and we are actively searching for those who funded his operation.

"To them, I say 'Run and hide.' No matter where you go, the claws of the Panther will find you. The fists of the Panther will punish you, and the fangs of the Panther will end your worthless lives. No longer will we let the rest of the world live as it would, as we enjoy our idyllic lives here in the Golden City. We will stride boldly forth, and bring our brand of justice to those who would enslave and endanger our brothers and sisters around the world.

"We will fight for justice, and we will win."

T'Challa thrust his fist into the air and looked out over his madly cheering people. "This is the new age of the Black Panther, and may our enemies weep!"

THE END

ABOUT THE AUTHOR

JESSE J. HOLLAND is the author of the bestselling *The Invisibles: The Untold Story of African American Slaves in the White House* and *Black Men Built the Capitol: Discovering African-American History In and Around Washington, D.C.* A longtime comic book and science-fiction fan, he is also the author of the children's novel *Star Wars: The Force Awakens—Finn's Story* and co-author of the late, lamented-by-no-one-except-a-couple-of-diehard-fans collegiate comic strip *Hippie and the Black Guy.* He spends most of his time as a Race & Ethnicity reporter with The Associated Press in Washington, D.C., where he also completed the trifecta by working as a White House, Supreme Court, and congressional reporter. He currently lives in Bowie, Maryland, with his wife, Carol, his children, Rita and Jamie, and his dog, Woodson Oblivious.